AIR SERIES   BOOK 6

FRACTURED WORLDS

AMANDA BOOLOODIAN

DEDICATION

Dedicated to silver. You forever help me. I'll forever help you.

CONTENTS

CHAPTER
ONE

My breath rushed in and out of my lungs at a frantic pace. One foot in front of the other, moving forward, not looking back.

Running.

Not being allowed to do my job unnerved me. My partners didn't need me at the time, but they would. The thing was, when they needed me, they weren't going to be able to call me up and say, 'Hey, come help us out.' It didn't work like that. Being an agent at the Agency for Interdimensional Regulation means that when you need help, it's generally right now or not at all.

A heavy, pounding cadence punched into the ground with each footfall.

When I went back to work, I wanted to be at my best. Mentally, physically, and with my powers reined in.

I wasn't sure all that was possible, but I was damned well going to try. The sun glittered through the canopy of leaves, hinting at a happy day. The truth was, I was lonely.

Well, as alone as you could get at the Sanctuary. Travis was around the entrance somewhere. He had waved me through with little in the way of small talk. The fairies lived on the other side of the park. I knew someone was living in the lake, but I had no idea who it might be. My first guess would be mermaids, but they tended to prefer warmer waters. It was nice and warm, but in a few months, the lake would cool along with the rest of the temperatures in the Midwest.

What was missing out here were my friends, mainly Rider. He and I used to go hiking, but he hadn't had much to do with me in a while.

As for my other partners, I don't think Logan runs unless it's toward something. Elves rarely exercise for sport, or even to keep in shape. It's not a rule, but in general, if they are rushing around, there's a reason for it. I'm fairly certain Vincent runs, but I doubt he would let me join him now. He'd been keeping his distance, trying to avoid upsetting Ethan.

Not that it mattered much, because they were all at work.

Picking up the pace, I felt the sweat trickle down the small of my back. Ethan would run with me. Being ex-military and as the current Lieutenant Detective of the local police force, it's possible that my boyfriend did exercise to keep in shape. Although, he'd also been avoiding me lately for all the same reasons that concerned Vincent.

Not telling him Vincent had a part of my soul might have been a mistake, but how did one normally broach that kind of thing with a man you were seeing. 'By the way, my partner stole my soul, and even though I got it back, he ended up keeping a piece.' It's not something that rolls off the tongue, and it's certainly not a topic for date night.

It's possible that I was making another mistake by not telling him I had a small part of Vincent's soul as well, but I had an excuse ready there. It's never been proven.

No one's seen it, and if they could, they'd have seen the

host of other soul fragments running through my system and they wouldn't know if it belonged to Vincent or not.

I know it's there.

It's an excuse, not a good one, but I could use it if needed. Not that it's something that would slip out. He'd need regular contact with me in order for something like that to come up.

It didn't help that he was at work as well.

With no one with me, it was tempting to stay at home. I had plans with Ethan tonight though, which meant no Krav class. That was one of the few things that forced me out the door.

My breath turned ragged, so I slowed my pace, first to a jog, then to a walk. I had abused my body enough for the afternoon. The parking lot came into view as I rounded the bend.

Between all the self-defense and running, physically, I was ready to return to work. My body was in better shape than it had ever been in my life.

Mentally, I was fine. The agency had their rules, though. Rider and Vincent had been cleared to return, and Logan had never been stood down. As the last straggler, it was my turn to get approval. Hopefully, tomorrow I'd be cleared. Rider had almost died, which seemed way more traumatizing than being kidnapped, right?

Blowing out a huff of air, I took a few moments to stretch. The crunch of tires on gravel announced someone driving down the winding entrance road to the Sanctuary. It must be agents or someone with high clearance.

Or one of the Lost. Most mythological creatures had permission to use the Sanctuary.

Unfortunately, I was sweating profusely and wearing clothes for running, not for work.

Seeing the large SWAT-style vehicle made my stomach twist. Speak of the devils and they shall arrive.

Vincent parked the truck. When he got out, I saw his face, which to most would look expressionless. It showed me hints of anxiety, but a smile hid in there somewhere.

Waving, I forced a cheerful attitude. Rider hung back, which was sad, but not unexpected, while Vincent closed the gap between us.

"Hey," I said, trying to hide any apprehension that might slip out.

"It's good to see you." A hint of sincerity in Vincent's voice helped me relax.

It also managed to draw out a real smile. "It's good to see you, too. Both of you." I raised my voice slightly for the second statement, but with werewolf hearing, Rider would have been able to hear anyway. "Coming out to check on Essy?"

"Yes, but I wasn't expecting to see you out here," Vincent said.

I shrugged. "It was a nice day to spend in the woods."

"How is everything?" Vincent asked.

"It hasn't been that long since we've seen each other." It had been over a week. It was hard to believe it had been that long. "I'm the same. How about you all, and work? I noticed Logan wasn't with you." I tried not to ask too much at once, but the truth was I wanted to know everything that had been going on.

"Logan had a meeting at the office. Kyrian called him in."

"Sounds like fun." My stomach squeezed tightly wondering if they were discussing my return. Logan would stand up for me, right? "Anything else going on?"

"Nothing," Vincent said. "You could join us, though, to visit Essy."

Glancing over, I saw Rider pointedly look away. "Yeah, I don't think I should." How was it that Rider, who was supposed to be my best friend, could make me feel so unwelcome?

Vincent noticed the look. "It would give us a chance to talk."

My heart beat faster with that prospect, but Rider wanting nothing to do with me, dampened the effect. "Maybe next time. I'm not exactly dressed for work or anything."

Vincent grinned. "I don't think it'll bother Essy."

Once again, I was struck with Vincent's brighter attitude. From the day I met him, he had always seemed closed off. Had always kept himself at arm's length. For the past few weeks, he had been more open. Lighter somehow.

"Rain check," I said, "I've got a few things to take care of."

"If you're sure." Vincent looked back at his partner. "You know, at some point, you two are going to have to get over whatever this is."

"I'd have to know what it is before I can get over it." I really didn't want to be bitter about the situation, but there was no use hiding it. "I should go."

Vincent looked torn, but I didn't give him a chance to say anything else.

"I'll see you... sometime, I guess." I started backing away. "Good to see you, too, Rider," I added loudly, but with no real conviction.

"Yeah, sometime." Vincent spoke so softly I almost missed the words.

Keeping a normal pace back to my car wasn't easy. All in all, the encounter was mixed. Rider still wanted nothing to do with me, but bumping into Vincent was nice.

Seeing him was enough to make my heart beat faster, which naturally led to guilt. When I drove off, I didn't look back. Nothing I could see would make me happy.

My phone started to ring. It was tempting to pull over and

dig the phone out of my bag. It could be the office. Instead, I dismissed the idea, knowing I could check it soon. The drive home wasn't long, but when I arrived, I felt grungy enough to want to jump into the shower right away.

"Gran, I'm home," I said, entering the house.

"In the kitchen, darlin'," Gran called out.

The warm air of the kitchen washed over me causing me to sweat again, despite the AC running.

"You've been busy, I see." The counters were filled with cupcakes, mini cakes, and cookies. "Is all this for Logan and the kids? I'm pretty sure this much would even give elves some sort of insulin shock."

"These are goin' all over." Gran slid over a small plate. "Help yourself to a cupcake."

"I should snag another for Ethan. He's supposed to stop by tonight."

Gran looked at me uncomfortably.

"He's not coming over, is he?" I felt deflated.

Gran shook her head. "Not tonight, sorry."

"Did he leave a message, or..." I let the question drop.

"He hasn't called the house."

"You're sure?" I shook my head. "Sorry, that was a silly question." Gran was a psychic, and when she saw the future, that future happened.

"I haven't seen your partners in ages. Maybe you could invite them over for the evenin'," Gran suggested.

"It feels awkward since I'm not working with them. I ran into Vincent and Rider earlier, though. And Logan's here almost every morning." I threw the last part in to deflect any questions about Rider and Vincent.

"Things will get better for you," Gran promised.

"Got a timeline on that?"

"If I get one, you'll be the first to hear. On that note,

however, you are going to want to be at work no later than 7 am tomorrow morning."

"Sure, I can do that. Maybe it's a good thing Ethan had to cancel. I can get to sleep early."

Gran went back to packaging up her baked goods. "Make sure you give Frank some attention. I worry about him being cooped up in a cage all the time."

"I opened the cage once and he wasn't really interested in jumping out. I'll make sure he gets around more, though, once I know for sure he won't turn everyone into a zombie or give them some awful disease."

"Poor little thing."

"I could bring him down here where he'll have company more often." I had made the suggestion earlier this week as well.

"We'll see what Dr. Taylor says." Gran didn't meet my eye.

I nodded and picked out a cupcake, purposely choosing one with lots of icing. "I've got to check my messages and take a shower."

"I'll be gone when you get out and I'll miss you in the mornin'," Gran said. "Chin up tomorrow, and make sure you're early."

"Thanks."

On the way upstairs, I listened to my voicemail. Both were from Ethan saying he would be working late tonight. Again. Somehow shoving the cupcake into my mouth didn't make the evening any better. It had been worth a try, though.

HAVE you ever walked into a room and felt everyone's eyes turn to you? The moment I stepped into the control room, I could feel the other agents looking up. Luckily, at seven am the office wasn't exactly bustling. The nightshift was leaving or had already left and the dayshift was barely pulling themselves out of bed.

There were enough eyes to make a girl uncomfortable, though. For a moment, I had been tempted to hide out in my office. Logan and I shared an office in the building, but he always preferred sitting in the control room. There were always empty desks and other people to chat with.

Logan wasn't here, but since we hadn't used the office in ages—not since Vincent had stolen my soul—I stuck it out in the large central room.

Hank, our handler, wasn't in yet, which seemed odd to me. He always got to the office before everyone, except maybe Kyrian.

Instead of settling into a desk and trying to look busy, I went down the hall to find Kyrian, the Director of the Midwest offices. The light was on in her office, so I steeled myself and knocked.

"Come in," Kyrian said.

I took a deep breath, told myself to be confident and pleasant, and opened the door.

"Good morning." It came out much too quickly. It sucked feeling this nervous at work.

Kyrian had glanced up and then back down to the tablet on her desk. "Ms. Heidrich, you're in early today."

"Yeah, I guess so." My tone showed a lack of confidence, but I didn't retrace my steps. "Someone needs to sign off on my return."

"Ah, yes."

"I'm assuming that would be you?" I hadn't meant to turn that into a question, but it was there.

"Yes and no," Kyrian said.

Not very helpful. "Who should I see first?"

"You've been cleared, but there's paperwork before you get reinstated. Hank will—"

Someone knocked on Kyrian's door and her sigh was audible.

"A moment, please," Kyrian said to me. "Come in," she added louder.

"Good morning, Director." A man had opened the door and stepped in, but he was someone I didn't recognize.

"Good morning." Kyrian's whole attitude changed. She practically glowed. "Agent Heidrich, this is Agent Boone. Agent Boone, this is Agent Heidrich, whom we've discussed."

Ugh, that didn't sound good. "It's nice to meet you." I stuck out my hand, which he shook.

The man bore no hint of a smile, though he didn't appear unpleasant. In fact, I wouldn't mind looking a lot longer, but his expression was serious.

"It's going to be a pleasure working with you," he said. When he stepped back, I noticed he stood with his hands clasped behind his back.

Parade rest. Maybe ex-military. That might explain the muscles.

Wait, working with me? I gave Kyrian a questioning look, but her eyes were mostly on Boone.

"Agent Boone met with Logan yesterday." The chipper voice Kyrian used felt out of place. "He's here on special assignment and will be shadowing your team. Starting today, correct?"

"I'll be meeting with Agent Seale in an hour in town," Boone said.

"Excellent. Agent Heidrich, could you excuse us? I'm sure you'll want to meet with Hank," Kyrian said.

"Sure." The feeling of uncertainty I hadn't expected.

"Thank you for your time. Agent Boone, it was nice to meet you."

What the heck was that about? I walked out, trying to shake the bewilderment. Why had no one said anything to me about this?

Back in the control room, I didn't catch sight of Hank, so I went to the break room and made coffee. That, at least, was something I was good at and something I could do while waiting around. Looking busy was almost impossible since I didn't have valid credentials for the computer system. My access had been taken away sometime after my forced extended vacation had started.

Once I had fixed my coffee, stalling long enough to add copious amounts of sugar, I looked for Hank. Once again, I felt eyes move to me, then back to their appointed tasks again. Worse, Hank still wasn't in yet.

Nodding to a few people when I caught their eyes, I made my way out of the room. I'm not sure why Gran wanted me to be in early today. Not with everyone staring at me and nothing to do. My office would be my safe haven until Hank arrived.

Remembering I hadn't left him a note on his desk, I pawed through my purse and found my phone. At first, I considered sending him a text, but texts are easy to put off replying to, but calls aren't as easy to dodge, so I dialed Hank.

"Cassie, I'm running a few minutes late this morning, but I've made it through the gates," Hank said.

"Thank goodness. What can I expect for today? Kyrian mentioned we were working with someone. Agent Boone?"

"Yes. We found out about Agent Boone yesterday," Hank said.

Flipping on the lights, I saw swirls of dust rise from the air I had disturbed, but it was nice to be away from prying eyes.

"Boone will be following Logan, Vincent, and Rider today.

Tomorrow, some specialists are coming in. Boone will work with them for a while, then he'll be riding along with you and Logan or some variation of the four of you."

I thumbed through the papers on my desk. "Does this have anything to do with me returning to work?" I asked, but I wasn't sure I wanted to hear the answer.

"Actually, he's interested in seeing how your team works. At the moment, you are the only team in the company made up solely of Lost and humans with special abilities. Most of the time the teams lean more heavily to the human side."

Muscles I didn't realize I had clenched started to relax, but my curiosity was piqued. "We're the only ones?"

"It's not unheard of to have teams like yours, but at the moment, you all are the only ones."

A crash sounded down the hall and I jumped. Thankfully, no one was there to see me. Someone dropping something wasn't cause enough for anxiety.

I tried to tell myself that it had been startling, not a case of nerves. Nothing would derail me from starting work again.

"I guess our team kind of fell together more so than it was formed. Are teams like ours usually formed intentionally?"

"From what I understand, that's why Boone's there," Hank said.

Something else clattered in the hallway, so I went to check it out.

"He's baseline human, but he'll be leading a group that's not strictly human," Hank said. "I don't know much more than that."

"Will I be joining the team later today?" I poked my head into the hall and didn't see anything, but I walked in the direction the noise had come from.

"Today, there is paperwork," Hank said. "Electronically speaking."

A few offices had doors open in the hallway, but I noticed none of them were occupied as I walked by.

"I'm at the building," Hank said.

"I'm in my office."

Hank hesitated. "Everything okay?"

I shrugged, but then remembered he couldn't see me over the phone. "People seem uncomfortable."

Hank didn't say anything right away. Seeing no one around, I moved to go back to my office.

"Things will settle down quickly," Hank said. "No one's sure what to say."

'Hi,' or 'welcome back' would have been a start. "So they pass the awkwardness around?"

Two doors down from my office, I stopped. The door was shut, but something dark oozed out from under it. I knocked on the door.

"Something like that," Hank said. "Lucky for you, the looks stop after a day or so."

"Um, do we have any new Lost around?" Thick, dark liquid spread out into the hallway. With no answer, my heart began to beat faster, and I knocked again.

"No one new. I'm here; I'll meet you at your office."

"Wait, do we have anyone or anything around that oozes?"

"That's a heck of a question," Hank chuckled. "Nothing on record that oozes is in the area. Not for almost a year now."

"Crap. You might want to hurry." I tried to open the door, but it was locked. Pounding on the door only made my hands hurt. "Everything okay in there?" I called.

"What's going on?" Hank's voice turned serious faster than a gnome runs.

"Not sure, but something's coming out from under the door, and it doesn't look like water."

CHAPTER

TWO

An agent entered the hallway. "Everything okay?" He recognized me, and then hesitated.

"Can you open this door?" I asked.

"Agent Heidrich, it's good to see you back." His awkwardness was noticeable, but I didn't have time for that.

"Thanks, but listen, I think there's someone hurt." I kept my voice firm.

Hank spoke in the background, though I didn't hear what he said. I gestured to the floor, and the agent came closer and checked it out.

It only took a moment's look before he, too, began to pound on the door. The fluid pooling appeared to be blood.

"No one's answering." Did he think his pounding would produce different results than mine? "Do you have a key?"

"Stand back." The agent motioned me away and stared at the door.

I stepped away and turned my attention back to the phone. "Hank, do you have a key to the offices? We need one here."

The agent rammed into the office door with his shoulder. It

sounded as painful as it looked. He hunched over and resorted to pounding on the door again.

"Screw this," I said. "Hank, I'm opening the door."

I closed my eyes and reached for the Path. Mentally, I stretched passing everything I knew about the known world, then it jumped into a large black chasm where excitable shards of soul, mine and others, skittered around. When I opened my eyes, I was deep in the raging Path.

Thankfully, it came easy to me. My control, not so much so.

"Stand back," I told the agent. When he didn't, I gently nudged him away. Looking at the door, there were only a few options I could think of off the top of my head.

Most people wouldn't think that a door would have a Path. However, everything leaves its mark on the world. Even a piece of wood—long since dead—and metal, had a ghosted Path of its travel through the world. In this case, the movement was strictly back and forth, which made it ingrained. I grabbed the door's Path and pulled.

The door bulged, not ready to leave its frame. Calling harder to the Path of the door and adding in the lock, I gripped hard. As a Reader, it was time to make myself known. In one fast movement, the door crunched its way open. It swung around on the hinges, bounced against the doorstop, and then tried to bounce closed again.

It didn't have much luck closing. Once opened, the body of Clancy fell out and to the floor.

From reading Clancy's Path, I could tell we were too late. It had been too late before I had taken a step out of my office.

A hand landed on my shoulder and I was shunted aside. Hank had arrived. He spoke into a comms unit and leaned in to check for a pulse.

Clancy. One of the few other humans around this place that had an ability. He was a clairvoyant, or he had been. We had worked together from time to time. Clancy could see in objects what I could see in their Paths. The hall filled with people, agents mostly, and I stepped further back. All those Paths racing around began to make me feel nauseated, so I closed my eyes and pushed the Path away. I hadn't used much power, but I felt tired.

Looking at Clancy, I knew the feeling had very little to do with being worn out.

Alarms rang throughout the building. Even being toward the middle of the building, you could hear the shutters rolling down over the windows and doors. Other doors to the outside were being automatically bolted. The subbasements would start to close. Thinking of the dark, enormous evidence room below, I hoped no one had gotten trapped inside. Surely, that was one of those things that gets closed off, though, right?

My brain locked in on those lines of thought. It was the only way for me to handle the fact that I was looking at the body of one of my coworkers. Hank organized a team which started going from office to office, beginning with the closest offices.

Kyrian and Dr. Yelton arrived together. There were far too many people in the hallway, so I moved into the doorway of my office.

Hank put together another ad-hoc team of agents and set them to work. Kyrian spoke to Dr. Yelton and Hank. Her eyes flicked to me and the other agent every now and again throughout the conversation.

What should I be doing? Unfortunately, I think I was doing exactly what I should be, which was standing around and not touching anything. Technically, at least at the moment, I wasn't active. I had been the first one on scene, though.

What had I heard? It had sounded like someone had dropped something.

Had I seen anything? From the time I entered the hallway, to the time that agent walked into the hallway, I hadn't seen anyone.

"Agent Heidrich, you're with me." Hank's voice was gruff and he didn't bother waiting for a response before stalking off to the control room.

This wasn't the first time I'd been in the building during an official lockdown. Cell phones, sat phones, and landlines would be down. Internet would be minimal and access would go through Hank. The last time this happened, we had been after someone too. A demon had created a portal in the control room and escaped into its own dimension with our former director in tow.

The enemy had been obvious that time. It had been screechy, angry, hostile, and impossible to miss.

"I need to know your exact movements from the time you entered the building this morning." Hank's intensity radiated.

The tone of his voice tripped me up. "What? Uh, okay. I haven't even been here for that long."

As we strode through the control room, I took Hank through my morning. Once ensconced at his station, he pulled up security videos, first of the hallway outside my office. Currently, Kyrian reviewed the situation with a few others. Hank started rewinding.

Seeing myself pull the door open, only in reverse, made me wince. Do I always look pissed off when I work with the Path? It was a fleeting idea. Once the video backed up to the point the other agent joined me in the hallway, static erupted on the screen.

Hank looked stunned, but he pulled himself together at once, getting the security footage of multiple other locations across the screens.

Everything from this floor showed nothing. From the time I

stepped into the control room with my coffee, moving toward my office, until the time we were trying to get into the room, the footage was nothing but static.

Hank pulled up programs and other footage. "I need the techs."

"Want me to get anyone? Is there anything I can do?" I asked.

"You are hands-off at the moment. Completely. One hundred percent hands-off. If I could get you to sit in a chair and not move, I would, but I know you better than that."

That was unfair, but I kept my mouth shut. Crossing my arms and glaring spoke volumes for me. At least it would have if Hank had been looking at me and not his screens.

"You," Hank called out to an agent, "Kyrian is in the west hallway; tell her I need you to go be cleared. Then head to the fourth floor. Find Marty and tell him to meet me in security."

The agent looked like he was going to say something, but Hank snapped, "Now!" and the agent was off at a trot to the nearest set of stairs.

"You're seriously not going to let me help you with anything?" I asked Hank.

"At this point in time, I'm going to be lucky to keep you out of the interrogation room."

"What did—"

"What do you have, Hank," Kyrian called when she entered the room, cutting me off.

"We have blank video." Hank stared at his screens. "I'm running the footage through a filter now to see what kind of blank we have."

Kyrian's cheeks turned pink, but she kept her voice level. "I cleared Donaldson for the fourth floor. He'll be bringing Marty down to security."

"The checks?" Hank asked.

"About a fourth of the building has been cleared," Kyrian said. "At this point, we don't know what we're looking for. That is, unless Agent Heidrich has something to share with us." She looked at me expectantly.

My stomach was sinking, but I kept my voice level and talked her through everything I had done, seen, or heard from the time I left her office earlier that morning to when I had found Clancy.

"And we have no one that can corroborate, aside from Agent Watts, who's with Dr. Yelton?" Kyrian asked.

I gestured at the static, trying not to look too hopeless. "I was talking on the phone with Hank, but unless there's a way to see my location without video, I guess there isn't."

"I've put Paulson in charge." Kyrian looked around the room, watching the agents bustling with intent. "Hank, I'm giving him to Red for now. I need you on security."

Hank nodded and got up. "I'll be in security. Agent Heidrich, grab that laptop and follow me."

"Paulson will want—"

"Paulson can pull her out of security, but you and I both know he isn't going to need her right away." Not only had Hank cut Kyrian off, but he was also disagreeing with her.

"You're positive you want to play it this way? It lands on you if you're wrong." Kyrian didn't look at me, but she didn't have to.

"She'll be with me," Hank said.

Kyrian nodded. "I'll send Agent Paulson when he's ready."

Hank hurried away. There was no choice but to trail after him.

Once we were out of the control room, I couldn't hold back any longer. "Does she think I had something to do with this?"

"No more than anyone else," Hank said. "But the only thing

we do know is that whoever did this is someone with access to this building."

"Thank you for sticking up for me back there." It had to be said, though awkwardness hovered around us.

"I know you didn't do this," Hank said.

I nodded, but didn't say anything.

The security room was a small room with more monitors than the control room. A skinny man sat in a swivel chair.

Hank sat down with his laptop and docked it. Within moments, screens began running programs and showing static.

"Is there anything I can do?" I know I had asked before, but I hated not being able to help.

"Not at this time," Hank said. "Until we are off lockdown, you are still officially on leave."

"This sucks." I crossed my arms. "There's got to be something I can help with."

"I've got solitaire on this tablet," Marty suggested, waving it in the air. "It's not connected to anything at work."

I shook my head and slumped into a chair.

"Until Agent Paulson has interviewed you, you're with me," Hank said. "There's no way I'm dealing with your partners if they hear otherwise."

That coaxed a grin out of me. "I imagine they're pretty anxious by now."

"Well, luckily, we're locked inside the building," Hank muttered before falling into his work.

Right away, I regretted turning down the offered solitaire game. I felt the need to be helpful, but since that wasn't an option, I was antsy. Instead, I got a few looks from Hank when I got up and started pacing, stopping only to look over his or Marty's shoulder.

Kyrian came in for a check-up after about forty-five

minutes, but even with the dozens of programs Hank and Marty were running, they didn't have much to share. At that point, the building was almost forty percent cleared.

Not long after Kyrian left, Paulson showed up.

"Agent Heidrich." Paulson shook my hand. "It's good to see you back in the office. Hank, do you have anything for me?"

"We've managed to rule out a few methods that might have been used to extract the information. That doesn't get us very far in knowing what they did use, however."

"Can you have all the footage of the past twenty-four hours before the incident, through now, sent over to me?" Paulson asked.

"The network is limited until the building is cleared and the lockdown is over," Hank said. "If you leave me a tablet or laptop, the files can be manually loaded."

"Thanks, I'll send someone over with one," Paulson said. "Agent Heidrich, would you mind coming with me?"

My stomach started twisting itself into knots. "Sure thing."

Agent Paulson and I didn't know each other well, which wasn't surprising, considering I didn't know many people well that were outside of my team. It was an issue I really needed to resolve.

"First day back?" Paulson asked.

"Yeah. You probably already know, but the systems went down before I went active," I said.

"Thanks for the heads up. No one had mentioned that yet, but things are only now starting to settle."

We went to the control room, and the moment Paulson was spotted, someone came over and started to give him a rundown of everything checked.

"The first, second, fourth and fifth floors are cleared and all except the first and the clinic are locked down."

"Thanks, Anderson. Have you met Agent Heidrich?"

Anderson bobbed his head in my direction, but he was obviously lost in his own little world. "Nice to meet you."

"And you," I said.

He carried on with his report as though there had been no interruption. "Once we finish with the third floor, we'll start on the basement and subbasement levels."

"We don't have many cleared to work below the first subbasement," Paulson said. "At least not many in the office. Come and see me before you move any farther down than that level. Keep them locked off for now."

Anderson nodded and walked off.

Paulson took some time looking around the room, making sure no one was vying for his attention. Seeing he was in the clear, he nodded me toward the hallway that led to my office. "I'm going to have you walk me through everything that happened."

"Um, sure," I said, frowning. I looked back at Anderson. "First, though, what about the roof? It wasn't mentioned."

"If anyone is trapped up there, at least they won't be trapped around people."

It took a great deal of effort not to look at Paulson as if he was an idiot, but he was certainly overlooking some things. Instead, I shrugged. "As long as it's nothing that can fly out, I guess."

"You may be on to something there."

"The last incident we had in the office was with a person who could fly. Not that he tried to run that way."

"Wait here," Paulson said.

He walked over to Anderson, though I didn't watch their short discussion. Did that make things look bad for me? Like I was deflecting?

Reminding myself I hadn't done anything wrong was

getting tiring. If my partners were here, it would have been easier. I was sure of it.

"Thanks," Paulson said, returning. "Let's get going."

The next two hours were taxing, aggravating, and tedious in turn. Paulson and I went over everything, walking around the hallway to show my movements. Then he matched it up to the video Hank had loaded to a tablet for him. Once we were wrapping up, Watts was released from the clinic with his arm in a sling, and we started over, Watts filling us in on what he did.

As far as I could see, Paulson had nothing. No clues, no witnesses, and without video or audio, he was going to have a tough time.

Back in the control room, Paulson began setting people up with tablets and having those that had been cleared go through video footage. He was trying to find the movements of everyone in the building throughout the morning. He asked me about Boone twice. Since he had never met the man, and he had left the building before Clancy had been found, I could tell Paulson was trying to make that stretch. However, Boone had walked out of the building around the time I had reached the hallway to my office for the first time that morning.

After all the questions, explanations, and walk-throughs, I still wasn't allowed to touch anything or help in any way. Asking if he'd like me to try to read the area Clancy died got me a few odd looks, and even a polite 'no thanks.'

Which made me feel like crap. Did he not want me to help because I wasn't active duty, because I was a suspect, or because he was leery of me using my ability? From the looks I was getting, I was betting on one of the latter two.

Looking back on it, Watts had given me a few funny looks as well. The last thing I wanted to do was to stay available to all the stares, so I left the room and returned to the little security office where Hank and Marty were settled in for the long run.

Hank looked at me when I walked in and he frowned. "Things not go well?"

I shrugged and sat thinking over the reactions of Paulson, Watts, and the others around me.

"That bad?" Hank turned to the other guy in the room. "Hey, Marty, can you grab us a few sandwiches and a drink. I'm starving, and I think we've earned a little break."

Marty left, then Hank got up and stretched.

"How bad does it look?" Hank asked.

"They can't find anything so far," I said.

"Something happened."

"I don't think I'm a suspect or anything. At least no one is treating me like one, but... Can you bring up the footage of the hallway, right after the static went away?"

"Sure thing." Hank leaned over and clicked a few buttons, putting the footage on one of the large screens.

It played, but instead of watching myself this time, I watched Watts.

"People here know what I can do, right?" I asked.

"Most everyone knows you're a Reader," Hank said. He played the footage again. "It could be that they don't know what exactly that means."

"Maybe not. I asked Paulson if he wanted me to read the Path in the hallway. I'm not sure I could find anything from this morning, but I figured it would be worth a try."

"Makes sense," Hank said. "Is it because the paperwork isn't signed yet?"

"That didn't seem like the reason he said no. Besides our team and Clancy, are there any other humans in the building with something a little extra going on?"

Hank frowned, but didn't answer right away. "Not full

time. A few people would come in if called and one part-time woman that works similar to Clancy, a clairvoyant. Right now, though, I think you and Vincent are the only full-time agents that are human, plus a little extra. At least since this morning."

Both of us were drawn to the video, which had paused on our discovery of Clancy.

THREE

"Is that odd?" I asked. "That we'd be the only ones?"

"Not really," Hank said. "We have several Lost agents. Believe it or not, being human, but having an extra power, is rarer in the Midwest than the Lost are. Since we have room to spread out, there's lots of space for the Lost to work and live, yet remain undiscovered."

"That makes sense, I guess." It was a lie—I didn't get it at all. Gran and my mom were psychics, I'd met a Palm Reader, and there was Neil with his super brain. "There are a bunch of humans with extra traits in other offices?"

"I'd be hard pressed to find out that kind of information about other branches. Even around here, I don't know everyone at the substations. Do you think this is relevant to what happened to Clancy?"

"No." I sighed and slumped in the chair again. "I don't think I realized how others felt, is all."

"Don't let today be—"

Marty entered with two vending machine sandwiches and two sodas, and Hank stopped talking abruptly.

"Thanks, Marty. Sorry, Cassie, I didn't think to ask if you wanted anything," Hank said.

"Thanks. I'm not hungry," I said.

The hours passed by in a gloomy stupor. Once the agents and each floor of the building down to the first sub-basement was cleared, some of the restrictions were lifted. My office was still off limits and there was no way I was going into the control room and put up with the stares, so I stayed put.

On the plus side, right before the lockdown was lifted, Hank had me digitally sign some paperwork and I was officially an active agent again.

It felt like a huge let down after the day, though.

Around seven-thirty that evening we were allowed to leave. My cell phone sprang to life when I reached my car. Texts and messages started feeding into my phone, but I ignored them all.

A shower, a bed, and maybe some brain bleach would scrub out the images of Clancy falling back into a pool of his own blood. Shivering, I left the Farm as quickly as I could, not caring what it might look like. Once outside the gates, I rolled up my car windows, turned the radio up as loud as it would go, and blasted an eclectic blend of music you could loudly sing with.

It was a cathartic release, but mostly it filled my brain with the sound, which pushed out the thoughts and images. When I entered our little subdivision outside of town, I turned the music back down on low and rolled down the windows until I reached my house.

Entering the house, I dropped my purse with a clunk next to the door. "Gran, I'm home," I called, going straight to the kitchen since the light was on.

"She's out."

"Oh." I pulled up short, surprised to see Vincent sitting at the table. "Hey."

"I hope you don't mind that I let myself in through the back," Vincent said.

"You know you're always welcome. You have a key, after all. And, you made coffee." I smiled and poured myself a cup. "If you broke down the door, it would be okay as long as there's coffee made."

"I'll remember that."

I fixed my coffee and slid into a seat across from Vincent. "So, what have you heard?"

Vincent shook his head. "Not much. We received a few texts saying there was a lockdown, but until Hank texted Logan, we didn't even know if everyone was okay."

"Sorry. On my way home, I should have called or something. It was a long day, though."

Vincent didn't say anything, but waited for me to go on.

"It's... there was a murder at the office," I said. "Someone killed Clancy."

Vincent's face drew in, looking somber. "What happened?"

"No one knows yet. The surveillance video for the entire first floor had about ten minutes scrubbed clean."

"Deleted? How?"

"No one knows anything yet. Clancy had been stabbed. There was a noise, and I went to see what it was."

Vincent frowned, but didn't say anything.

"There was nothing in the hallway. No one was around, but when I went back to my office, there was blood coming out from under a door." I held back any waterworks that wanted to come out. "The door was locked. Agent Watts showed up while I was trying to get the door open. He tried to break it down, which didn't work out too well for him."

"I'm not familiar with Agent Watts," Vincent said.

"Me either, but he'll be the one with his arm in a sling." I tried to force a grin, but it didn't work. "Um, after that, I think I might have made a mistake."

This time, Vincent tensed. Not only could I see it, but also the air around him stilled.

I cleared my throat and played with my coffee cup. "We didn't know who was on the other side of the door or if they were alive. It seemed like the best way to move forward." I knew I was trying to justify what I did. "I used the Path to open the door."

"That doesn't sound too bad," Vincent said.

"Yeah, but, it was rushed and I didn't think I had time to be creative or use any sort of finesse."

"I'm not sure what you mean."

"Apparently, I don't either. I ripped the door open."

"When you say rip..."

"It was still on its hinges."

Vincent let out a huff of air that screamed frustration and disappointment.

"That's not fair," I crossed my arms defensively. "The first time it didn't budge, so I had to try a bit harder the next time."

"And Watts saw this?" Vincent kept his voice remarkably level.

"Yes. And everyone else that has seen the video." Which at that point was probably everyone in the building.

"People know what you do, though. How bad was it?" Vincent asked.

"It was more than I should have done, but it could have been a lot worse. I thought, well, we thought that we might be able to save him. But, then Clancy was there, and I could tell right away that we were too late."

"It was a tense moment. I'm sure everyone will assume the strength came from adrenaline or something."

I nodded without enthusiasm. I'm pretty sure it wasn't common knowledge I could do anything like that.

"Are you—"

A knock on the door cut Vincent off.

"I'll be right back," I said.

Once I cleared the kitchen, I sniffed and wiped the corners of my eyes to make sure I had kept myself in check.

Opening the door, I found Ethan on my doorstep.

"Hi." I forced myself to smile. "I'm surprised to see you."

"I hadn't heard back from you, so I wanted to stop by."

I ushered him through the living room. "Sorry, it's been a long day. I haven't had a chance to check my messages yet."

"That's okay, I—" Ethan stopped as he stepped into the kitchen.

"Good evening," Vincent sounded a bit stiff and formal, but polite.

"Sorry," Ethan said. He looked unsure about what to do, so he stayed where he was. "I should have waited for you to call. Is now a bad time?"

"No," I said.

"I should go." Vincent stood. I might have been the only one that could see it, but he looked reluctant. "Will you be here in the morning?"

"I'm not sure, but I'll need to be in the office early tomorrow," I said. "To make sure I'm in the clear."

Vincent nodded. "I'll see you tomorrow, then. Let me know if you need anything."

"Thanks," I said.

"Good evening to you as well, Ethan," Vincent said. He left through the back door, leaving silence in his wake.

"I'm glad you stopped by," I said after an awkward moment. "Do you want some coffee?"

"No, thank you," Ethan said rather stiffly.

"At least have a seat."

He stood there, looking uncomfortable, and then he glanced at the back door. "I don't think I should stay."

Sighing, I leaned back in my chair and tried not to get aggravated. "It was a difficult day at the office. Vincent was here to find out what happened."

Ethan nodded. "I understand."

"You're going to see Vincent and me together. He's my partner."

"I know." Ethan finally sat next to me. When he reached out and took my hand, I had a hopeful feeling.

Then I looked into his eyes.

"You're not going to be okay with this, are you?" I asked.

"This is something I don't think I'll be able to get past." Holding my hand, he rubbed the top with his other hand.

My eyes burned. "After everything you've seen? Frank? Meeting a bigfoot? You faced a fairy."

"It's been an amazing couple of months."

"And Vincent and I aren't... I mean, we're not..." I didn't know how to finish.

"I know you're not, but you share a soul." Ethan looked down and cleared his throat. "You share a soul with another man. I'm not sure how to handle that. It's not... I don't know. It's not normal."

"Huh." The lonesome chuckle fell short. "Has anything about me been normal?"

"I'm sorry, Cassie. I wanted it might be possible to move on, but seeing you two together—"

"Sitting in my kitchen, talking." I tried to keep the sarcasm out of my voice. Now wasn't the time.

"Even that. I'll be wondering what it is he's feeling from you. Wondering what he can sense that I can't." Ethan shifted in his seat. "When we're together, what is it that he feels?"

The question took me by surprise. "I can't answer that. It's not something we talk about on a regular basis. This is something that I can't change. Neither can Vincent."

"That is the problem."

I felt my face turn red. Before I had an outburst, he rushed on.

"It's not your problem. It's not even Vincent's problem. It's mine. I know that, and I hoped we could make it work, but I'm sorry, I don't think I can do this."

If he had gotten upset or blamed Vincent or me it would have given me something to yell about, but this? He sounded sad. Heartbroken, even.

Gently, I pulled my hand away.

Ethan sat back, looking down, not meeting my eye.

It had been moving toward this. I knew that, but it didn't make it any easier. Despite my best intentions, tears fell.

"So, this is it?" My voice cracked.

"It has to be," Ethan said. "If we went any further, it would feel like I was lying to you."

I nodded.

"I'm sure our jobs will cross paths." The trepidation in his voice was obvious.

"They will. Vincent and I both may run into you."

"Will you be okay with that?"

I forced a half grin, through the tears. "Will you?"

"I don't have anything against Vincent, and you know I have feelings for you. That hasn't changed. So, yeah, it'll be awkward, at least at first."

Sniffing, I nodded. "I'm sorry." Dammit, my voice cracked again.

Ethan stood and took my hand. When I stood, he pulled me into a hug. "I'm the one that's sorry." His voice was soft and sincere. "I really wish I could make this work."

I half laughed. "Me too."

We stood there, hugging, neither one of us wanting to be the first to let go. When you let go, it's over. We'd be done.

Ethan was the first to pull away. "I should go."

I nodded, not trusting my voice to say anything. He must not have been ready to let me go completely, because he kept my hand in his until he reached the door.

"Goodbye, Cassie. I'll see you around."

"Yeah," I said. "Take care."

"You too."

Watching him get in the car and drive away was like a special kind of torture to myself. However, karma paid me back immediately in the form of Gran coming home. Ducking my head, I wiped my eyes before waving to Dee Dee. Gran had two bags in her hands, so I went to relieve her of the packages.

She patted me on the arm and turned to Dee Dee. "Tomorrow morning, right?"

"You bet. I don't want to miss the view." Dee Dee cackled and waved again. She waited until we were in the house before driving away.

"What view?" I asked, taking the brown paper bags to the kitchen. My voice was almost as morose as my mood.

"Dee Dee has a new man she's chasin'," Gran said. "I don't know what she's thinking, since the man must be nearly eighty. I told her he's too old for her, but he has his own hair and teeth, so she thinks he's hot stuff."

I nodded, not paying too much attention.

"How are you feelin', sugar?" Gran asked. "No, don't answer that. That's a silly question. I've got wine and ice cream. Once we get settled in front of the TV, you can let it all out."

The tears that had died away started to come back. "You brought ice cream?"

"Of course," Gran said. "Ben and Jerry's is the first step to get over any break-up. No woman should have to get by without those men in her life. Although, you could make do with wine. We've got both."

"Thanks, Gran. How much do you know?"

"Never mind that. You tell me what you need to, but first, go get in your pjs. We're going to do this right."

Gran busied herself pulling out bowls, spoons, and wine glasses. I interrupted her with a hug, which she returned before shooing me upstairs.

And we did it right. No one could do a break-up like Gran. Even Mom would have agreed with that. We talked for a while. Once I got the worst of it out, I was forced to admit I knew this was coming. And while, yes, I was sad and my heart hurt, I wasn't devastated. After Ethan had walked out the first time, when I told him about the Lost, I had been bracing myself for the time when he would walk out for good.

My world was too much. Remembering the look on Agent Watts' face on the video when I opened the door, and Agent Paulson's face when I asked if he wanted me to read the Path at the office, I had come to the conclusion that even for people in my world, dealing with me might be too much. Shattered soul, powers that were stronger than anyone could expect, fragments of other souls littered through me, and the memories of I don't know how many Lost mixing with my owns.

No one deserved to have to deal with that.

Before I went to bed, Gran said something that took me by surprise.

"None of us know what's going to happen tomorrow. Not even me. We can't give up before we start." Then she looked lost in thought. "That's truer than even I thought. I don't see what's going to happen tomorrow."

Her distant look made me uneasy. "Everything okay, Gran?"

"Well, I was visiting your mother today. It's her house. All those fake plants she insists on keeping around sap the future right out of me."

"How's Mom doing?" I asked. Visiting Mom wasn't typical, especially considering the fact that it was a workday. Mom never misses a workday unless it's serious.

"She's having a hard time, I think," Gran said.

"With Bob? What's wrong?"

"Bob's been sick lately, and your mom needs help with a few things."

"Oh," I said, not knowing what to say to that. "Is there anything I can do? Does she need anything?"

"Not yet, but I expect she will," Gran said. "You should run and get some sleep. You have a full day tomorrow, right?"

"Yeah. I'm not sure what to expect."

Gran chuckled. "Even I don't always know."

CHAPTER
FOUR

Unsure if I was still a suspect in yesterday's murder, I went into the office early. The command room was more crowded than usual, but the atmosphere had calmed down. It was subdued compared to the frenzy of the hunt the day before. Now, everyone was more resigned in going about their business.

Gone were the stares of yesterday as well. There were a few glances, but my return to work was yesterday's news.

"Hey, Hank," I said, going straight to our handler. "I didn't get the chance to get my computer access yesterday. Um, is there anything new?"

"Yes and no." Hank leaned back in his chair and I saw the deep, dark circles under his eyes. "We know more about how the recordings were scrambled, but there's not much we can do about it."

"Is there anything I can do?"

"No, we've got our techs, and techs from Washington, going over the footage. I'm not sure if Paulson has anything new, but I expect we'll find out sometime today."

"What's on my agenda for the day? Do I join Logan again?"

"Later today. This morning, you're with Boone."

"Agent Boone? Why am I with him?" The idea of working with an outsider made me uncomfortable. Besides MyTH, I'd never worked much with someone outside of my team.

"Paulson is going to be interviewing your team this morning. Standard procedure, but who knows when he'll get to them. Boone met them yesterday. This morning, he's joining the specialists that will be sealing the gremlin portal."

Despite my unease of working with someone new, this piqued my interest.

"It'll give you two a chance to meet and you can both join up with Logan later today."

"Do you know how they close the portal?" I asked.

"From what I hear, they're a bit like you and Clan... Well, you and Vincent now, I guess." Hank clicked a few keys, uncomfortable with thinking about Clancy in the past tense.

I couldn't blame him. It was hard to believe he was gone.

"Anyway," Hank said, scrubbing his face with his hands, "this portal was forced open and it's clearly unstable. They use their abilities to seal the world away at that point."

"Rider's going to miss the gremlins." The attempt at lightening the mood wasn't great, but it did the trick.

"Yeah, who would have thought a werewolf would look forward to catching gremlins. Maybe it's the chase?"

Not having thought of that, I grinned. "That could be."

"Let me get your log in information and you can get caught up with whatever you can this morning."

Hank took a tablet from his drawer and after what seemed like one hundred taps and swipes, he had me enter a password and scan my thumbprint.

"Here's your cell phone back. You're good to go," Hank said. He took a moment to look around the room. "Your office is open this morning, but everything past that is closed. It looks like we have a few desks out here still unoccupied. I'm not sure when the night shift will go this morning, but day shift is starting to show up early today, so they're filling fast."

"Thanks, Hank."

There was one desk off to the side this morning. It seemed like everyone wanted to be here, but no one wanted to be in the middle of things. At least that's how I felt, so I chose a place at random. I didn't have to go far, but I noticed an office worker not looking at me, walk around the desk I was passing, giving me a wide berth. Shaking my head, I sat the tablet down, claiming the desk, and looked around. No one stared like they had yesterday, which was a relief. Maybe he was being polite and giving me space.

For some reason, when Hank said, 'catch up,' I thought he was joking. Turns out, he wasn't. There were reports from the team to read from while I was gone and what seemed like a thousand emails.

Reading through the emails, my brain started to blank on what I was seeing as I clicked mindlessly through the list.

"Good morning, Agent Heidrich."

I had expected Agent Boone to track me down, but Paulson found me first.

"You look beat," I said without thinking. We knew each other, but he had always been a coworker in the background until he had taken over a case for the team a month or so ago. "Sorry, I mean, you should take a seat."

"I think I will." He dragged a chair over from the desk behind me. He rolled it over—beside me instead of across from me—and sat, watching the room.

He didn't seem inclined to talk at the moment, so I clicked through a few more emails, mostly announcements that were no longer relevant, and let him sit.

Peeking around my monitor, I noticed Paulson was getting the stares I had received yesterday, although never when he was looking directly at anyone.

"Sorry, Agent Heidrich," Paulson said at last, turning to me. "I got lost in my thoughts for a moment there."

"It's no wonder," I said, "and you can call me Cassie."

A ghost of a grin flitted across his face. "Thanks. Everyone is more formal around me today instead of less."

"Oh." Should I have offered my first name or stuck with the agent? Too late now.

"I'm not sure if I'm the pariah, or if they're afraid they're going to be labeled one." He sounded sad as he spoke and I felt for him. Having to interrogate your own coworkers couldn't be easy.

"Don't worry about it," I said, wanting to try to lighten the heavy load he put on himself. "I got all the stares yesterday; it's just your turn today. Once this is over, it'll be someone else."

"Could be. Not the first day back you intended, is it?"

"Not in the least."

"Were you close to Clancy?"

Was he questioning me or did he ask to be nice? Either way, the answer was the same, but hard to explain. "Not close, but..." I tried to put words around the relationship. "I mean, we worked together when we needed to on a case." Even though my feelings on the subject were strong and raw, it was hard to put my thoughts into words.

"You were going to say something else." He sounded interested instead of questioning.

It could have been a tactic to interrogate coworkers, but again, it didn't matter. "It's a little different." Feeling awkward, I glanced around and leaned in, not wanting to have others hear. "He was a clairvoyant and I'm a Reader."

He interrupted before I could continue. "They're different though, right?"

"Yeah. I mean, there's some crossover, but not much. The thing is though, we're both, I don't know, outsiders. We're different. Vincent too. Coworkers treat us differently, and they're sometimes leery of us." I shrugged, trying to play it down.

Paulson looked like he thought hard on what I said. "I guess I didn't realize."

"You see it with the Lost too. They have something in common that others don't relate to. Some humans don't like them. And I know you've seen people steer clear of Vincent."

"Vincent's another story. You and Clancy are normal, though."

I shook my head and looked around. There were a few office workers and agents in the small kitchenette area off the control room. One of them was the same guy who had walked around me earlier.

"Vincent's no different than the rest of us. I'll give you an idea of what it's like." I sighed, turned off my computer screen, and stood. "Watch me and the others."

I plastered a small smile on my face and went straight to the coffee machine. "Hi," I said brightly as I approached.

The smiles were courteous, and I received a few nods and a good morning before the room cleared out of all but one agent. He also smiled while I mixed up my coffee.

"It's good to see you back in the office," the agent said.

In my periphery, I noticed his eyes look me up and down. It took everything I had not to roll my eyes.

"Thanks," I said.

He leaned closer, taking the coffee pot and brushing against my arm. Getting coffee for both Paulson and myself, I went back to my desk.

He had his arms crossed and was frowning.

"I wasn't sure how you like your coffee, so I brought some cream and sugar," I said.

He nodded and took a cream and sugar, not saying anything.

My computer screen stuttered to life and I logged back in. I scrolled through a few more emails before looking at Paulson. Once again, he watched the room.

Maybe I shouldn't have said anything. Oh well, too late now. Besides, how was that something he had never noticed before?

"It's always like that?" he asked after a while.

"With some people," I said.

"And there's always people like that around the office? I wouldn't have expected it with all that we see."

I shrugged. "Just because you're in this job doesn't mean you're comfortable with everything around you."

"Yeah, but you get used to it." He was quiet again for a minute. "Have I ever... I mean we've worked together some and..."

I thought of his reaction yesterday when I had offered to read the Path and shook my head. "Don't worry about it. Honestly, it's rare that I even notice anymore. It's the way things are, and like you said, you get used to it."

"I have to ask this for the case. Have you ever noticed anyone who was more uncomfortable with you or Clancy?"

Giving the question due consideration, I tried to run through anyone that had stood out. "Not that I noticed."

"Did Clancy ever mention anyone giving him a hard time?"

Frowning, I thought about the few times I had seen Clancy on the job with others around. "I think a few people didn't like it when he told them not to touch anything. But that could be because they didn't think they needed the reminder."

"You think like I do. It's hard to look at your coworkers and not give them the benefit of the doubt," he said.

"Are you positive it is someone who works here?" I asked.

Looking weary, he rubbed his hands over his face again. "No, but it's the most likely option. What do you know about Agent Boone?"

"Only that he's an agent who's here to watch our team. Logan, Rider, or Vincent could tell you more. They were with him yesterday."

"I keep finding myself looking at him, but he had already left the building when Clancy was killed."

"Do we have a time of death, then?" I didn't actually want to know the answer to that, but needed to know all the same.

"It's only an estimated time of death. A window, but the doctor was there early enough to make the window short. We think when you heard the noises was when the incident occurred."

Nodding, I swallowed hard and looked away, concentrating on my computer until I knew my tear ducts were once again under control. Why had I asked? It was my exact worries come true. He had died while I listened from the other room.

"There's no way you could have known," Paulson said.

"You don't know that," I said.

"Now that you do know, what do you think the noises were?"

Thinking about the sounds, I couldn't place anything. "It was a storage closet. Had things fallen off the shelves?"

"One thing looked like it had been knocked over."

I thought back and frowned. "Did the person clean up after himself?"

"Not that we can tell."

"Nothing else was out of place?" I asked.

"A vent duct cover that had been knocked off."

"Do you think the person went through there?" Why was he talking to me if he had a lead?

"Not that we can tell. It would have to be someone really small, likely not human, and there's still dust in the duct."

"Is it smaller than anything we have on the Farm?"

"No, but I have teams out interviewing everyone."

"Is there anything I can do to help?" I asked, wondering why he had sat down here.

"You've already helped. I know more now than I knew yesterday. I'll catch up with your team today to get information on Agent Boone, but I'm afraid that's a dead end."

"I'll be out with him this morning. If I see anything odd, I'll let you know."

"You're going out without your team?"

"Guess so. Only for the morning."

Paulson frowned, but didn't say anything.

"I know I asked yesterday," I said, pushing the idea once more while he was distracted. "But the offer still stands. If you want me to read the Path in the hallway, let me know. I'm not sure what I can find this far out, but if I'm lucky, I might be able to see everything."

"I'm not sure what you mean."

It was my turn to frown and feel confused. "It's what I do. Read what happened at the location. Find a Path and track it if I can."

"Is that what you did to the door?"

"Something like that. It was the adrenaline, though. It had to be." I could feel my face blushing, which sucked. I was usually a much better liar than this. "But somehow, I was able to see the door's Path and pull on it."

He nodded, but didn't reply.

Oh well, I had made the offer. It was strange, he didn't take me up on it, but I let it drop.

"Looks like your team has arrived," Paulson said.

Looking around, I saw Logan and Rider entering the room. Vincent wasn't far behind.

"You were wondering if you ever treated us differently." I was pushing things, knowing I shouldn't. Office politics could be like putting your finger in a beehive.

"Yes?" Paulson asked, watching Vincent come our way while Logan and Rider went to see Hank.

"Think about how you look at Vincent."

"Vincent's different."

"Is he?" I asked. "You saw him a few weeks ago in the field, injured and exhausted after taking on a threat. Much like you are now. Well, not the injured part. He's different because he's treated that way, along with rumor and myth."

Vincent was close enough that Paulson didn't reply beyond a nod. His reaction spoke volumes, though.

"Morning," Paulson said when Vincent walked up.

"Good morning," Vincent replied, barely giving the man a glance.

It had been done so often to him that I think Vincent expected Paulson to walk away, but he didn't. Vincent kept his emotions so closely guarded that no one around seemed to be able to see beyond the indifferent mask he always wore. I could read him like a book, though, and when Paulson didn't walk away, Vincent looked wary.

"Would you like some coffee?" Paulson asked, raising his almost empty cup. "I was on my way to get more."

"Thank you, but I'm good." Vincent's tone was careful and calculating, as though he was trying to discern what angles Paulson was playing.

The coffee was going a bit far. Asking a Walker to take coffee when he didn't know you well was a little like offering a fairy food. If they didn't trust you, they'd dust you and chase you away, assuming you were trying to poison them.

Paulson nodded. "I'll need to interview your team, but I'll grab you all sometime this morning so you won't have to stick around here all day."

"We'll be here until you need us," Vincent said.

"Thanks again, Cassie." Paulson looked more exhausted than he had before he sat down. "Let me know when you think of something else."

"Sure," I said. "And try to get some rest. I know from experience that Dr. Yelton will track you down and make you if you don't do it voluntarily." It was a stretch and we all knew it, but it got the point across.

Paulson smiled and patted my arm. "Thanks again. I'll see you later." He headed straight for the coffee pot.

Vincent leaned against my desk and watched him go.

"Everything okay?" I asked.

"Anything I should know before I meet with him?" Vincent countered.

"Not that I know of."

"What were you all talking about?"

"He's asking everyone about Clancy. Standard stuff."

Vincent chuckled with what sounded like real amusement. "Standard? I don't see him thanking me and patting my arm."

I rolled my eyes. "Cute. I've seen you get a pat on the back before."

"You're right, though," Vincent said, ignoring my comment. "He looks like he could use a break. I'm surprised Hank hasn't said anything."

"Hopefully, he'll take one today. Hank's not his handler on this, though."

Vincent nodded and looked around the room. "It's a packed house today."

I nodded and went back to flipping through emails.

"I wanted to apologize about last night," Vincent said.

"For what?" I asked.

Vincent looked uncomfortable and kept his eyes on the room. "I'm pretty sure me being there upset Ethan. It wasn't my intention to cause a disagreement."

Reminders about Ethan were like a stab to the heart, but I tried my best not to show it. "You should know he doesn't have anything against you."

"Huh," Vincent scoffed.

"He was sincere."

"Why should Ethan have anything against Vincent?" Rider asked.

I hadn't seen him approach, and I wasn't appreciating the accusatory look he gave me.

"He shouldn't, and he doesn't," I said, sounding a bit too defensive.

"I would if I was him," Vincent muttered.

Shaking my head, I went back to my emails.

"I do not understand," Rider said.

"It's okay," I said. "No one's upset with Vincent."

Vincent made another noise of disagreement under his breath, and I narrowed my eyes at him.

"You're not helping," I said.

"*You* are not helping," Rider said.

Rider had been pushing my buttons for what seemed like ages, and the moment I realized his comment was directed toward me, I lost my cool.

I squared my shoulders and narrowed my eyes. "You know that—"

"Agent Heidrich."

We had company, great. Looking up, I tried not to frown too hard at Agent Boone as he approached.

CHAPTER

FIVE

"We met yesterday morning," Agent Boone said.

"Yes, it's good to see you again." That sounded like a lie, but Rider was getting under my skin.

"You too," Boone said, rather formally. "I spoke with the director and she said you've been released from the inquiries today. She asked that you take me and the other out-of-town team to the portal they'll be closing this morning."

"Yeah, happy to help." Happy to get the heck out of here was more like it.

"You can use our truck." Vincent dug out the keys. "It hasn't been used in a few weeks, but there's still plenty of plastic in case of gremlins."

"Thanks," I said. The anger toward Rider dissipated, but the disappointment in the direction our friendship was taking stuck with me.

"The others are in with the director now," Agent Boone said. "They should be a few more minutes."

"I'll bring the truck around in a minute and meet you all up front," I said.

"Thank you. Vincent, Rider, we'll join you and Logan this afternoon," Boone said.

"Will this work with the four of us together?" Rider asked after Agent Boone walked away.

Vincent shrugged. "There's no reason why it wouldn't."

"Really?" I crossed my arms and looked pointedly at Rider. "Because I can think of a few things that aren't working now."

"Cassie returned to work only yesterday," Rider said, taking a sidelong look at me. "I am not certain everyone will mesh well."

"Is this the way friends act where you're from?" I snapped at Rider. "Because this friendship appears to be sunk."

Rider looked upset. "I do not know what you mean."

"What?" My temper was building. "Cause where I'm sitting, things are far from friendly anymore."

"Let's take a step back," Vincent said.

"No," I said, feeling hurt. "I'm taking my steps elsewhere." I stalked off to the parking lot, leaving my team behind me.

Regret welled up the moment the front doors clicked shut, but I forced myself to move on. Rider had been either ignoring me or growling at me almost every time we'd gotten together and it had to stop. But I had no idea what I had done to raise his hackles.

It was worse when I got into Vincent and Rider's SWAT-style truck. They'd been riding with Logan while I was off work, but the scent of Rider still lingered in the air. Not strong, but the clean, woodsy smell was never strong. Instead, it lingered wherever he made himself comfortable for long periods of time.

It must have been a werewolf thing. The truck growled to life and I drove up to the entrance to meet Agent Boone and whoever else would be joining us. I found Logan waiting for me. I hadn't seen him outside of my house in weeks and my mouth dropped open.

Letting the truck idle in park with the AC on, I climbed out.

"Howdy partner," Logan said, tipping his hat.

How had no one warned me about the cowboy hat? "Is that a Stetson?"

"You bet," Logan said. "They match the boots."

Looking down. I saw that, sure enough, he was wearing cowboy boots. "They look new."

"Haven't had a chance to break them in yet."

"They look good."

Logan grinned. "Thank ya kindly."

Seeing the elf smile was infectious, and I felt the corners of my mouth turn up, despite my best efforts.

"Quite the ruckus inside," Logan said.

Blowing out a loud breath, I looked at the sky. "I know. I shouldn't have been upset with him."

"Well, seems to me it's a long time coming. The timing's not great, though."

"Yeah, I guess. It's been a bad couple of days, but I should have explained things or talked to him or something instead of getting upset."

Logan nodded. "I think what happened yesterday has everyone out of sorts."

"I've got to run these guys over to the gremlin portal and spend the morning working with Agent Boone. Will you let Rider know I'm sorry? Tell him we can talk after work or something, if he's still willing to talk to me."

"I'll let him know. I'm not sure you're the one in the wrong here, though."

"Overall, I don't think so, either. But I shouldn't have said what I did."

"It'll be good to work together again this afternoon," Logan said.

"I'm glad someone thinks so. Anything I should know about Agent Boone before I go out?"

"Seems a good sort. A bit stiff, but easy to get along with."

"That's good. Know anything about the others?"

"Not a thing. They came in today and have kept to themselves. I'd join you, but I think Paulson would have my ears if I left before talking with him."

"Could be."

"Sounds like the team you're escorting is on its way," Logan said.

"I'll take your word for it." Even with his ears curled away, Logan's hearing far surpassed my own.

"It's good to have you back on board. I'm going to mosey." He tipped his hat again and then walked out to the parking lot.

Before I could get back in the truck, Agent Boone exited the building with two other men, one tall and blond and one short and brunette. The pair looked odd standing next to each other.

"Agent Heidrich," Agent Boone said, "these are Agents Dempsey and Walden. They're going to be closing up the portal today."

"Nice to meet you," I said, offering my hand to shake. The tall man gripped a bag tightly and looked at the shorter of the two, which I think was Walden.

Agent Walden only nodded and got into the truck without saying anything. Looking nervous, Agent Dempsey followed suit, nodding and getting into the back of the truck.

"They're not very talkative," Agent Boone said.

"I see that," I said. "Are we all ready, then?"

"Yes, I think we're set to go."

"Alright," I said, going to the driver's side and getting in. "If it gets too warm back there, let me know."

Once again, Dempsey looked to Walden, but neither said anything.

"As you know," Agent Boone started, "I met with your teammates yesterday. It gave me a chance to get to know them and get a feel for the team."

"That's good." I said it because I had nothing else to say. My concentration was still back at the office and with my team.

"Today, I'd like to ask you a few questions and see how you work before we join your team."

"Do you mind if I ask you something?" I asked.

This appeared to stump Agent Boone. "This exercise is about me viewing your team, but if it helps, I can answer questions as well."

He didn't sound happy about it, but I didn't much care.

"What's this for?" I asked.

"Most of that is confidential." Agent Boone's eyes strayed to the rear-view mirror, but at his angle, I don't think there was anything he could see. "What I can tell you, however, is that I will be overseeing a group of talented individuals that has been formed to complete certain tasks for our organization."

"That doesn't sound ominous or anything," I muttered.

"I'm sorry?" Agent Boone frowned.

"Sorry, it's nothing."

"I suppose you've had a difficult time the past twenty-four hours," Agent Boone said. He didn't sound happy, but since he was making an excuse for what I had said, I supposed I was still in the clear.

"What types of tasks is this new group going to perform?"

"I'm not certain that's relevant."

"I guess that depends on what it is you're looking for in our team."

"I think I understand why you're asking," Agent Boone said. "But I'm reviewing the teamwork and interaction, not the execution of orders."

"Do you think the type of cases, or orders as you put it, affect the interactions?" I asked.

"No." He was adamant with his answer, so I didn't press the issue.

He was wrong, of course, but I could tell from his attitude that he was uncomfortable with my line of questioning and starting to grow agitated, so I let it drop.

"You could be right," I said. "What types of questions did you want to ask?"

"Let's start slow. Tell me about your teammates."

"Okay, but you've met them."

Agent Boone cleared his throat and took a moment to respond. "I have them, but I would like to hear what you have to say about them from your point of view."

"You asked them these questions?"

"Yes."

"With everyone all together?" I asked.

"Yes," Agent Boone said, a little more forcefully.

It seemed strange to think anyone would ask someone to tell you about the guy standing next to him, but I answered anyway. "Logan was my mentor. Still is. We mostly work together as a team. When a larger case comes along, we team with Rider and Vincent."

Agent Boone didn't say anything for a few moments. I'm not sure if he was expecting more, but that was all he was going to get.

"How do you feel about the traits the members of your team have?" Agent Boone asked.

"Traits? I don't feel any particular way about their traits."

This wasn't going well. I could feel the frustration rolling off Boone, even with the Path closed.

"Do you feel that being a member of the Lost has affected the work of Logan or Rider?" Agent Boone's voice was starting to become clipped.

Trying to do better, I thought the question over. "I think they have more empathy than other agents might have. I've never worked for long with a human partner, though."

"I see," Agent Boone said. "Do you feel not having a baseline human partner has affected the way you work?"

"The way that I personally work? Um, I don't think so. I think that having Logan as a mentor has made me a better agent than I would have been if I had been matched with anyone else."

"What makes you think that?"

This was beginning to feel like a nightmare pop quiz where I didn't know the answers. The urge to look down and make sure my pants were still on was strong.

However, I resisted and tried to come up with a decent answer. "Agent Seale has more experience than most agents, not only with this world, but with other dimensions and the Lost. He has a good rapport with those he works with, both Lost and human. Even after a year, I learn something new almost every day."

Sure, some of those things were how to drive cattle and what a modern-day dude ranch looks like, but Agent Boone didn't need to know that.

"Tell me about your relationship with Logan," Agent Boone said.

"He's my partner and mentor. I already said that."

"But you live almost next door. Are you friends outside of work?"

"Oh, sure. He stops by before and after work most days and his kids come over and spend time with my grandmother."

"Has your relationship ever been intimate?"

That question took a few moments to sink in, but when it did, I started laughing. "Are you serious?"

"Yes, I am serious. These are serious questions," Agent Boone said.

His sincerity caused me to laugh louder. "No," I was finally able to sputter out. "Not intimate. He's a bit old for me, don't you think?"

"I wouldn't know," Agent Boone said.

"Did you ask the others this?" I asked, striving to rein in my amusement.

Agent Boone rubbed his forehead and didn't reply.

Biting my lip, I tried to let the laughter die away. "We're almost there." I looked back at the men in the back seat, noting Agent Dempsey looked nervous. "We have to park off the gravel road up here, and then there's about a two-mile walk. You might want to start checking your pockets now."

"Checking our pockets?" Agent Dempsey asked, sounding as nervous as he looked.

Agent Walden frowned at the man, but didn't say anything.

"There's no gremlins out here right now," I said. "But if any come out while we're here, you're not going to want to have any metal on you."

No one said anything else, but I had a feeling Agent Dempsey was new at what he did. He looked to be in his early thirties, but humans with abilities sometimes got a later start in the job. Either that or this was something new he'd learned or was still learning.

I parked the truck and dug out one of the gremlin-safe field bags. There was some metal stored away inside, under layers of plastic, but the majority of the bag contained nothing metallic, including the bag construction.

"In case of emergency," I said, jingling the keys in my hand, "these will be here." I indicated a magnetic key holder. "Which will be above the front, driver-side tire."

"That's metal," Agent Dempsey said. "What happens if the gremlins get the key?"

I grinned. "If the gremlins get to the truck, you're not going to have to worry about the key anymore."

Agent Boone was still not looking amused, but this time, his attention was on Agent Dempsey. I almost felt sorry for the guy.

"Since you are familiar with the terrain," Agent Boone said, "do you have a suggested formation?"

"It doesn't need to be so formal," I said.

Agent Boone didn't look happy with that response, either, so I tried not to roll my eyes while coming up with something better.

"Two by two will work here," I said. Glancing at Agent Dempsey, I thought about that. "With me and Agent Dempsey in the lead. Although one by one also works, with me in the lead and Agent Boone in the back." I had a feeling Agent Dempsey and Walden were specialists, not your average field agents. As much as I didn't care for Agent Boone, I'd feel better with him bringing up the rear, rather than the others.

Agent Boone seemed to approve. Instead of being happy about that, it only aggravated me. I didn't need his approval here.

"Agent Boone, I'm going to call and make sure we're logged. Do you want to make sure everyone's ready to move out?"

"Yes, ma'am," Agent Boone said.

I walked to the other side of the truck and down the road a bit to try to get out of earshot while I called Hank.

"This is Hank."

"Hey, Hank, it's me," I said. "We've stopped and are getting ready to walk to the portal."

"Things going well?"

"Not that I can tell."

Hank chuckled.

"Listen, do you know anything about Agent Dempsey?"

"Not a lot," Hank said.

"Is he new to this job?"

"No, he's been working with portals for almost ten years now."

"Is his partner new?"

"He's been training Agent Walden for over twelve months now. Why do you ask?"

"No reason." Maybe I had gotten their names mixed up.

"Cassie, what's going on?" Hank asked.

"It's nothing. I just want to make sure you've got us logged."

"Are you sure?"

"Yeah, we're fine."

"I have you logged. Is there anything else I need to know?"

"I'm not sure how long it takes these guys to work, but we have to leave the phone behind."

A voice chimed in behind me. "It should take us around an hour."

I jumped and saw Agent Walden not far away. "You startled me." I laughed it off.

"Hank, Agent Walden says that it will take them around an hour," I said.

"Right," Hank said. "With the walk, I expect to hear back from you within two and a half hours."

"It sounds like we should be back by then."

"I'll have a satellite in that area as well."

"I doubt that'll be necessary," I said.

"Maybe we'll get some interesting readings."

"That's a good point. Talk to you in a few hours."

I hung up the phone and turned back to the group at large. "We're logged, and Hank's expecting contact within the next three hours."

"Sounds good," Agent Boone said. He was standing behind the others and taking in his surroundings. His gaze kept falling back on Agent Walden.

"Is everyone metal-free?" I asked.

"Yes, ma'am, as much as possible, " Agent Boone said.

The others stayed quiet.

I'm not sure what Agent Boone meant by saying they were as metal free as possible, but if he was holding on to some piece of metal, I wasn't going to argue with him over it.

"Let's head out, then." I tossed my phone back into the truck, put the gear bag on like a backpack, and walked into the woods.

We'd been here so frequently in the past nine months that there was a visible path. They didn't need me to lead, but I felt better doing so. It must have been Gran's influence. They were guests and it was my job to show them around. The trail started out flat, but it wasn't long before we were skirting a small bluff and going up and down some rather rocky hills.

I called for a break about three-fourths of the way there. Not for myself, but because Agent Walden appeared to be more out of shape than he looked.

"Once we get there, what are you two going to do?" I asked, trying to make small talk.

"What do you mean?" Agent Dempsey asked.

The man needed meds or something—his anxiety was through the roof.

"She means," Agent Walden said gruffly, "how are you and I going to close the portal."

"Oh," Agent Dempsey said. "Uh, mostly—mostly, the only thing you'll probably notice is us standing around, staring at nothing."

"And while you're staring at nothing, what are you actually doing?" I asked.

"With a reoccurring portal like this," Agent Dempsey said, "to me, to us, it's as if the portal is still there, only buried slightly. That's because the pathway between worlds is still there, but doesn't have enough power to stay open all the time. We shift things around a little until we can close the entire connection between dimensions." By the time Agent Dempsey was done with his explanation, he seemed calmer.

Since Agent Walden appeared to have his breath back, we moved on.

"What do you think that looks like between the worlds?" I asked Agent Dempsey.

"That's an interesting question," he said. "We've often speculated about that. There's a nexus point in the Antarctic with enough energy to keep a portal permanently open. We haven't found a way to close it. The major theory is that the portal burrowed a permanent hole through the area between dimensions."

"That sounds interesting," I said. And I meant it too. I didn't know much about the area between dimensions, but the idea of some sort of natural wall or tube cutting through it sounded like it would be interesting to see.

"It does. It would take a Walker to tell us for sure, though, so I doubt we'll ever know," he said.

"Why don't you ask one?" I asked.

Agent Dempsey chuckled. There was a hint of nervousness behind it, but he was obviously more comfortable talking about his area of expertise. "I'd rather keep my soul, thanks all the same. Even if you found a Walker, who would talk to one?"

"What?" My voice was shrill, even to me, but I didn't care. "Why wouldn't—"

"Agent Heidrich," Agent Boone interrupted.

It was a good interruption, because I was steamed. It was that kind of prejudice that makes Vincent so closed off. There's also the possibility that it was the type of thinking that had gotten Clancy killed.

CHAPTER
SIX

"Yes, Agent Boone?" I asked, trying to maintain some sense of professionalism.

"As interesting as this is," Agent Boone said, "I was wondering if we were nearing our destination, and if we are, what is our plan?"

"Excellent questions," I said, moving quicker, not caring if the others kept up. "We're getting close to the location. Before our *friends* here," I made the word friend sound as sarcastic as possible, "do their thing, we're going to make a wide circle around the location and drop some metal filings. If we have any rogue gremlins, that will lure them out."

"Is it likely there are any in the area?" Agent Walden asked.

"No," I said. "There's nothing on satellite. Even though they're small, we check the area regularly. The nearby junkyard and the surroundings have shown no activity, and there have been no reports of odd things happening in the tri-county area that may be gremlin related."

"Then why the filings?" Agent Walden asked.

I gritted my teeth, but didn't turn around. "Before you

shut the doorway to someone's home, you should always double check, no matter how sure you are there's no one left behind."

"That's fairly standard procedure," Agent Boone said with a hint of accusation in his voice.

"Most teams tend to make sure that the site is ready for us by the time we arrive," Agent Walden said defensively.

"We've cleared the area recently," I said. "And no portal has been opened since then, but it's best practice to make one last check." No one argued, but I could feel the tension building behind me. "We'll start circling around here."

Slinging the bag off my shoulder, I dug out a tightly sealed plastic jar and dumped a few small pieces of metal. Dropping a few at a time, I made a wide circle around where I knew the portal opened. Every now and again, I'd pause to listen for activity before moving on. When our circuit was complete, I closed up the metal in its encasement once again.

"You don't make a trail closer to the portal?" Agent Boone asked.

It wasn't an accusation, but a genuine question.

"We don't." It was a chore to keep my voice level. "If the portal opens at any point while we're here, we don't want to lure any gremlins over. Although, our soil is usually enough to make them curious anyway."

"Sensible," Agent Boone said approvingly. "I've never worked directly with gremlins."

"If you want to learn more about their reactions and behavior, Rider would be a good source," I said. "He takes as many of the gremlin calls as he can."

"I might do that during my stay," Agent Boone said.

"The portal opens here," I said, pointing to an area where the ground was scored.

"Uh, we'll get started, then, I guess," Agent Dempsey said.

"Will Agent Boone and I be in the way?" I asked. Now that I was out here, I had no idea what I should be doing.

"Actually," Agent Walden said, "you both may be of some use here. Dempsey, why don't you position the agents?"

Agent Dempsey hesitated. "Are you sure you want me to do this?"

"Yes, of course." Walden must have seen the nervous look on my face. "Don't worry; he knows what he's doing. You won't have any real involvement. You're more of a focal point."

Agent Dempsey was eyeing the marks the portal had left. Grooves had been bored into the soil.

"Agent Boone, can I have you stand right here?" Dempsey asked.

The spot he indicated was about a foot in front of the portal.

"Isn't that a bit close?" I asked.

"Not at all," Agent Walden said. "We're closing the portal, after all, not opening it."

I shrugged. I was sure they knew their job, but I didn't think I'd want to stand that close, and I was thankful they didn't try to put me there.

"Agent Heidrich," Agent Dempsey came over, staring at the ground, looking from Boone's feet then back to mine, "I need you right around here."

"Sure," I said. I was left facing Boone, who was maybe five yards away. How we would be used as focal points wasn't obvious, but I was curious.

"That's it, then. Agent Walden will stand over there to the left of the portal. I'll stand to the right and we'll get this closed," Dempsey said.

As I stood there, a thousand questions started to form in my head, but Agent Dempsey was already sweating and looking anxious. I didn't want to add to his stress level.

Besides, maybe I could get some answers on my own. My eyes shut automatically when I took a deep breath. The meditation was starting to pay off. When I reached the edge of my knowledge of the world, I looked out into a black abyss, ready to make the jump into the Path. Glittering shards of soul, both mine and others, lay stretched out on the blackness. I was getting used to seeing it. The leap to the Path was becoming easier.

When I opened my eyes again, it was to a shimmering overlay of our own world. The colors were vivid, and everything flowed as though moving through a river. Concentrating a bit harder, I dammed up that river until there was only a stream.

I'm amazed I had never thought to open the Path when taking one of the gremlin calls. I had seen portals before; we had several at the office. When those portals were open, however, they dragged the Path down, with my power alongside it. I had seen a natural portal like this one once before, but I hadn't known what I was looking at, at the time. That one was long past closed.

The portal itself had a Path. There was a glowing ring standing inches away from Boone. It was shiny white and had balls of light, power maybe, flowing around the circle of the portal.

It was beautiful. I could sit here, watch those little balls of light zip around their circle for hours, and be amused the whole time. It wasn't what I had expected when Dempsey started to work. I saw his power billow out in front of him. Instead of strands like around the portal, it appeared as a cloud rushing toward the portal.

I turned to Walden, curious to see if the power worked the same in both agents. Agent Walden's Path looked normal. I didn't see a flow of power reaching out. He did appear anxious, though. Without looking at his intense expression, I could read the anxiety in his Path. Maybe he wasn't as sure of Agent Dempsey's work as he had made it sound. Dark yellow sparked out, showing his uncertainty, before flaring and turning to a ghastly yellow green of mistrust.

His part must come at the end. Dempsey's cloud of power was reaching the portal. The little white lights zipped faster and faster, as though cutting the air.

Which is kind of what they had done. Carved a hole between worlds.

Pressure began to build and I put my hands over my stomach, suddenly nauseated. This, I had felt before too. Whatever portals did when they opened, it didn't mix well with my power. Most people didn't appear to notice the power of a portal, but for me, it felt like I was being pushed down and squeezed tight at the same time.

Being this close sucked, although I think the Path being open might have been making it worse.

"Are you alright?" Boone asked.

I nodded, but didn't trust myself to talk at that moment, worried that more than words would come out.

Had I ever been around a portal closing?

Swallowing hard and taking a few deep breaths, I hazarded a few words. "Do you have to get the portal close to opening to close it?" I asked.

"What?" Dempsey asked.

"Do it now," Walden growled.

Dempsey's power wavered and he looked at me, not watching his work.

"Now!" Walden shouted.

Dempsey jumped and focused again. A burst of power exploded out, creating a blinding light, brighter than the Path.

Shading my eyes, I watched through slits in my fingers as the portal opened.

Wind rushed through the area, expanding out from the power of the portal.

"Why is it opening?" Boone had to raise his voice to be heard over the rush of air. He took a step back.

"Don't move!" Walden shouted.

Boone froze to the spot. The portal appeared to waver, although it could have been a trick of the light. Looking lower to the ground, I watched for any small shapes, worried the gremlins might jump through.

"You have to close it off," I said. I had to repeat myself louder.

Dempsey was covered in sweat now and visibly shaking. His face paled.

He was using too much power. I'd been close to burning myself out a few times and it wasn't a pretty sight.

"Finish it!" Walden screeched.

The portal wavered again, and then jumped forward.

Boone fell through. I ran on instinct alone and threw a strand of power out looping it around Boone, forming it into a solid rope.

It had him. I knew the power was wrapped around him, I could sense it. Nevertheless, Boone was gone. I rushed forward to the portal.

What did I know about portals? My thoughts hiccupped as my brain tried to work again, but it was in panicky disorder. Could I yank him back? Would that kill him or leave him in some sort of limbo?

My stomach clenched. Or would that leave him between worlds? It was an awful thought.

Then my brain kicked into gear. Gremlins came out of this

thing all the time. Boone should be able to move back through as well.

Looking up, I caught Dempsey's horrified expression.

"Keep it open!" I yelled, "I think we can get him back."

Dempsey shook his head, and then his eyes grew wide. He started to say something, but something slammed into my back.

Sharp bright light surrounded me. My lungs seized up.

A blur of color greeted me before I hit something face first.

Staggering, I fell to the side and landed hard on the ground.

Spots of light dotted my vision, but around it, I could still see the intense brightness of the portal. The little balls of white lights were starting to slow. The light dimmed. In moments, the portal winked out.

I jumped to my feet, but wavered when my head swam and sat back down again, hard on the ground. The Path flowed unevenly and the colors swirled in odd patterns. A bright spot in my situation presented itself. My stomach wasn't ready to toss up breakfast.

Then I realized what that meant. The portal was closed.

Someone cursed a few feet away and stalked around. By sound, I knew it was Boone, but I was still light-blind from the intensity of the portal. Taking my time, I stood shakily to my feet and moved closer to what had been the portal.

"What just happened?" I wasn't asking anyone in particular, but I felt like it had to be said all the same.

Still reading, I went to the ghosted outline of the portal. The balls of light were still there, but so faint they could barely be seen. I probed the Path, nudging the little ball. It didn't move and faded further still.

"It's almost closed," I said.

A torrent of curses was Boone's reply.

The lights in my eyes were starting to fade. When I turned away, I saw Boone. Frowning, I looked behind him to the meadow of grass that hadn't been there when we came to the portal.

"How do you know it's closing?" Boone demanded.

I rubbed my head. "The Path is fading away."

Something was wrong with the grass. It was green, but the wrong color of green. Could grass turn blue?

A part of me knew what was happening, but my mind threw up as many roadblocks and denials as it could grasp hold of.

"Can you stop it from fading?" Boone asked.

"Um..." I looked at the portal, but all that was left were its ghosted remains. The forest that had sprung up behind the portal was a bit of a distraction. "I don't know."

"Then try, dammit!" Boone barked the command.

I glared at him, but knowing my chance was fading away, I didn't argue. We were stuck in the wrong world.

No, I shoved that thought down. Those words would lead to nothing but panic and I was running out of time. Closing my eyes for a heartbeat, I released the holds on my power.

The Path glowed strongly around me and the ghosted Path of the portal brightened considerably, which gave me hope.

The problem was I knew nothing about how portals worked. Energy was the key. I knew that. Massive amounts of electricity were used to open the ones at the office. I remembered Logan and Rider talking about portals. That seemed like a lifetime ago, but they had mentioned there were others in their worlds that could open portals. Logan had even theorized that I might be able to open one if I put enough power into it.

I was probably remembering wrong.

Still, if energy were the key, I'd try my hardest. Gathering as much power as I could, I started to feed it into the portal.

For a few moments, nothing happened. Slamming more

power into it, the tiny glowing balls of light started to glide gently around their circular trail. I watched one move agonizingly slow, and I wavered.

"Can you open it?" Boone was obviously used to giving orders and expecting immediate answers to his questions.

"Shut up," I snapped, not liking the tone of his voice. Gripping the aggravation, I fed that touch of extra power into the portal. The little balls of light jumped a few inches, and then stuttered to a stop.

No, no, no, this was not happening. I thought about Gran and Mom. Rider and Logan.

Vincent.

I shook out my hands and circled around the portal until I stood back in front of it. I had no idea what to do. It looked more solid and adding energy caused movement, but nothing like the zipping balls of light that Agent Dempsey had created.

"This is going to suck," I said, more to myself than anyone else. I took a deep breath and began to draw in power. Paths around me bent and started to flow toward me. After a few moments, it felt as though I was vibrating in my skin.

"What are you doing?" Boone asked. This time, he sounded weary.

Looking at him, I saw I had unintentionally pulled on his Path. "Sorry." I adjusted in order to drop his Path and keep his swirly strands of energy separate from everything else around me.

When I couldn't take in another hair's breadth of energy, I let it go. All at once, I slammed the power toward the portal. The sound of wind rushed past me, but the air was still. Bright lights started to pop in my vision. For a moment, I thought I might be achieving some success, but the lights weren't coming from the portal.

I ignored them and drew more power through me until I swayed.

What would Gran do if I didn't come home? The thought added a renewed surge of energy. The edges of my vision started to blur.

Rider and I hadn't made up yet.

My eyesight narrowed until there was only the portal and me. The little balls of light slid around. They were moving.

This would work. I felt lightheaded, but began drawing the Path out of the ground, adding it to the flow.

What would Vincent do if I didn't come home?

I started feeling detached and my vision narrowed into one shining dot. I kept track of it as it made laps around the circle.

There was pressure on my arm. I didn't need to look to know it was Boone. I wasn't sure if he was holding me up, or trying to get me to stop. It didn't matter, though, because this had to work.

Would Vincent sense I was gone? Would he come after me?

That was stupid—how could he come after me? The shiny ball of light began to slow.

Would he leave the others? He had a life before we met. Would he go back to it?

I blinked and struggled to open my eyes again. Something wet, sweat maybe, rolled down my face, but I ignored it, trying to find the remains of the portal. I spotted it in time to see it stop.

Then it winked out and I was left in darkness.

A MIXTURE of warmth and cool air was the first sensation I felt. Then I realized my head felt like it was splitting in two. My groan was involuntary. My hands went to my head, pressing to hold it together before I opened my eyes. Firelight flared in the darkness and when I looked at the light, my head pounded. I closed one eye in an effort to minimize the effects. There was no way I was closing both. When you wake up lying on the ground, there are priorities that rank higher than nursing a splitting headache.

"You're up," Boone said, stating the obvious.

Grimacing, I sat the rest of the way up and looked around. "I guess you could call it that. What happened?"

Boone yawned. "You'd know better than me."

"Huh." Still rubbing my forehead, I looked around. We were at the edge of a meadow where I recognized nothing. "How long was I out?" I needed an answer, though I didn't know if I wanted one.

"At least twelve hours."

I groaned again and rubbed my face with my hands, wanting this nightmare to end. "Where's the portal?"

"Gone. It used to be over there," Boone said, pointing into the darkness.

"Gone?" I blinked sadly into the night where Boone had indicated.

"I went through, although I'm still unclear as to how, and when I tried to return, you pushed me back. Before I got to my feet again, it was gone. Want to fill in some blanks?" There was a bitter edge to his voice.

A deep melancholy began to settle in, and I stared into the darkness where the portal had been, attempting to will it back into life.

Boone raised his voice. "Agent Heidrich?"

"Something hit me in the back and I fell through."

"Why were you next to the portal? It was obviously unstable."

I shrugged and immediately regretted it. Through the

headache, I hadn't noticed the stiffness in my muscles. "Why do you think? I thought I could help pull you back through."

"So you weren't a part of this?" An accusatory sourness was in his voice that told me he already blamed me for something.

"A part of what?" I had a feeling my brain needed to catch up and the faster the better.

"I'd like to know that myself. What else happened?"

"Dempsey was holding the portal. Something hit me and I fell through. That's all there was to it."

"I meant after you got here."

"Oh." The blanket mental denial was the first thing I thought of. "Um, I was Reading, and I could see the remains of the portal, but they were fading fast."

"You mentioned that you could see it. You were pretty non-responsive beyond that." Again the bitterness.

"That wouldn't possibly have had anything to do with you trying to bark orders at me, would it?" I rolled my shoulders trying to work out some of the aches. "What made you think I could reopen a portal?" For that matter, what had made me think I could?

Boone sat quiet for a moment. "What were you doing after that?"

I guess I couldn't begrudge him ignoring my question. Still, I was getting aggravated about the third degree. "The portal was going away, so I did what I could to try to stop it."

"Agent Heidrich, I can't see what you see, and I know very little about Readers. Could you add more detail?" It sounded like he was biting off each word.

I was used to describing what I could see, but I was used to it with my partners, not a stranger. Sighing, I told Boone everything, starting from the very beginning.

"And you passed out because?" Boone asked. His words

were more subdued at this point, but it did little to dampen my aggravation with him.

"I gave it everything I had," I snapped. "What else could I do?"

Boone was silent again and we were left with the crackle of the fire. I took the opportunity to stretch out. Most of my muscles protested at the action.

A small part of me wasn't ready to accept what had happened. "How well do you know Agent Dempsey and Agent Walden?"

"I've met them before," Boone said, "but I wouldn't say that I know them."

"Should they have been able to stop this?"

"Could they have? It's possible. I don't think they had any intention of doing so, however."

That ripped away the last of hope. "They're not going to try to reopen the portal, are they?"

"That is highly unlikely."

"How can you be so calm about this?" I hadn't intended on raising my voice, but I had all the same.

Boone shook his head. "We're in a world that we know nothing about. The only way, Agent Heidrich, that we are going to survive, is to keep a level head and think things through."

Keep a level head? The only thing filling my head was thoughts of home. I turned toward the night, unsure if I could stop my eyes from tearing up. There was no way I was going to let Agent Boone see that.

It took a few minutes before I could speak again without betraying my fear and frustration. "You asked if I was a part of this."

Boone nodded, but said nothing.

"So you think that Dempsey and Walden did this on purpose?"

"From what you've said, that's what I believe. At least, if I believe your account of what happened."

My head whipped around and I glared at Boone. "Why on earth would I do this? Do you think I want to be here?"

"You don't have to want to be here to have been a part of this." Boone's voice started to become louder as well.

"What's that supposed to mean?"

"If you were in on this, and they felt they were done with you, what would be a better way to get rid of you than to send you to another world?"

My fists clenched. "What did you do that made someone want to get rid of you? What did you do that I would even care about?"

"Do you know why I was observing your team?" Boone looked like he was studying me, but he was clearly pissed off.

"Hank mentioned it yesterday." *Hank, would he be organizing a way to get us back?* "You're going to be working with a group of Lost, or people with powers, or both."

"Something like that," Boone said.

"And apparently my team is the only one set up that way." *Would they be working on a way to get me back?*

Why was I thinking about my team? Boone was right about one thing: to survive, we were going to have to stay calm, and thinking about home wasn't going to work.

"Right," Boone said.

I cocked my head and waited for more—when none came, it did nothing to improve my mood. "Why on earth would I give a damn about your team?" Earth? Was this considered earth anymore?

Boone shrugged. "You tell me."

My hands balled into fists, but I forced myself to relax them again. After taking a few measured breaths, I sat back down, one eye on where I thought the portal might have been. I was done talking with Boone. How had I ended up trapped here with him? Whatever the reason, it was obvious he wasn't going to tell me. Why couldn't one of my teammates have been with me? It was my first day back and they had let me go away with another team.

Before I realized what I was doing, I sniffed. I really didn't want to cry in front of this man. I closed my eyes and took a few moments to meditate. Home, my family, and my team, it all had to be shoved into the recesses of my mind. It took longer than I expected. Thoughts kept bubbling to the surface despite my best efforts.

"Do you know anything about this world?" I asked.

When I didn't get an immediate answer, I looked over and saw Boone watching me.

I rolled my eyes and shook my head. "We're going to have to trust each other."

"I think you're mistaken about that." He didn't sound angry anymore, but there was a hint of sarcasm. Still, I guessed that was improvement.

"Right. Can you at least trust the fact that we're going to need help from each other to survive?"

Boone shrugged.

That was the best I was going to get. I rubbed my head. The ache had started to fade, but Boone's attitude was making it come back.

"Is there any trace of the portal still left?" Boone asked.

"Would you believe me if I gave you an answer?"

I hadn't expected a hesitation. "I trust that you want to get back to our world just as much as I do."

I sighed. "You're not wrong about that at least." Turning inward, I concentrated on the small amount of energy I had built back up while I had been asleep. It didn't look good. "I'm not sure I can check." I didn't raise my voice much louder, mostly because I didn't want to admit I had reached my limits. "I'll give it a try."

Sitting crossed-legged, I closed my eyes, took a deep breath, and made the jump into the Path. When I opened my eyes, I swayed. The Path here twisted and moved in a way that agitated my stomach. It still had the beautiful, glittering glow, but the flow was different, and there were eddies and blockages. In some areas, the Path swirled in circles, and in others, it flowed downward instead of from side to side. It made me dizzy to watch.

"Agent Heidrich?" Boone called. He sounded farther away than he was.

"Right." I focused in on the area where I thought the portal lived. *Was there anything left?* Without thinking, I tried to stand, but didn't get far before I slumped back down to a seated position. "I don't see it, but there is something there."

"I don't know what that means." The words were each cut short.

"If you gave me a more than half a second, I'd say more," I snapped. The Path fell away and my vision grayed around the edges. My body felt like it was weighted down. "There's nothing there to see. The circles of power are gone, but the Path itself is still there." Seeing Boone was going to talk, I raised my voice slightly and talked over him. "What that means is there is something there, either hidden behind the Path or imprinted on it somehow. It could just be the memory of the portal."

"So it's gone?"

I shook my head and rubbed my hands over my face. "It means that the Path remembers it. If someone tries to reopen the portal, I think it will be pretty easy for them."

"Can you reopen it?" Boone asked.

"I'm not sure what I need to say to make you understand that I don't know how to open or close a portal." I wanted my voice to drip with acid to let him know how aggravated I was. Or at least sound angry. Instead, it came out listless. I was too tired to work up any real emotion.

We both sat silent, lost in our own thoughts. I watched the fire grow smaller and tried not to think about what was going on back home. There had to be something I could do to put off wondering and worrying about what the others might be up to.

A plan was what we needed. I'm not sure what needed to be done. Maybe we needed a plan for a plan? When I turned my attention back to Agent Boone, he was asleep. My questions and planning would have to wait. I'd been camping before. Sure, it had been in my own dimension, surrounded by people I could trust, but I knew what needed to be done. He was asleep, so it was my turn to take watch.

The trouble was, I never found out what it was you were supposed to do when it was your turn to keep watch. Somehow, my partners seemed to know what to do instinctively. The best I could do was to stay awake and wake up Boone before he got eaten by anything.

Shoot. That was worse than thinking about home. What else lived here aside from the gremlins? I didn't remember anything else coming through the portal, but it was my understanding our soil was enough to lure the gremlins over. They wanted the minerals and metals. I don't remember anyone talking about anything else that came through. The gremlins kept us on our toes. I'm sure I would have heard if there was anything else.

The woods were full of shadows. The snap and crackle of the dying fire was the only thing I could hear. I covered my mouth to stifle a yawn. Last time I took watch I had leaned against a tree. Here, I wasn't willing to step far enough outside the firelight to get close to a tree. We hadn't had a fire the last time we had camped. We were too worried about giving our position away.

Shouldn't we have worried about that here? Maybe Boone knew something I didn't. I wasn't willing to wake him up to find out. He was aggravating enough without being tired and cranky on top of everything else.

The ground was rough enough. Maybe if I kept myself busy, I wouldn't fall asleep. Looking around, I saw Boone had our bag next to him. That was annoying. It wasn't that I couldn't take an inventory what we had; it was more the idea that he didn't trust me.

Did I trust him? Maybe it didn't matter.

My eyes started to get heavy.

A snap came from the woods. I smiled, thinking of Rider stepping on a twig to announce himself in the dark. Then my brain kicked in. Rider wasn't here.

Straining, I tried to hear hints of other sounds. Still, I had an uneasy sensation I was being watched.

It was just my nerves, right? Gremlins weren't exactly the type of creature to stalk someone. They were almost annoying in the amount of energy they had. They didn't walk anywhere. Instead, they ran, jumped, and swung around on things.

That line of thought wasn't helping. What were my choices here? I could investigate, but that thought had stupidity written all over it. It didn't matter if it was a squirrel—whatever it was would have an advantage over me. I could wake up Boone, but that thought wasn't appealing, either.

Taking a deep breath, I decided on door number three. I did nothing. I still listened intently for any hint of a sound, but aside from that, I sat and watched the fire die down to embers.

Time seemed to go by slower than it should. The noise had probably been my imagination. Either that or it was something that wasn't interested in us.

When the sky began to lighten, I relaxed. With the firelight gone, my eyes had started to adjust to the night. As the sky became brighter, I could see into the forest and make out individual trees. Some of them were large. Massive, even. My eyes felt weighed down, but I watched the woods until Boone started to stir.

"Did you sleep?" Boone asked.

"I kept watch." My voice was scratchy.

Boone nodded and didn't ask anything else.

"I heard a noise, a twig snapping, I think. It happened about an hour or two ago," I volunteered. "But I didn't see anything. We may want to avoid a fire, unless you know what kind of animals we're dealing with, that is."

Oh, crap. Animals. It hadn't crossed my mind until that moment. Animals didn't like me. One of the downsides to a shattered soul was that predators wanted to take me out. The last time I ventured into the woods, Vincent had become irate when he found out I hadn't had a weapon.

"What else?" Boone asked.

"What do you mean?" I tried to push the thoughts away.

"It looked like you had more to say."

"That's it." It was a different world. Who was to say the creatures here would react the same way.

Except every Lost had treated me the same way. Some didn't want to kill me. The smarter ones knew something was wrong and couldn't figure it out, and those that were too self-absorbed to pay much attention to those around them hardly noticed.

Predators were predators. It didn't matter who or what you were.

Boone shook his head, aggravated.

"We do need a plan, though," I suggested.

"That's something we can agree on. Are you able to check the portal?"

"No." I hated it with every fiber of my being that I couldn't. Any time I reached a limitation, I had a hard time dealing with it.

He seemed to take me at my word, at least, because he didn't push.

"Okay," Boone said, "our plan for today is to scout the area. You need to stay here and—"

"I'm not your lackey. When I said we needed a plan, I wasn't asking you to tell me what to do. We need to work together on this."

Boone gave me a hard look, but I only returned it back to him. There was no way we were going to start out by him ordering me around.

"You have a plan?" Boone asked.

I rolled my eyes. "No, we need to make one. Together." I said the last word slowly, as though he were slow or hard of hearing. He acted as if he was both.

"Agent Heidrich," Boone looked like he was having a hard time keeping his temper, "I have ten years of experience in hostile environments. I've been dropped into some of the worst places you can imagine and survived, getting myself and others out."

"A, I'm not one of your troops. B, we don't know if this is a hostile area, and treating it as such could turn it into one. And C, we need to take stock of what we have so we know what we need."

Boone stood and rubbed the back of his neck, taking his time to look around. When he spoke, he was much calmer. "I know what we have. I took an inventory last night. Our priorities are water, food, and shelter so we can stay alive long enough to get home."

I shook my head and shifted around, trying to find a comfortable position.

"You disagree?" Boone asked. He looked surprised and genuinely interested in my reaction.

It was a shame he had ticked me off so badly. I glanced him over from head to toe, paying special attention to his shoes. "I'm beginning to think it doesn't matter if I disagree."

"If there is a legitimate reason—"

"What possible reasons could I have? It's obvious you know what you're doing. Go for it."

He sighed and rubbed his hands over his face, but he sat back down across the dying fire from me. "This isn't going to work," he said at last. He looked tired.

I tried to pull my frustration and sarcasm down to simmering levels. "It will if we work together."

"Okay. What survival training do you have?"

Training? "Um, I've gone camping with my partners."

Boone's face looked strained.

My response was to give him a warm smile and say, "Twice."

His hands balled up and flexed a few times. "Okay," he said, "where do you think we should start?"

I had to give him props for his attitude, so I replaced the large, fake smile with a smaller, but much more real one. "We're better off than we were before. I know you have some sort of survival skills, and you know I have none."

Boone nodded.

It looked like he was having a hard time forming his next question, so I went ahead and beat him to it. "What I was going to suggest is to take a full stock of what we have."

"I told you I already checked," Boone said.

"You did, but you were looking for survival stuff, right?"

"And you're looking for?"

"My first thought is to comb through our supplies and check carefully for metal. Did you look for metal?"

Boone looked surprised. "I didn't."

"Yeah, I guessed that. But I thought I'd be nice and ask."

"The bag was specifically meant to be used for gremlin patrols, right?" Boone pulled the bag over to him.

"Yep. Plastic zippers and snaps."

While I watched him paw through the bag, I felt a little smug, but I let him go through it all the same.

"We dumped the metal shavings. It doesn't look like there's any other metal in the bag. What I also don't see is more than a liter of water or much in the way of food. I'm suggesting we get the lay of the land and start to find those things."

It was obvious he thought he might have overlooked something, and now, once again, he thought he was right and I was wasting time.

I sighed. "We have more than what's in the bag."

CHAPTER

SEVEN

Boone sat the bag down and patted his pockets.

"Your shoes," I said, putting an end to my game. "When we run into any gremlins, they're going to swarm you. If you want to get by unscathed and keep your feet warm, you're going to have to take the metal out of your boots."

Boone let out a sharp burst of air and shook his head. "You're right."

"We should both check our clothes for any signs of metal as well. Zippers, snaps, anything."

While he looked himself over, I did a quick inventory of my own clothes, wanting to make sure I caught anything before he did. Luckily, I had answered a few gremlin calls in the past year, so I had come prepared.

There was probably a way I could have made myself useful, but I laid down. While Boone worked on pulling the metal lace holes out of his boots, I fell asleep.

When he woke me, I was thirsty, but I felt much better than I had that morning.

"How long have I been asleep?" I asked.

"About an hour, but it's hard to tell here."

I nodded. "We have water, right?"

Boone handed over the bottle.

"How much should I drink?" I asked.

"What?" Boone asked.

"How much should I drink? You're Mr. Survival. I'm hoping you know how to ration."

"No more than an inch."

I nodded and drank, handing the bottle back to him. "No more metal in your clothes?"

"None. You?"

"I'm good."

"What about your, um..." Boone pulled at his shirt.

"What are you, twelve? You can say bra. It's an item of clothing like anything else."

Boone grinned, but didn't say anything.

"There's no metal in this one."

Boone only nodded. "That's fortuitous."

"Not exactly. I did mention this wasn't the first time I've been around gremlins, right?" I could feel my face turn red from the memory and turned away.

"You mentioned that, yes."

"Last winter I broke my leg. The office had been dealing with the gremlins for more than a month by the time I went on my first call."

The look on Boone's face was almost worth the story. I could tell he knew where this was leading, and he was trying not to smile.

My own smile started to come out, despite the blush. "That time, I had wire in my bra."

He snorted and I continued, pretending to ignore it. "Needless to say, the gremlins were very excited to get their hands on something beyond the metal shavings we were using to catch them."

"They took your bra?" Boone asked.

"Yes." I took a deep breath, knowing my face couldn't get any redder. "But they had to get to it first, so they took the shirt."

He laughed, and I could see his own cheeks reddening.

"What did your partners do?" he asked.

"Logan dumped the shavings into a pile, which distracted most of them. Rider just picked them up one at a time and held them up, taking pieces of my clothes back before using the plastic zip strips on them."

Boone laughed again and I couldn't help but join him.

"After that day, I've been very careful about what I wear at work. We get calls all the time for the gremlins." That sobered me up. We used to get calls, but the portal was closed now.

I looked at where the portal should be, and as Boone followed my gaze, his laughter died away. He didn't look aggravated or upset anymore at least.

"I'm sure the whole office was more careful after that," Boone said.

"You'd think so," I said. "But someone else wore jeans a month later. I got off lucky."

Boone chuckled again.

I tore my eyes away from the portal and looked around. "Okay, metal is out of the way. Did you keep hold of it?"

"I put it into one of the plastic containers the metal filings were in."

"Good idea. I'm sure we'll want to use it sooner or later. What do you think we should do next?"

He still smiled, but I saw the uncertainty in his eyes.

"It's fine," I said. "We need to work together, which means we consult each other. As long as we treat each other as equals and don't start ordering one another around, I think we'll be fine."

"I'll do my best," Boone said.

"Don't worry, when you slip up, you can count on me to point it out."

He laughed again. "Well, I doused the fire. You're right about that. If we can help it, we shouldn't start one. Last night was a special circumstance."

"Special circumstance?"

"Well, I had a virtually unknown, comatose woman with me. I wasn't sure how you'd react if you woke up with a stranger watching you in the dark."

I thought that over. "That was probably a wise course of action."

Boone nodded. "Now, I think it's time to find water and scout the area."

I nodded, but I didn't feel good about the idea of splitting up. "How does this work?"

"That's a good question. I'm not sure if we should leave the area unattended."

"Do you think they'll get someone else to reopen the portal?"

He looked uneasy with the question and didn't answer right away. "Opening portals is a pretty rare gift. It may take them a while to find someone."

"I hope Dempsey and Walden are locked up in tight cells."

"Do you think they will be?" He watched me carefully again, as though he was ready to weigh my answer.

"I think the longer we're trapped here, the more pissed off my partners are going to be."

"That's true." The thought seemed to unsettle Boone.

"You look worried. Don't be. Logan's not going to let anyone kill Dempsey or Walden. He'll keep the others in line." I thought about that a little further. "Well, in line may be stretching it."

"The problem is when they returned to the office, they only have Dempsey and Walden's word for what happened."

My stomach sank. "But I don't think they can say anything to convince my partners not to come looking for me."

Boone shrugged. "I don't know them well yet, but I hope you're right."

Could they say anything that would stop my partners from trying to get me back? Thoughts raced around my head.

"Don't worry about it now," Boone said. "You'll drive yourself crazy. But be on your toes when we get back. We can't assume the others will know what happened or that they will take our word for it."

"Do you think Dempsey and Walden will try to convince them the portal can't be reopened?"

"I doubt it. I think with enough power, used the right way, any portal can be reopened. I don't know if they can transport much power to where the gremlins break out, but there may be other ways."

That should have made me hopeful and it would have if Boone had sounded even remotely convinced.

"So, one of us stays by the portal and the other looks for water?" I asked.

"For now. I'll go out first. If it opens, take your chance and leave. Make sure you yell as loud as you can first, though."

"You want me to leave you here?"

"Yes. Reopen it if you can find someone who will."

Yeah, if he thought I would leave without him... well, that wasn't going to happen, but I didn't say anything. "Should I check out the immediate area?"

"As long as you can still see the portal."

"Sure thing. Take the water with you."

"I could be gone for a while," Boone said.

"Good. You can bring some water back with you when you return."

Boone handed me the bottle first, and I took a drink before he left.

The sounds of the breeze and the forest were the only things I was left with. And the bag. Well, at least I could finally take inventory. Boone had a lot to learn before he and I were going to get along, but at least he was trying. The bag was a typical gear bag except for the weapons. Boone had been right, nothing metal remained in the bag, but we had a first-aid kit, paracord, a few power bars, and a few plastic containers, one of which held the metal from Boone's boots.

He should have taken it with him. Gremlins can swarm over someone even if they didn't have metal. It's less likely, but they are enthusiastic little buggers.

Then I found the most wonderful commodity of all, tucked away in the first-aid kit. Caffeine pills. Someone must have thought of me and added them, just in case. It was tempting to take one now, but I beat down the idea and put them back in the first-aid kit.

With that done, I stood, stretched, and took in my surroundings. The woods were close, but I wasn't about to start there. Vincent's warning about always keeping a weapon on hand was still rattling around in my head. It's possible I should have let Boone know about my little affliction, but we were getting out of here soon, right? There was no need to tell him what he didn't need to know.

Besides, if I told him, he's likely put it into an AIR file some-where and I'd be benched or out of a job. There was no way I was going to let them stand me down for something I couldn't control.

Away from the woods in the other direction, a field

stretched up a small rise. I moved up the small hill, but I consistently looked back to see the portal. It was surprising that the grass wasn't high. The color struck me as interesting. When I had fallen through the portal yesterday, I had spotted it, but I had had other, more pressing issues to consider at the time. The grass was a blue-green color instead of our typical green. I plucked a blade and twirled it around in my fingers, finding it was softer as well.

As the ground sloped upward, more of the meadow stretched out. The tree line was just that, a line. Roughly drawn, but the ground went straight from field to forest with no in-between. Standing this far back, I took the opportunity to look for movement in the woods, though with the steady breeze blowing, it didn't lead to results.

When I topped the rise, it didn't give me the view I had hoped for. Nothing would give me the view I had hoped for until I was back home, so it wasn't like my surroundings here had much chance at wish fulfillment.

The land straightened out until it bumped into another stand of trees. Not quite the dense forest that we had slept by, but nothing that screamed civilization. I watched for a while, unsure of what I was looking for, then I gave up and went back to the campsite.

With this many trees, there had to be lots of water around. The wind blew light, but steady. Maybe between the two columns of trees this area acted as a wind tunnel. It was hard to tell.

Looking up, the sky was a bright blue color that I'd never really seen at home—Not in the United States. At least the sky was similar. I'm not sure I could have handled a red sky or something along those lines.

I stood back at our puny camp, unsure of what to do. We had nothing. Each time I had gone out with Logan, Rider, and

Vincent, they had packs filled with what seemed like hundreds of odds and ends that they had deemed necessary to bring.

How do you do this with nothing?

A void began to build in my stomach. I swallowed hard and tried to focus on what I could do and what we did have. Well, at least what *I* could do, since we had almost nothing I could work with.

The only thing I could do was read. Maybe making an attempt at Reading the Path would tell us something. At the same time, saving my energy for an emergency might have been a better idea.

Wait, we're living the emergency. I shook my head and closed my eyes. When I stretched to the edge of my mind, I stopped for a moment, taking in the state of my soul. If we were here for much longer, I'd have to warn Boone about that, at least. If something else managed to gain control of my body, we'd both be in big trouble. He hadn't said it since last night, but I was sure he still didn't trust me. If I attacked him or started speeding around the woods looking like I was on meth, it might cause an issue.

Everything looked fairly normal. Normal for my soul, anyway. Since our fight with Einar more than a month ago, there had been less activity. It felt like there were fewer shards of soul than there had been before. It felt like my own personal shards were there for the most part, but some of the others had been taken and released.

Maybe, I wouldn't have to tell Boone. I'd love to force them to stay settled down, especially the minotaur soul, but there was no consciousness there. Only tiny shards of essence that had once belonged to another person.

Satisfied my soul was in the best shape it could be, I stretched into the Path. Since I had been intent on my soul, jumping into the Path felt like a punch to the stomach. A roaring tide greeted me, and every muscle tightened as though the weight of the Path were slamming physically into me.

It burned through energy too fast. I did what I could to dam up the flow, but it wasn't enough. Not wanting to get worn down this early in the day, I took a quick look around. The irregular flow of energy had me baffled. *How do you read this mess?*

I went to the portal, knowing Boone would want to know what we were left with. It was the same as yesterday. A hint of the circular portal was all the Path remembered. A white glow with beads of energy that looked ready to be set into motion. Knowing how hard it was to get those little suckers moving, I didn't bother trying.

Maybe when I had saved all my energy I could try again.

Knowing the longer I stared at it, the more power I burned, I looked around the woods, trying to see if I could find anything else of use. There were other Paths of a sort. Animals, maybe. They weren't the light colors of brown and green of our animals, which had very little thought beyond instinct. They still had that light, filmy look, but the colors were blues, yellows, and purples, and they shifted in quicker succession than I would normally see in our world.

I had no idea what lived out here. Shaking my head, I took one last look around. A solid swirl of color caught my eye. I itched to run over to it, but something told me a slow approach was better.

Cautiously, I walked a few yards and stopped. I rolled my shoulders and looked around. It felt like I was being watched. The Path wasn't that old and it was complex—something that a person might leave behind. Worried about moving any closer, I started to circle wide around the remnants.

Someone had stood there. Remembering the twig snapping last night, I wondered if that person had been there at that time. An involuntary shiver ran through me, and I hastily looked around to see if anyone else was nearby, but there was nothing else.

My head started to ache, and I realized I had almost run through any meager energy reserves I had built up. The spot where the person had been should be easy enough to remember. There was a circle of trees where they had been standing. A few other landmarks stood out, so I studied the spot one last time and closed my eyes, ready to push away the Path.

The Path didn't want to be closed. When I struggled to push it back, it built up and overwhelmed my attempts. Knowing this could only mean trouble, trouble I wasn't sure I could get out of, anxiety sprung up along with the power of the Path.

My breathing increased and I moved to grip the side of a tree. I'm not sure what leverage the tree could give me, but I felt better grabbing the rough bark, almost as though it were an anchor, holding me to the spot.

Power buffeted me from all sides. Panicking wouldn't help, but that didn't mean I could stop it. I took a few deep breaths and thought of the meditations Vincent and I had tried. Remembering his voice, telling me to breathe in and out, slowly—the comforting timbre of his voice steadily moving me through me the process of nearing the abyss which held my soul and backing away again—it all helped.

I could practically feel him here with me.

After taking those few meditative breaths, I concentrated hard and shoved my way through the resistant Path.

When my attention snapped back to the real world, I sagged against the tree. There was no other noise apart from a small rustle here and there. I listened intently for a while, trying to let myself go numb, not daring to move until I knew I could stand on my own.

Even with him being gone, Vincent was able to help me. An empty feeling spread out inside that kept continuously reminding me he was gone. They all were. I was alone with a stranger in a world where I didn't belong. There was no help and no backup if my powers spun out of control.

In that moment, I was certain if we didn't find a way home soon, or if my partners didn't find their way to me, I would die here. And they would never know.

I slid to the ground and hugged my knees, allowing myself a few minutes to grieve what I might be losing. Logan, Rider, and Vincent, Gran and Mom, Gran's cat and my bunny, Hank and everyone at work. They were all gone.

Except they weren't.

Gran would know if I was coming back. She had to know. Sometimes, she knew when someone else was on their way from another world, so I would be no different. She'd keep hope alive for the others. Besides, my partners wouldn't stop looking for me. Even if they thought I was dead, I'm sure they'd want some sort of proof. Some evidence.

I sniffed and rubbed my face, catching stray tears which annoyed me to no end. Tears wouldn't help anything.

What would Dempsey and Walden tell everyone? I couldn't think of anything my team would accept. They'd question them, surely, maybe even keep hold of them until we got back. In the meantime, there had to be other people that could open portals.

We would be okay. What we had to do right then was stay alive. It was obvious we weren't alone. I wasn't sure if that was a point in the survival column or a point in the 'we're screwed' column. But it was something we hadn't known yesterday.

What else did we know?

EIGHT

The portal remnants hadn't faded any further, but I wasn't certain we could count on it to remain that way. Another person living here, much larger than any gremlin, could mean there was more than one intelligent species in this world.

If others could survive, so could we.

Still, I wasn't in a hurry to rush to my feet and back to the camp. Boone might be there. It had been a moment of lost hope and now it was gone. No need to let him think I couldn't hold it together. The last thing I wanted was to give him an excuse to start ordering me around.

Looking out over the forest, I heard the rustling again, but never saw anything. No other noises indicated something alive. It was eerie.

No birds. That was what was missing. Nothing chirped in the trees or flew around. No squirrels, either, which you'd never see at home, not with a patch of woods this large.

It wasn't that I expected all worlds to have little furry creatures, but wouldn't there be something replacing them? Something else that foraged the area? Feeling uneasy once again, I pushed myself to my feet and looked around, this time for any physical indication something was alive.

I saw nothing.

What would keep animals out of a place like this?

The only thing that came to mind was a predator. Could something have claimed this area and scoured it of food?

Maybe it was the portal. It affected me poorly; maybe it did the same to the creatures here as well. That had to be it.

I was almost able to convince myself.

On the way back to the portal and our, for lack of a better word, campsite, I started checking the ground for sticks—something that might hold up if I had to use it to defend myself.

I found a few options and took the best. Whether or not it would stop a raging monster that might be lurking in the woods was another story.

Ugh, there are no raging monsters. Come on, Cassie, get a grip on yourself. Stick to the facts. Instead, I needed to think over what we needed, water, food, shelter, and a way home. Back at the camp, I once again surveyed items we had on hand.

Food and water I couldn't do much about, unless I stumbled onto something.

Shelter and a way home, that's what was left. I glanced at the portal, but looked away quickly. There was nothing for me to try there. Best not think about it. That left shelter.

It sucked to think about it, but Boone was going to be the one to come up with a shelter as well. If I got started, he would probably laugh at the results if I didn't beat him to it. Since I had no idea what to do, building would have to wait. Besides, building a shelter would have given Boone an excuse to order me around. That might lighten his mood for a while, but then he'd tick me off and we'd both be in a bad mood.

I hated being useless. Looking around, nothing jumped out at me as needing to be done.

What would he make a shelter out of? It wasn't like there was lumber lying around. In shows about deserted islands, you see fake shelters made out of palm leaves. None of them was there. There were large leaves on the trees. Very large, in fact, but they weren't exactly building materials. That left grass and sticks. I doubted the soft, smooth grass would do anything, so sticks it was.

Besides, wasn't that always one of the first things the guys did when we camped? Even the times we didn't build a fire, they'd still gather up a pile of wood. There had to be a reason for it.

So, I set out, walking the edges of the forest, looking for sticks and choosing the longest ones that could double for some sort of lean to, or whatever it was Mr. Survival would come up with. It still felt creepy if I walked more than a few feet into the woods.

I also looked for food. Not the running kind, since I hadn't seen any signs of real animals, but my growling stomach had me looking for berry bushes, mushrooms, or anything else that seemed like it might be edible.

This was definitely not a movie. In the movies, you typically don't get someone smelling the bark of sticks while they gathered them, just in case something was edible.

Scouring the area caused me to break out in a sweat. I'm a terrible judge of time, but it had to have been a few hours of work. By then, I had found all the nearby large sticks, medium, and even small ones, and started making a stack of twigs. I knew I was taking the gathering overboard as an excuse to keep busy.

I also started to feel pretty gross. Both because of the sweat and dirt that covered me, and my stomach protesting due to the lack of food.

Sweating? Shoot. I didn't even think of the fact that I was wasting water. And of course, as soon as I thought about it, my throat became unbelievably dry.

The bag was there, and there were protein bars in it, but I had no idea how much to eat. That was something I should have asked Boone before he left. I sat down at the camp and tried to think of my next move. My eyes strayed repeatedly to the bag, which distracted me.

Where was Boone? I thought he wasn't planning on staying away long.

Except we had decided together, hadn't we? I rubbed my head. Or had he thought of that on his own? Not remembering made me cranky. Or maybe the foul mood was because I caught myself staring at the bag again.

Shaking my head, I stood and moved closer to the portal. There was a line on the ground under where the portal had stood. It was as though the whirling mass of light had run directly through the ground. I sat down nearby. When I did, I heard a small crunch. Looking around, I saw that the grass was dead immediately around the portal.

Was it killing the plants? I plucked a few blades and rubbed them between two fingers. The grass crumbled and dropped from my hand. It looked like the area of dead plants started near the portal and had spread out several feet.

That was something to consider. If the portal was killing the area, did it survive because it stole energy from the surroundings?

There were too many unknowns. The other side of the portal, the side we should have been on, had plants that still thrived around the portal, although it had cut through the ground the same way this one seemed to.

"See any changes?"

Even from a sitting position, I managed to jump. Thankfully, my throat was too dry for the squeak that had been forming to find a way out.

"Don't scare me like that," I snapped.

Boone looked amused, but when he saw my face, he hid it pretty well.

"Here, drink this," Boone said.

I took it and started drinking, forgetting to ask how much I should consume. It took a few moments for me to notice the taste. When I stopped and took a closer look at the contents, I saw the water wasn't as crystal clear as it had been when he left.

"You found water," I said, surprised at how happy that made me.

"Yeah. Have you had anything to eat?"

"No, but I think it's past time." I took another drink before capping the bottle and standing. "We didn't discuss how we should ration the food. For that matter, I also forgot to ask how the water should be rationed."

"We have water," he said, walking back to our camp with me trailing behind. "As for the food, we don't have much and we have a lot to do."

That didn't sound promising, but I didn't say anything.

"At the same time, there has to be food in the area," he continued. "Eat this." He tossed me one of the power bars.

Once again, I found myself sitting on the ground. "The whole thing?" I asked.

"Well, you look like hell."

I rolled my eyes. "Gee, thanks." Still, I didn't argue and

planned to take my time eating, thinking I wouldn't finish the whole thing.

It disappeared despite my efforts.

"Now, fill me in what happened here. Anything new with the portal?" Boone asked.

I told him how I had spent my day, pointing out where he could find the wood, which I had placed a little ways into the tree line and well away from camp. Even I knew that stacks of branches drew animals wanting to use it for shelter.

He didn't look happy about the lack of activity at the portal.

"Tell me what you saw that made you think someone was watching us last night," Boone said.

I had to remind myself Boone knew almost nothing about Readers, or me for that matter, so I patiently explained what I had seen. After which, he wanted to see the evidence for himself. Sadly, my food was gone, so I showed Boone the way.

When I approached the spot where I had spotted the figure, once again I became uneasy. "It stood in the middle of that stand of trees," I said, not moving forward.

Boone strode around me, heading for the spot. I threw out my arm and stopped him. He looked at me, eyebrows raised, waiting for an explanation.

Unfortunately, I didn't have one. Not a real one anyway. "I'm not sure why, but I get the feeling something is wrong here."

"Is this a feeling or something you read?" Boone asked.

I shook my head. "It's not as easy as that. The two are tied together."

"I'm going to need more than that to go on."

I let out an exasperated sigh. "That's all I've got." My partners would have gotten it straight away. Or at least they'd believe me.

Boone stared at me, apparently expecting more.

The only response he got was a return stare from me.

"I can't see anything from here," he said.

I shrugged. "Do what you want, but be careful. I'm staying right here until I know more."

He looked a little uneasy, but he studied the area more carefully before moving forward. He only took a few steps before stopping again.

"Grab a branch for me," he said.

"A nice 'please' wouldn't be too hard," I muttered under my breath, but I snatched up a long stick, giving him a dirty look when I handed it to him.

"Thank you." If he heard me, he didn't let on.

He dragged the stick across the ground in front of him. There was a snap, like a broken twig, and I moved aside so I could see around Boone.

"What is it?" I asked.

Boone squatted down. "Some sort of snare."

"Some sort? Like what sort? For an animal?"

"I doubt it was for the trees." He sounded more thoughtful than sarcastic, so I let the comment slide.

Besides, I doubt I would have treated the question any differently. "I meant, do you think it was for hunting or for something like us."

"No idea, but it works for both." He picked the contraption up and moved the stick around on the ground more slowly this time before continuing forward.

"Don't move any further," I said after a minute or so of watching his antics. If I hadn't been so tense and worried, it might have looked comical. "I think whatever it was stood in front of your stick."

Boone squatted down again and took a closer look at the ground.

"What do you see?" I asked impatiently when he said nothing.

"There's not much to see. There are more fallen leaves in this area, but I can't tell if they fell naturally or were intentionally laid to hide these." Boone waved the contraption through the air. "But there was something out here at some point."

"Is there anything else you can tell? Like what it might have been?"

Boone shook his head. "I don't even know what kind of animals or people are here aside from the gremlins. It could have been them, maybe, but I didn't get the idea they were crafty enough to think of traps."

"It's hard to tell with gremlins," I said. "Is there any metal in the gadget you're holding?"

Boone took one last look and walked back the way he came. "No metal."

"Then I doubt it was gremlins," I said.

"Do they only work with metal?"

"That's all I've seen them use. And they'll go pretty far to find it, too. Can I see?"

Boone handed over what he had found and started back for the camp. I studied the thing as best I could, being cautious so I didn't trip over anything, including my own feet.

The thing was wooden, but the wood was flexible. Smooth, too. There weren't any sharper bits like one might find in bear traps, but I could see where the general idea of the contraption might be the same.

Back at the camp, Boone looked around, much as I had earlier in the day. He seemed like he was trying to figure out what to do next. With so little at our disposal, I wasn't sure there were many options.

"Do you have any idea how this works?" I asked.

"No," Boone said. A general grumpiness was in his voice that had me inwardly groaning.

Somehow, I managed not to roll my eyes at him and dropped the trap next to our bag.

"We need to decide our next steps," Boone said.

"How long will our food last?"

Boone looked down the corridor of grassland. "Through tomorrow."

It wasn't a promising prospect. "Did you see anything resembling food while you searched for water?" I asked.

"Nothing."

"We know there are gremlins here. They have to eat something."

Boone shrugged. "I could explore a bit farther." His eyes strayed back to where the portal should have been. "If they tried to open the portal, would you be able to tell?"

"When it's opening, yes."

"I mean before that. If they were working on things from their side, would you see it? You could check before I leave."

Where could I even start with a question like that? "I have no idea if I'd see anything. I don't even know if anything changes unless it's opening. Right now, though, I don't think I should try. Not without sleep."

Boone sighed.

My face heated up as my temper swelled. "If there was something I could do I'd be doing it," I snapped.

He didn't say anything. It took a great deal of effort for me not to get more agitated.

Then self-doubt started to peek through. *Was* I doing everything I could? It had been stupid of me to read the area earlier. My power had run away from me. I could check the portal again, but I was almost tapped out. Looking for a few seconds wasn't going to help, but if I looked and lost control, it would put us in a tight spot.

However, I was more than a Reader. There had to be something else I could do.

"I think we should stay here for the rest of the day," I said.

"Why?" Boone asked.

"If this was some big mistake, it's likely Agents Dempsey and Wallace will regain their strength before long. If it's not," I continued before Boone could interrupt, "and there's someone else in the area that can open a portal, they'd be able to reach us. Also, it's getting late. We have no idea what we're dealing with in this world, but it'll be easier for us to see what's coming when it's full daylight."

Boone didn't say anything for a while.

For something to do, I grabbed the water bottle and found a spot to sit down. I took a quick drink and then examined the water. Maybe there would be fish in the water. When Boone walked away and up the short rise in the meadow, I pointedly ignored him.

A cool breeze streamed through the grassland, dragging a sweet smell along with it. The sky turned violet as the sun fell lower. To forget my animosity toward Boone, I laid back, stared at the alien sky, and fell into the breathing patterns Vincent and I did while meditating.

Any thoughts of what my partners were doing, I shoved away. That was no more than a guessing game that threatened to twist my stomach. Wondering what they would do if they were in my place wasn't helping either. *What should I be doing?* That was the question.

We didn't know how to communicate with the gremlins, but we knew they would fall over each other for metal. They'd fall over you, as well, if you were holding some. Never in a mean way. They had never attacked anyone to my knowledge.

Gremlins were enthusiastic, was all. Without metal, I wasn't even sure if we'd see them.

Well, we had a little metal. That might help bridge some sort of relationship.

Was that a good thing? Would it be useful?

Although, with no gremlins around, the point was moot.

The sky grew darker and took on the appearance of dark velvet. Pinpoints of light started to appear. In a way, it was serene.

"How would you go about finding food?" Boone asked, walking up.

Serenity tried to flee, but I held on tight. "Ordering takeout always worked best for me."

"That's helpful," Boone grumbled.

I sighed and sat up. "It was a joke. Well, sort of. I was thinking about the gremlins."

"What about them?" Boone asked in a guarded tone.

"Like I said before, they have to eat something. If we could find a way to communicate, maybe we could find out what they eat. They might be willing to help us find food."

No moon rose, and with the sun gone, the landscape turned pitch. Even with good night vision, I had a hard time seeing Boone settle on the ground.

"Any ideas how to do that?" Boone asked.

"Not really," I lied. The Path might have been useful here, but it would have taken too long to explain to Boone.

"They haven't been around. We'd have to find them first."

"Hopefully we can find them the same way they find the portal," I said. "Through the metal."

"With the number of gremlins you all had, I'm surprised they aren't nearby."

"They didn't come through the portal every time it opened," I said. "Maybe they roam around more."

"Possibly. We should get some sleep. I'll take first watch."

"Sure," I said, not moving. Sleeping on the ground wasn't something I looked forward to, and there seemed to be no use trying to find a comfortable spot. It was the ground. Nothing was comfortable.

Boone wasn't quiet for long. "As a Reader, how long do you need to sleep to... to build up your strength?" The last five words came out uncertain, as though he was worried about offending me.

"Honestly, it varies. I'll be okay in a few hours, but I'll burn out fast without more sleep." Restful sleep was what I needed, and I didn't think I could find that on the ground. There was no way I was sharing that with Boone, though. It might have been Logan's influence, but I was starting to be leery of the idea of the agency knowing more about my power than they already did.

"Is there anything else that helps?" Boone asked.

"Coffee definitely wouldn't hurt." I yawned.

Boone snorted a short laugh. "I'll be right on that. Get some sleep."

The moment I tried to sleep, my body decided it was time to point out every patch of rough ground and every ache. I twisted and turned a little before I closed my eyes and meditated once again. It didn't take long to fall asleep after that.

Light crept into the darkness of sleep, and I opened my eyes to thick fog. It took me a few moments to remember where I was. Depression tried to loom over me, but it didn't have time to make itself comfortable.

A shadow started to take shape.

My heart beat faster and I sat up. Listening intently, I looked around for Boone.

An unknown light source grew brighter and the shrouding

began to burn away. I didn't reach for the Path, but I braced myself, ready for the jump.

Then I heard the muttering. The very familiar muttering of Gran's sweetheart of old.

The old man's voice grew stronger. "... not my fault... traipsing around indeed..."

The voice began to fade and I jumped to my feet. "Don't go!"

CHAPTER
NINE

Silence dropped, but the sense of movement became stronger and the shadow more pronounced. Wisps of cool clouds swirled and began to blow away. An old man stepped into a rapidly clearing bubble of air.

"You've scared the life out of your grandmother," the old man snapped. It was hard to read his expression under the long white beard, but it was easy to read his tone.

"Are you really here?" I asked, wondering if I had dreamed him or up or if he had dreamed himself here, which he was known to do.

The man snorted, and with a craggy voice he asked, "Does it matter?"

"Yes!" I tried not to get overly excited. The man was crazy, but if he was here, then there had to be a way back home. "You're here to help us get back, right?"

"I'm here because your grandmother, my Margaret, is upset."

That made me feel morose. "Have you seen her? Is she okay?"

"She will be." He sounded a little smug about this. "Once she hears from me."

I tried to feel good about that. "Are the others alright?"

He looked confused. "Others? Others..." He grinned, causing his beard to twitch. "Don't know, don't care. I've seen you, now I'm off."

"Wait, you can't go!"

He let out a short cackle.

"That's not funny. How am I supposed to get home?"

He shrugged, which looked wrong on the man. His shoulders and back seemed to move independently under his clothes.

I tried to hide my aggravation at his dismissal. "You could help me."

"I don't do portals."

"But you could still help!" I struggled with what to say to the old man that might make him care. "Gran will want me home." No reaction. "And you need me for something. You and your friends." It wasn't a guess. During the few times I had encountered him, he had hinted there was something he wanted from me.

He made a 'tut-tutting' noise and sat down on a rock that hadn't been there a moment before and certainly wasn't in the real world. "You make the mistake of assuming we need you. Humph. You could help us, true enough. But it does not have to be you." He pulled out a long pipe and began to smoke. "You jump around far too much. Far too reckless."

"I'm not reckless."

Mad laughter was the only response, which didn't help my mood. He gestured around, indicating the world in which I was trapped.

I crossed my arms and glared at him. His laughter broke into a spastic cough.

"You shouldn't smoke. It's bad for you."

He caught his breath and chuckled. "We can't change how we're made."

"If you're not going to help, go away. When I do get back, and you had better believe I will, I'm letting Gran know you wouldn't help us."

"Huh." He began muttering again, but he raised his voice enough for me to hear the word, "tattletale."

Knowing I had him, I tried to suppress a grin, but I don't think I managed it.

The old man gave me a calculating look, which turned into a devilish grin. "Fine, fine. I will help."

"You will?" Seeing the look on his face, I felt doubtful.

"What help I can."

"Great," I said, trying to squash back the hope that had begun to rise. "Maybe you could get a message to my team."

"No, but I will tell my Margaret that you are alive."

My chest tightened. "I thought you meant you'd help me get back."

"Oh, yes. I don't do portals, but I know something that does. You know, too." He seemed more animated now and jumped off his rock, which promptly disappeared. "I will lure it here. You must get it to take you home."

"Can't you get it to open the portal and let us through?"

"It will come from another world. When it nears this place, it should sense our world and should try to get to it."

"Who is it that you're asking to come here?"

"You don't ask, not without a bargain. And you don't bargain. There's no help for you if you do."

A chill began to settle in the air that had little to do with the fog. "What are you sending here?"

He chuckled. "You have other things to worry about first."

"I'm sure we'll find food tomorrow. And we have water."

"Water. Lots of water. Best to lash yourself down."

It sounded like crazy gibberish, which didn't exactly surprise me. "What are you talking about?"

"Good luck. Try not to die."

He disappeared.

"Tell Gran not to worry!" I shouted into the night.

The fog disappeared, and I was still firmly trapped in the gremlin world. It seemed brighter now, even though it was still very much dark. But this was a dream. I guess it didn't actually matter if it was lighter or darker than the real world.

Something rumbled in the distance and I looked down the meadow and into the night. It sounded like a truck coming, or maybe a train. I sighed and settled back onto the ground. The old coot was gone and Boone and I were alone once again.

Nevertheless, I had hope now. The old man was going to send someone to help. Although he hadn't said send... he had said lure. Why lure?

The rumbling grew louder and I looked up. The wind picked up as though it were running away.

Telling myself it was only a dream, I laid my head back again. Moisture filled the air. I closed my eyes and listened to the roaring noise come closer. Drops slashed against my face and I opened my eyes again.

This time, it was darker, but the sound was there, still growing louder. I sat up, wiped my face, and tried to look at my hand, though I could see nothing in the darkness.

"Good, you're up."

I jumped. Boone stood near me with the bag in his hands.

"I was about to wake you."

"What's that noise?" I asked.

"Storm, maybe," Boone said. "It's starting to rain, so I thought we'd move into the woods. Maybe we'll avoid the worst of it."

"Sure," I said, getting to my feet. "Do we need to worry about lightning?"

"I haven't seen any," Boone said as the rain started to make itself known.

The rumbling sounded closer and the wind picked up.

I looked around to make sure we had everything, but it was more habit than anything else. Everything we had was in the bag.

"I'm right behind you." I had to raise my voice some because it was getting louder and Boone had started to move through the trees.

My clothes became heavy as the rain soaked in.

"Stick close by," Boone said. "I can see pretty well in the dark."

I meant to say, 'me too,' but my thoughts were still spinning over what the old man had said. "Best to lash yourself down."

"What?"

"In my dream, an old man said there was lots of water and we should lash ourselves down."

"Right." It appeared Boone planned on ignoring what I said. "I think we'll be good here."

Despite the thick trees, the wind was fierce. I stood beside a tree, but no matter which side I was on, the blast of air pushed me around.

"Maybe we should move farther in," I suggested. I had to raise my voice to make myself heard.

"I think we need to stay here," Boone yelled back. He was nearby and pushing himself against a tree, trying to keep steady. "It'll pass."

He might have known how to rough it through storms, but would he know these storms?

Raindrops became thicker and heavier. The amount

doubled, and then doubled again. The wind threw me off balance, forcing me to grab a tree to steady myself.

The curtains of water made it impossible to see Boone. It became difficult to breathe without inhaling liquid at the same time.

Then the storm hit.

It felt as though I was drowning. Wind tried to pry me away from the tree, and I tightened my grip. It wasn't long before I stood in ankle-deep water. It might have been higher, but my feet were starting to feel numb from the cold. Even the noise pressed into me, threatening to grind me into the tree or down to the ground.

Is this what a hurricane felt like? A tornado? How are the trees still standing?

Something slammed against the back of my legs and my knees buckled. Trying desperately to hold on, I slid down the tree. Bark scraped against my skin, but I tried to hold tighter as my legs were swept out from under me. My face plunged into floodwater before my feet found the ground again.

Panicking, I reached for the Path. The thought of stemming the tide didn't come up and the full power of the Path roared around me stronger than the storm, because of course, it held the storm and everything else.

Then it didn't.

As though someone had cut a cord, the storm stopped. The rain died, the wind stilled to a breeze, and the clamor of the gale started to subside.

My feet found purchase on the ground and I stood. Despite the fact that I was no longer being buffeted around, I felt unsteady. Holding the Path wasn't helping. After a short struggle, I managed to force it away and lean against a tree.

"Boone," I called, not looking around.

"Over here," Boone said.

Sighing, I pushed myself away from the tree and splashed through the receding flood. The shadows grew lighter as the sun contemplated an appearance. I found Boone sitting in few inches of water, leaning against a tree.

I tried to see if he was okay, but he looked as disheveled as I felt. The water sloshed when I joined him on the ground.

"You hurt?" I asked. I hadn't realized I was out of breath until I tried to say more than one word.

"No. You?"

"No."

We sat in silence and watched the water flow away, leaving mud and debris behind.

At some point, my eyes drifted closed. When I opened them again, Boone was snoring and the sun was bright.

Every bit of myself hurt. My arms were covered in scratches. My body was waterlogged from head to toe.

Miserable was the only way to describe how I felt.

Using the tree as leverage, I pushed myself up as quietly as I could. It didn't work, though. By the time I had moved more than an inch, Boone was awake.

He didn't say anything, which was good. The last thing I wanted to do was try to make small talk.

"I'm going out into the sun to dry off," I said.

The meadow was closer than I had expected. Last night, it seemed we had walked farther into the woods.

The blue-green grass laid flat and looked deceptively soft. When the sun beat down on me, I pulled off my socks and shoes and set them aside to dry before I laid down. The warmth of the sun made me realize how cold I was. My skin broke into gooseflesh as I soaked in the warmth.

Boone joined me. He handed me half of a protein bar before removing his own socks and shoes.

Sometime later, after he, too, sprawled on the ground

drying, he said, "We should have gone a bit deeper into the woods. It was a bad call on my part."

I shrugged, even though he couldn't see me. "It's not as though either of us knew."

"You knew."

"I guessed. Had I known, I would have pressed the issue."

"Huh," he said. He was quiet for a while longer. "Lash ourselves down?"

I stifled a groan, knowing it wouldn't help. "It was a dream."

Boone wasn't going to let me off that easy. "Is that something that happens to Readers? Dreams that come true?"

"No, that's my mother's territory. In my dream, a friend of my grandmother came and said he would help."

"And that told you there'd be a storm?"

I sighed. "No, he said he would send someone who could open a portal. Then said we'd have plenty of water and that we should try not to die."

Boone was quiet for a minute. "I have no idea what to say to that. Are you being serious?"

Knowing how crazy it sounded, I shrugged. "It was a dream. There's nothing to say. After last night, we may need to rethink where to set up a shelter."

Boone took the hint and was probably relieved by the change of subject. "Maybe. Did you notice something strange about the trees?"

"You mean that they're still standing?"

"Something like that. They still have their leaves and branches. Most of them, anyway."

"Pretty impressive trees," I said, not caring.

"I tried to pull a leaf off and it wasn't easy."

"Interesting." I didn't bother trying to sound convincing.

A skittering sound could be heard at the tree line. I bolted up, but Boone moved slowly. It was the first sound I'd heard beyond the rustling noises of hidden creatures.

Boone put on his socks and shoes, so I followed suit. They were still wet, but I felt better with them on. We watched the woods for a few minutes. There wasn't a sound.

"I guess we should get to work," I said, not happy with the prospect.

"Yeah. Do you want to check the—"

A rustling noise in the woods sounded out like a warning. Boone whipped his head around, and we wordlessly moved closer together as we watched the forest line. The noise came again, farther away, then again, closer than the first.

This time, I didn't bother to keep the groan in.

"What is it?" Boone asked.

I sighed. "Grab the bag and get the can of metal ready, but don't open it."

"Gremlins." He sounded resigned, but he grabbed the bag, and without taking his eyes off the woods, he pulled out the plastic container which held the metal. Then he pushed both bag and jar into my hands.

Wordlessly, I slung the pack over my back and out of the way. With the amount of noise they were making, there seemed to be a lot of them.

When I glanced back to Boone, he had a knife out.

"What are you doing?" I hissed. "Put that away!"

He ignored me.

"It's not metal, is it?" I asked. There was almost a pleading in my voice. "Please say you don't have any more metal on you."

"It's a type of plastic," Boone snapped. "Can you keep it down?"

"What?" I shrieked, though I tried to keep my voice low.

There was an increase in the amount of noise from the hidden gremlins.

"You heard me."

"Put the knife away." It was an order, and I put as much demand into it as I could. Even to my own ears, it sounded different.

Boone sheathed the blade, then blinked a few times and glared at me. "What did you do?" he spat, pulling the knife once again.

The noise in the woods died.

"I didn't do anything, you idiot." Internally, I frantically tried to figure out what I had done. It sounded like an order. One that I'd only heard a werewolf give. "But if you don't put that knife away, I am going to make you regret it."

"And what is it that you suggest?" Boone asked, pouring sarcasm into his voice.

"I'm not suggesting anything!" I was losing my temper, but I didn't care. "I'm telling you. Those are Lost in those woods. They aren't the enemy, and they aren't animals."

Screeches and strange howls broke out again.

Boone rolled his shoulders, and after a few moments, he put his knife away. "We don't have anything else."

"We shouldn't need anything else unless you do something stupid." Now that the knife was away, I looked myself over again. If I had had metal, they probably would have swarmed us. I patted my neck and checked my ears for jewelry, everything I could think of.

Then I looked over Boone. He looked metal-free, so I relaxed some. At that moment, gremlins poured out of the forest. Boone stiffened and kept his hand on his hip, which I knew hid the knife.

"The sheath doesn't have any metal in it, does it?" I asked, somehow managing to keep the panic out of my voice. Closing my eyes, I reached for the Path.

Dozens of gremlins began to circle. They were screeching, yelling, and jumping all over one another. What I wasn't hearing was an answer from Boone.

"Does it?" I snapped. The jump to the Path was easy and caught me off guard. In my frantic state, I had assumed there would be a struggle, though I was able to hold back the roaring tide.

"I don't know," Boone snapped.

"Throw it away, then."

Then, the gremlins surged as one. Without thinking, I threw up a bubble of solid Path around us and moved closer to Boone.

He had his hands balled into fists. When the first gremlin sprang at him and rebounded off the air a few feet away, Boone jumped. I gripped his arm, pulled him in closer, and then shrunk the bubble of power around us to a more manageable size.

"You need to calm down," I said. Gremlins weren't predators, and they didn't have much of a reaction to my soul, so I wasn't worried. As another one bounced against our protection, I thought about that again. Well, not too worried.

"What's going on?" Boone asked, jerking back when another struck a few inches away.

"They're curious, that's all. They're..." I struggled to find the right words. "I think they're having fun."

"Fun?"

"Yes. They want to figure out what we are." The worn feeling came on again, which wasn't a good sign. Still gripping Boone's arm, I slung the bag off my back and pushed it into him. "Take this."

He took it and watched in amazement as the small creatures bounced around, over, and sometimes on, one another. I unscrewed the top of the plastic jar and took out a few small pieces of metal. I passed one to Boone, kept two, and resealed the jar, before also shoving it into Boone's protesting hands.

I half sat, half fell down. The nearest gremlin put his hands on the seemingly empty air and leaned as far into it as he could, pressing his nose to the invisible surface. I opened up a small hole and held out one tiny piece of metal. He screeched and snatched it excitedly out of my hand. Then he pawed over my hand, looking for another.

"Come down here. I can't keep burning through this much energy."

Silently, Boone squatted down next to me, and I once again shrunk our enclosure.

Not finding anything else, the gremlin hopped away and was engulfed by his friends. Then I repeated the act with another and motioned for Boone to do the same.

Two other gremlins claimed prizes before I began to sway.

"Is the lid tight on the metal?" I asked.

"Yes." He sounded in awe and he watched the gremlins as though fascinated.

"Good, because I'm dropping our barrier."

"What will they do?"

"Nothing, I hope. And if you pull out your knife again, I swear I'll make you regret it."

Boone grinned, but didn't look away from the gremlins.

I let go of the bubble of solid air, which I had held for far too long, and our shield got swept away. Then I realized my mistake. We should have stood again before I had let go.

Too late now. I pushed the Path away as the first gremlin jumped on top of me. Like they had done with one another, it bounced off again. One rolled in front of Boone, and I saw one take up residence on his shoulder like a parrot.

"You should stand up, before they knock you down," I yawned before the words got fully out.

He moved carefully so his new friend didn't fall off. It did take the chance to jump off before Boone fully stood.

"Come on." Boone held out his hand to me. His eyes were still fastened to the little, green, scaly people.

I sighed, knowing I'd be hard pressed to get to my feet.

CHAPTER

TEN

Resigned, I took the proffered hand and Boone pulled me to my feet.

"Thanks," I said.

"Did you know that would work? Giving them the metal, I mean?"

"It's metal. Of course, they were going to take it."

Boone shook his head. "That's not what I meant."

"I knew it was worth a try, and I knew I wouldn't be able to hold them off for long."

"How exactly did you do that?"

Feigning deafness, I kept my eyes on the ground, afraid I might step on any one of the scurrying gremlins. "They're leaving."

Boone looked in the direction I nodded toward. "Some of them are. Listen, Agent Heidrich, I think—"

"Cassie," I said. "Call me Cassie."

He seemed caught off guard by my statement.

Before he could rally, I did my best to steer the conversation in another direction. "Do you think they live nearby?"

"I think we're going to find out," Boone said.

Gremlins pulled on his pant legs, and moments later, they began to do the same with me. Some were urging from behind as well, bumping into the back of my knees to get me to move forward.

"I'm not sure we should leave the portal," Boone said.

One barreled into the back of me and my knee buckled. It was difficult to keep my footing. "I'm not sure we have a choice."

Boone planted his feet, and one of the gremlins hissed at him. When another repeated the sound, Boone looked disconcerted.

"It's possible I'll know if the portal opens," I said. I was exhausted to my core, and I wanted nothing else other than to curl up and sleep, but the hissing gremlin had unnerved me as well.

After a few moments of hesitation, Boone relented and we were swept away in the tide of gremlins. Around us, they jumped, fumbled, and tackled one another. It was interesting to watch, but I was too tired to take more than a cursory interest.

"Do you mind passing me the first-aid kit?" I asked.

"Everything okay?" Boone asked as he began to situate the bag to a more comfortable position, trying to reach the kit.

"I need caffeine."

He stopped, kit in hand, and looked at me. "Caffeine?"

I rolled my eyes and held out my hand for the kit. He shrugged and handed it over.

"It's not standard issue for a first-aid kit," he said.

"It should be." After taking one pill out, I passed the kit back to him and he stowed it away.

"Do you and your partners take caffeine pills often?"

Sighing, I swallowed the pill before giving a response. "No, most of the time caffeine comes in the form of coffee or the occasional soda. If you have one of those, I'd gladly take it over this."

"No such luck."

"Then I'm stuck with what we have."

He shook his head and re-situated the bag on his back. I knew it was the exhaustion that made me feel cranky, but Boone wasn't helping matters. Soon, the caffeine would give me a bit of a boost. I'd never relied much on caffeine in pill form, so I crossed my fingers and hoped it would be enough.

We walked in silence for a while. Well, Boone and I were silent. The gremlins sounded like they were having a party. The caffeine started to kick in, which was a bonus. If I needed to, I thought I could manage the Path again, but I wasn't going to try it unless I had to.

And I hoped I wouldn't have to. I didn't like the idea of having to rely on Boone if I got myself into any trouble. Two nights ago, he had told me he didn't trust me. Now, I wondered if I could trust him.

How was it that I had never questioned that before? He was an agent and we were on the same side, technically, but that didn't mean I should automatically trust him.

Since we were stuck together for a while, it would be good to get to know him. "Tell me, Agent Boone, if you weren't here, where would you be right now?"

It was a subtle enough start.

He seemed to think about it for a while. "You can call me Boone. Um, hard to say. I'm supposed to be watching your team today. What would you all be doing?"

"I'm guessing Logan and I would be checking up on some of the Lost. Although Agent Paulson might still be interviewing people. If he needed us, we may have been stuck at the office."

"I think I was supposed to meet with him again the day we

went to the portal. It sounded like they didn't have any leads when we left."

"None that I'm aware of." What had Paulson mentioned about Boone? He had left the control room around the same time I had. "Were you at the office when Clancy..." I swallowed hard, not realizing how hard it would be to say Clancy's name.

"No, I had left shortly before," Boone said.

Remembering how I had found Clancy, I gripped a hand over my stomach. We hadn't been close, but it was still hard to believe he was gone.

"I can understand how you might want to look at an outsider," Boone said. "Your office has had a hard time of it this past year."

That pulled me out of my reverie. "What do you mean?"

"Wasn't it a year ago that your last director died in the line of duty?"

"Huh," I shook my head. "Right. Something like that." If being in the line of duty meant while trying to kill me, then sure. But that part had been redacted, and I wasn't allowed to share the truth.

"That was around the time the portals opened, wasn't it?"

The gremlins were bunching together in front of us, which forced us to stop. Amazingly, we were still in the meadow and the tree line was still there.

"Do you find it strange that things are lined up in strips here?" It was a lame question, but I didn't care as long as it changed the subject. I didn't like to dwell on the fact that my boss had hired someone to kill me.

"On the other side of the woods there was another field, a bit like this one. That's where I found the water."

"Over the rise, the hill slopes down and runs into another forest," I said.

"It does seem odd. Orderly, but odd. Maybe the weather sculpts the landscape."

Many of the gremlins had run away, though a few others milled around. It was late in the day and even with the extra boost from the caffeine pills, I was tired.

Making sure to find a spot clear of gremlins, I sat down on the ground. "You know," I said, "when I get home, I don't think I'll ever take a chair for granted again."

Boone chuckled. He came over and dropped the bag beside me. "It's not much, but you can try to lean against it to see if that helps." He looked around as though debating to sit, but stayed standing up.

I tried the bag and no, it didn't help. "Thanks." I leaned against the bag and watched the gremlins. One meandered over and plopped down next to me. Its leathery green skin rubbed against my arm as it settled in.

I watched it for a bit, and then looked around. We were surrounded by gremlins. A few dozed, and a few still had enough energy to bounce around.

"You know, being stuck in another world sucks," I said, "but the fact that we have a job where we meet with and work with people like gremlins is still pretty neat."

Boone didn't say anything.

"Which office do you work for?" I asked.

Outwardly, nothing about Boone changed, but an air of unease stirred. "I move around."

"Really? You're not based anywhere?"

"I go where they tell me."

"Oh, but you're getting a new team, right? That's why you're visiting here?" It immediately struck me what I had said, and I sadly corrected myself. "I mean, visiting our office, back in our world."

"Yes."

"All Lost and humans with special abilities?"

"Humans," he said. "At this time, they're all humans."

"Oh, for some reason, I thought there were Lost as well." Wasn't that the whole reason he was watching our team? "What types of abilities do they have?"

"That's confidential." His voice sounded clipped and tense.

I raised a questioning eyebrow at him, then shook my head and looked away. I tried to find a more comfortable position, much to the displeasure of the gremlin beside me, and laid my head on the bag. The sky was such a deep blue it once again amazed me. Then I closed my eyes, intent on blocking out everything around me.

Right then, I wanted nothing more than to be at home.

I'm not sure how long I slept, but it wasn't long enough. A chittering broke out among the gremlins, which roused me. When I looked around, I saw they were all looking toward the top of the rise. Soon a shriek came and gremlins scattered, several of them climbing over me in the process.

As soon as I was able, I pushed myself to my feet and looked around for the source of the commotion. I saw Boone doing the same.

"What happened?" I asked. Then I had to cover my mouth to yawn. Definitely not enough sleep.

"I'm not sure, but we might want to follow them," Boone said.

"You think?" I grabbed the bag and slung it over my back.

"If a flock of birds flies off suddenly, you take notice."

"Birds?" I looked around, not finding anything.

Boone let out a harassed sigh. "When animals flee, there's usually a reason."

My blood pressure instantly started to rise. "What? They aren't animals."

He looked confused. "What makes you say that?"

"The fact that they're intelligent, you ass." I could feel my face turning red.

"We're all animals. Never mind that, I think we need to move."

"They tend to run." The voice sounded like it came from behind me.

I spun around and stepped back at the same time, trying to distance myself from the speaker. Behind me, a woman stood. I'm a horrible judge of age, but the woman looked ancient. Way older than Gran or any of her friends.

Seeing her eyes, I backed up a few more paces. They looked like the eyes of a much younger woman. They were blue and crystal clear, heavy on the crystal part, and they sparkled.

My tongue had apparently fled with any sense I may have had. Boone grabbed my arm and pulled me further away.

"They are not animals," the woman continued. "They are old ones."

I shook off Boone, who was still gripping my arm. "Do you," I started, but I couldn't nail down any one of the hundred questions the woman aroused. "Um, I wasn't expecting to run into someone that speaks our language."

"More than gremlins travel through portals." The woman's head twitched. "I am Wyna. You are Cassie and Boone, yes?"

"Um, yeah." I wanted to take another step back, but I stood my ground. "How did you know that?"

"Our friends told me," Wyna said.

"Well, Wyna, it's nice to meet you." I made no move forward to shake her hand.

"It is," Boone said. He appeared to finally catch his tongue. "And I am sorry if I have caused offense with the gremlins."

The woman's smile looked too large for her face, which made my skin crawl.

"It is hard to offend them at their age. The younger ones

who are more formal," Wyna said. "The old ones still have sense though. They brought Cassie to see me."

"Why?" My voice was shriller than I would have liked. She was an old lady, after all, not some gun-wielding madman. She looked mostly human. Two legs, two arms, a head. Everything in between shaped womanly. Yet somehow, she managed to put me on edge.

"How well do you know gremlins?" Wyna asked.

I thought that over, not knowing what she was looking for. "Um, not well, I guess. They like metal and they build stuff with it. It's usually not what you'd want built, but, but it's pretty all the same. And they act like, well, like kids."

"They do build, but they also fix. Gremlins can fix anything," Wyna said.

"What does that have to do with bringing us to you?" Boone asked.

The woman grinned. "They want to fix Cassie."

Boone moved a step forward, so he stood closer to the woman than I did. He tried to make it look casual. The fact that I glared at the back of his head probably didn't help it look casual. I'm not sure what he intended, or what he thought was happening. I, on the other hand, was afraid of what Wyna might say at that point.

"I'm not sure we understand," Boone said.

Wyna looked curiously at Boone. "Fix her." Wyna patted her chest. "Soul."

"I'm not sure I follow." Whatever Boone had been expecting, it obviously wasn't this. He looked tense and sounded leery.

"It is obvious to me and them."

I could practically feel Boone wanting to turn to look at me, but like me, he didn't turn his back to this woman.

"You think there's something wrong with her soul?" Boone asked.

Wyna didn't say anything, but watched us both with interest.

I bit my lip. This was something I didn't want the office to know. I mean, it was my soul, after all. I'm pretty sure there wasn't anything in the rule book that said a soul needed to be whole.

"They think they can fix it?" I asked.

Boone stepped back so he could look at Wyna and me at the same time. He didn't look happy about the situation.

"They can fix anything but it is not easy," Wyna said.

My soul can be fixed. Something that Vincent had been researching for ages. No more rude waitresses or waiters, no one getting angry with me for no reason, and no one pulling a gun on me, without quite knowing why.

Well, I hoped for the latter at least.

I cast a nervous glance at Boone, but plunged on. "If the gremlins know about my soul, do they also know about the other pieces?"

Wyna nodded. "They know of these. They sense one of their own among you."

There was a gremlin inside me. "I'm sorry for the gremlin." The idea made my eyes burn and water. "Please let them know it wasn't me that caused it."

Do other Lost know when they looked at me that I had shards of their people inside me? The essence had been split by a mad man and had come to reside in me by accident. There were fewer pieces rattling around inside me, but they were always lingering, waiting to slip in and take control.

Wyna watched me until it became uncomfortable, but I didn't look away. I wanted the gremlins to know, wanted everyone to know that this wasn't something I had done.

"You give one of them passage. A life beyond this one. They do not look to place blame."

I shook my head. "The soul isn't whole. I didn't break it up, but I don't want them to think that it's someone living in me."

"A part of them all lingers on. The part you carry survives."

"I don't understand. It's only instinct that anyone seems to have."

"Sometimes that is all that is needed," Wyna said.

"So, what happens to it if my soul gets fixed?" I asked.

Wyna appeared to think that over or maybe she was choosing her words carefully. "There is no certainty."

"Then why would they want it fixed?" I asked.

"They have no certainty. At least the old ones do not."

"And the younger gremlins?" I asked.

Wyna didn't answer, and I could feel Boone's unease.

"We only want to get the portal open and go home," I said, trying to change the subject.

Wyna's eyes narrowed. "Is that why the creature comes?"

Did I miss a part of the conversation? "What?"

"It is late in the day and you are tired," Wyna said stiffly. "You will return with me and rest. Tomorrow, we make plans."

"We'll stay by the portal," Boone said, speaking at last.

"There is more comfort with me," Wyna said, still sounding curt.

"I'm going to stay by the portal. Agent Heidrich can do as she chooses." Boone didn't wait for a response and walked away into the dying sun.

I hesitated. "He's right. We need to wait by the portal. We shouldn't have left it for this long."

Wyna glowered.

"I'm sorry," I said before following Boone.

She didn't follow, and none of the gremlins joined us. I didn't bother trying to catch up with Boone. I was too tired, and quite frankly, I didn't want to talk about what had happened. Plus, there were a thousand things to think about.

For starters, which world had broken into this one? Would that be worth checking to see if it was ours? Then again, it could also be one of hundreds, if not thousands, of other dimensions around ours. It would have to be close, at least, if not ours.

The day caught up to me. The only reason I knew which direction to walk in was because I had followed Boone. As the sun went down and the sky began to turn purple, I lost sight of him. The Path was out of the question. After the day I had, there was no way I could stay in the Path long and still be standing.

Had there been days like this before my soul was broken? I was sure there had been. Times when I had grown so tired, I was unsteady on my feet. But it didn't seem to be the numbing tiredness I felt now. Before Vincent, I couldn't remember a time where I was so tired I lost consciousness or felt so tired I couldn't go on.

How far from the camp was I? Was staying at the camp any better than stopping here?

The light left the sky and stars popped out, brighter than any stars I had ever seen on earth. I stopped and stared at them, tottering on my feet. It was beautiful, and now something threatened the world.

But what could I do about it?

Once I stopped, it was hard to get started again. Two thoughts drove me forward. One, I didn't know what might crawl on me if I slept here in the grass, and two, I didn't want Boone to find me passed out because I couldn't handle the stress I had put on my own body.

"The camp is over here," Boone said.

I jumped. Had he not spoken, I would have walked right past the spot next to the woods.

Wordlessly, I sat across the fire from him. How had I not noticed the fire? Why was he burning one? I was too tired to ask questions.

Unfortunately, Boone didn't see it the same way. "It seemed like you and Wyna got along well."

I shrugged, not sure what he was getting at, and stared into the fire.

ELEVEN

"So," he started again, "all that talk about souls. That's something I didn't see in your file."

I rolled my eyes. "Will I see the state of your soul in your file?"

He didn't say anything right away. "If you can get the full file, I'm sure my history speaks to the state of my soul."

"It doesn't work that way. What happened to me was an accident. It's one I'd rather not discuss, and it's none of AIR's business."

"How does it work, then?"

I countered a question with a question. "What do you know about Readers?"

"I can't say that I know a whole lot about them. I don't know if anyone besides a Reader, and maybe those close to them, know much."

"But what *do* you know?" I asked.

Boone thought for a for a minute. "You read tracks people leave when they move around."

I raised my eyebrows, waiting for more, but nothing else

came. Bone-weary tiredness had truly settled in, but I could see Boone wasn't going to drop the subject.

"Everything leaves traces in the world. This and ours, although the Path here is difficult. When I read what's left behind, I'm looking at an overlay." My thoughts turned inward as I thought of the Path back home. "It's like a glittering stream that carries everything about the past, present, and sometimes I even catch a glimpse of the future."

"A glittering stream?" Boone said in a level voice.

"Yes," I snapped. "When something or someone moves around, I see the traces it leaves behind, which means I can follow someone back to where they may have entered an area or the movements they took in an area."

"That sounds like a pretty useful talent," Boone said. "What does that have to do with souls? Yours and whoever else you have with you."

I could see his lip curl back involuntarily at the thought and sighed. "I'm getting to that." I was wavering as I was sitting, but I wanted to get this out and sleep. "When I enter the Path, I mentally stretch out. It's hard to explain, but at the edge of my mind, I can see my soul or essence."

"Can you see anyone's soul?"

"No, I can read what traces you leave in the Path, and I can read your emotions when I try. Nothing else." I waited a few beats to see if he was going to interrupt again, but he held his tongue "I'm not sure what's left in the file about last year. On the case where our director died."

Boone shrugged. "Not much. At least that I can see."

"There's probably not much for anyone to see. Anyway, during the investigation, there was an accident. My soul split apart." There was no way I was going to mention Vincent. It would be bad enough if Boone wrote this down in a file somewhere.

Boone looked like he was trying to find the right words. "That sounds uncomfortable."

While yawning, I shrugged at the same time. "You get used to it. It didn't hurt, exactly."

"And Wyna is offering to fix it."

"That's what it sounds like." I tried to make it a throwaway comment, but the truth was, my sleep-deprived brain was still sluggishly trying to figure out what that meant and if it was something I actually wanted.

"She mentioned you have a gremlin inside you. What does that mean?"

"I suppose it's too much to ask that at least part of this could wait until morning?"

Boone said nothing.

"Right." I scrubbed my face with my hands, trying to wake myself up. "It's not that difficult to explain, I guess. It's much harder to understand. Since my soul is broken, it acts like a magnet to other soul fragments around me."

"You're pulling people's souls?" He looked uncomfortable again. "That's a Walker ability."

"I'm not taking out souls and I can't steal someone's soul. Even if your soul was broken, it's yours; I can't take it out of you." I tried to sound confident, but I wasn't completely sure of that fact. "If there are soul fragments lingering around, they are attracted to mine. They want to be whole, so they try to attach to me."

"You're saying there are fragments of souls floating around?"

"No," I said, getting cranky. "They aren't just lying around anywhere. But some really bad guy created them and now they're stuck with me." I tried to make it sound like that was the end of the conversation, but I was too tired to be direct.

"I didn't see that in your file, either."

"Judging by the look on your face, do you think this is something I want to write down where anyone can see? I'd rather it stay out of the files, if it's all the same to you."

"Don't you think this is something your coworkers ought to know?" Boone asked.

"My partners know everything—and in a lot more detail than I'll tell you. When you trust someone to have your back, they have to know who you are and what could go wrong."

In Boone's silence, I took the opportunity to lay down. I could tell sleep was going to be difficult, even through the exhaustion.

"I'd say we're in a pretty tight spot out here, and you haven't been very forthcoming," Boone said.

"You've already said you don't trust me. Has anything I said made you trust me more or less? I'm guessing it's the latter. And I don't see you volunteering details about your past."

"My past doesn't mean much here."

"Doesn't it? So far, you've done more than I ever could to keep us alive. I haven't grilled you about what type of survival skills you have or how you learned them."

He was quiet for a moment. "Fair point," he said at last. "But I'd disagree with me doing more. You knew about the trap in the woods, you kept the gremlins off us, and you can see the portal. Maybe even open it."

"I told you before, I can't open the portal."

"Maybe, but your skills are helping keep us alive all the same."

"Sure, right, until I push too far and kill myself."

"What's that supposed to mean?"

"You don't know anything about Readers, do you? It's how most of us die. We follow the Path, which burns a lot of energy. If we get caught up in it, it kills us, and chances are we won't notice until it's too late."

"I didn't know that."

"Really," I said, yawning again. "It seems to be one of the only things most people do know."

"Is that what happened a few days ago at the portal?"

"Has it only been a few days?"

Boone ignored the remark. "You tried the portal until your nose bled and you passed out."

I lifted my hands to my face automatically. "That's never happened before. At least not that I know. I didn't notice any blood."

"I wiped it off when I moved you here."

"Thanks," I mumbled, then shifted around, trying to find a more comfortable spot.

"Get some sleep," Boone said.

"You'll keep watch?"

"I'll be up."

"Wake me when it's time for my watch." I thought about that for a moment. "What do you do when you're on watch? I never learned."

Boone chuckled under his breath. "Go to sleep."

Sleep came quicker than I had expected.

I didn't remember much from my dreams. They were disjointed, and when Boone woke me up, they melted away. He didn't say anything, but he looked grumpy and lapsed into an uneasy sleep of his own.

This left me alone with a deep sense of homesickness. My thoughts wandered to what everyone would be doing this time of the day. Back home, I would be sleeping, that one was easy. Unless we were on a case, there was a good chance I would have been missing a sunrise.

Gran kept odd hours, so it was hard to say when she might be awake or asleep. I guess that depended on what she saw in the future.

Vincent was about as big of a morning person as I was, so he would still be asleep as well. Or would he be working on getting me home?

Logan and Rider were both 'early bird catches the worm' kind of people. Rider might be up and running at this time of the day. I had snapped at him before I disappeared, which had left our friendship on even rockier terms.

This was no good. At least Boone was asleep. Briefly, I wondered what he missed back home. Once again, tears threatened until I scrubbed my eyes to make them go away.

The first order of business was getting home. Forget Wyna and her offer.

What did concentrate on getting home mean? What did we need to do?

I stood and stretched, increasing my blood flow while staying as quiet as possible so as not to wake Boone.

The sad truth was the only thing we could do was sit and stare at where a portal should be and hope it opened, or at least showed some signs of life. Maybe if someone started to open it, just gave it a little push, I would be able to help it along.

My mind went to Vincent and wondered if he waited for me at the other end.

That's a stupid thought, though. He would be busy. They'd all be busy trying to get us back.

And if they weren't, they were going to get an earful from me when I see them.

The sun began to stretch into the sky. Boone had let me sleep most of the night, but since there wasn't anything for us to do, there was no use in waking him up. I thought about going to get water, but Boone's vague indication of where it was located was a recipe for disaster if I went searching on my own.

The rustling noises started in the forest. Something small had to be nosing its way through the underbrush. Now that the sky was getting light enough, I took a closer look at the woods and the meadow. No gremlins lurked in the trees, as far as I could tell. Since I'd shown them I had metal, they'd be back at some point.

Not that it bothered me. They were cute, in a way. It was hard to believe Wyna when she called them the old ones. They acted like toddlers on steroids. If that's what old age was like, it had an appeal.

I stretched and twisted, getting my muscles to move more after a night on the ground. The blue-green grass was a pretty sight to look at as I twisted one way, then the other. When I turned away from our camp, something sprouted from the grass.

Startled, I nearly tripped over my feet. The person was outlined in the sun, maybe a bit shorter than I was, but certainly not gremlin sized.

"Boone." I received no answer, so I stepped toward him and glanced down. "Boone." I dared to raise my voice above a whisper.

When I looked back at the figure, the person was no longer alone. Three figures stood there.

"What do we have?" Boone rose to his feet next to me and joined me. For all the noise he made, he must have been tiptoe-ing, unless he was part elf.

"I'm not sure." A tingling on the back of my neck made me turn around. There were more behind us. On the hill, it looked like others were rising from the ground as well.

"Where'd they come from?" Boone asked.

"I swear one minute the field was empty and the next someone was there. And now they're all around."

Boone took in the others before turning back to the first. I kept my eyes on the people behind us and tried my hardest to trust Boone to have my back.

Someone made screeching noises, but I didn't turn to see who it was.

"Whoever they are," I said, "they're trying to talk. That's a good sign, right?"

"That might depend on what they're saying." Boone cleared his throat and spoke louder. "I'm sorry, but we don't understand the language."

The sun had fully risen and was no longer hiding the features of those that surrounded us. They were people, most of them shorter than I was, which wasn't something I often see. They were also green and had an almost leathery look.

"Gremlins?" I asked Boone.

"Maybe."

The screeches began again. They wore clothes that looked handmade, but constructed well. If they were gremlins, then it seemed odd to think their old people went running around naked after spending their lives in clothes.

"They're moving closer," I said in a low voice the moment they started toward us.

"Here too," Boone said under his breath.

"Is Wyna around?" I called. "We can't understand you, but perhaps she could translate."

"I am here," Wyna said.

I jumped and banged into Boone. Wyna appeared seemingly from nowhere, next to the woods. She stood very near to where the portal had opened.

"Oh, um, hi," I said lamely. My focus was torn between Wyna and the still-advancing gremlins. "It's good to see you. Um, do you know who these people are?"

"They are young ones. Actually, middle ones, but they do not like the name," Wyna said.

"So, they're gremlins? That's good." I looked at the closest gremlin and saw that he had a weapon. "At least I think it is." The weapon wasn't in his hand, which I took as a silver lining.

"Do you know what they want?" Boone asked.

"Yes," Wyna said. "They are here for you."

"Why do they—" I started, but then wavered. I automatically reached out and jumped the darkness in at the edge of my mind, taking refuge in the Path. I tried to throw up some semblance of a defense, but the Path had altered in flow around us. Instead of smooth rivers, it ran away as if I were the center of a target which repelled it. It fled.

Some semblance of Path remained, but the awkwardness made it difficult to grab onto.

I couldn't shape the Path as it streamed away.

"Why do they want us?" Boone asked, taking over while I fumbled with the Path.

"They would like to speak with you," Wyna said.

"Okay," I said. "We'll talk with them."

"We will?" Boone asked.

"Why not?" I asked.

Boone sighed. "Okay."

Wyna made a screeching noise, but she kept her eyes on us.

As one, the figures stopped moving forward. The first person that had arrived, shrieked what must have been a reply. Back and forth, they went, and then there was silence. Complete silence.

The gremlins looked into the forest and the air appeared to freeze. The trees didn't blow, and the consistent rustling noise that came from the forest stilled.

Ominous. Foreboding. These words popped into my head. Something lurked in those woods. Whatever it was, no one looked ready to deal with it.

When I looked back at the gremlins that had flanked us,

many of them had disappeared. Looking around, only a handful of those that had ringed us in remained.

"What's going on?" I asked, keeping my voice low.

"The creature is moving," Wyna said. "You must go quickly."

The stress that we felt didn't seem to faze Wyna. She kept her back to the forest and looked as though she couldn't care less what was behind her.

However, there was nothing there. Even with the Path behaving oddly, I could see there was nothing close by.

Then, why did it feel like I was being watched?

"Where do we go?" Boone asked.

"They wish to take you to their city," Wyna said, calmly.

"How far away is that?" I asked.

"Many, many harrocks," Wyna said.

"What the heck does that mean?" I asked, still keeping my voice low.

"Far," Wyna said.

"We don't want to get too far from the portal," Boone said.

There was a keening noise, which came from what I hoped was very far off.

"Or maybe we do," I said, watching the woods nervously.

"They will settle on taking you to... a town. Not far from here," Wyna said. "With the beast moving, they will not stay long."

I could feel the indecision radiating from Boone behind me. The noise sounded far off, but it made my skin crawl. And from experience, I knew that the closer I was to any type of predator, the more they would want to find me.

Hopefully, it would remain far away. I closed the Path, wanting to save my strength for later.

"I think we need to go," I said to Boone.

"And if the portal opens?" Boone asked.

"If it opens once, it will open again. I'd like to be alive when that happens, though."

Boone shook his head. "I'll go, but we need to come straight back here." Boone looked hard at Wyna. "Make sure they understand that."

Wyna chuckled, which made my lip curl back in distaste. "They intend to return you. That is the point in fact."

"Then why don't we just stay?" Boone asked.

Wyna shrugged. "They wish you to have a chance at survival." She said it as though she couldn't care less one way or the other.

"We'll go," I said.

"Follow Aghrah." Wyna nodded at the person. "He is the leader for the group."

"You're not coming?" I asked.

"I will meet you there," Wyna said. She screeched again at the gremlin and he turned, walking up the hill.

"He's in a hurry," Boone said, scooping up the bag and tossing it over his shoulder.

"Yeah, I think we should be too." I wrung my hands. "Look, there's something else I need to tell you." I turned back to Wyna, intent on asking her if any of the gremlins could speak our language. "Where did she go?" She had disappeared. I didn't see or hear any trace of her.

"There's something about that woman that I don't like," Boone said.

"Me too." We followed the gremlins, but I repeatedly cast anxious looks behind us until we were over the hill and our little campsite was lost from view.

"What were you going to say?" Boone asked.

"What?" My brain still tried to wrap around the fact that Wyna had disappeared.

"You said there was something else you needed to tell me," Boone said.

"Oh, right." I frowned and tried carefully to line up my words. "This isn't going to help the whole trust issue we have, but we're stuck with each other, so there's more you need to know. About me, I mean."

"Okay." Boone's voice sounded cautious, but I couldn't tell if it was because of me or because he was keeping a close eye on the gremlins.

The gremlins, however, took very little notice of us.

So, I told him everything while we were led through another stand of trees. I kept my eyes on the gremlins as I spoke, but it was only so I could conveniently avoid looking at Boone. He knew about my soul, but I told him the effects I had on what Rider always referred to as predators. I told him about the tiny fragments of soul that sometimes wanted to make their way out—anything that could have a direct impact on him while we worked together.

"I know it's a lot to take in," I said when I finished my speech. When he didn't say anything, I felt the need to chat. "But we are stuck together and it's something you need to know."

"Your partners know all this?" Boone said after another long moment.

"Of course they do. We work together, I couldn't not tell them."

"None of this is in the files," Boone said.

"Yeah, I'd like to keep it that way if we could."

"You didn't ask me if I would keep this quiet."

I shrugged, resigned to my predicament. "It doesn't matter one way or the other. You need to know. If the others were here, maybe not, but they're back home."

"What do they do when something happens in the field?"

He kept his voice level, but I was still too anxious to look him in the eye.

"It rarely happens." I tried to stress that part without making it sound like it never happened. "But I make them carry around tranquilizers."

"They're okay with that?"

"I didn't give them much choice." The words weighed on me. The more information I gave him, the more the office would know. "But Logan's the only one who's had to use one."

Boone walked quietly for a while, so once again I felt the need to converse.

"If you tell the office, could you leave them out of it? Logan, Rider, and Vincent, I mean."

"Why are you telling me this?" Boone asked.

"I told you, you need to know if we're working together. I mean, I know this isn't work." I gestured to the surrounding woods. In the clearing up ahead, the beautiful blue-green grass stood out. "Or maybe it is considered work, I don't know. But if we're supposed to survive together, you need to know."

"What do you propose I do if you attack me?" Boone asked.

For the first time, I looked at him, and I couldn't help but think it was a stupid question. "You're a big guy. I think you could take me down without breaking a sweat."

"Take you down?"

"Do whatever you have to do." Maybe it had been a mistake to tell him everything. Still, if he relied on me, he had to know the extent of how far he could trust me, which I guess meant he couldn't.

It was a sad thought. Maybe my partners couldn't trust me, either.

We walked silently for a while. Since I was sinking into a slow depression, I didn't feel the need to fill the silence.

I should have kept my mouth shut.

Well, it was too late. One more person on the list of people that knew I was a big freak.

"Your powers," Boone said after a while. "When this other personality jumps out, what happens?"

"Nothing," I said. "If I'm not me, you don't have to worry about me Reading the Path. Or them. They can't touch it. At least as far as I've seen."

"That's good to know, at least," Boone said.

I didn't think it was possible for him to be less pleased with the situation, but he was definitely ticked off now.

"Yeah, I guess so," I mumbled.

A thousand different thoughts and scenarios moved through my mind, each one bleaker than the last. If we got back, I'd be out of a job and my partners would slowly move out of my life. People broke apart when they weren't around each other every day. Or, if I kept my job, there would be trouble for not reporting everything.

And all that was *if* we made it back. *It could be me and Boone, stuck here together, waiting for a door that might never open.*

CHAPTER

TWELVE

The gremlins started talking up ahead and one of them ran off. Mutely, I watched. I didn't bother trying to pick up the conversation with Boone again. I had already said too much.

"Here," Boone said, thrusting a water bottle in my direction.

I took it and drank, then wordlessly handed it back to him.

"If things go bad here, we need to figure out what we're going to do," Boone said.

"Honestly," I said, shoving the depression and worry away, "I don't think there's much we can do."

Boone frowned and I hurried to continue.

"This whole world is their home turf. If things go bad, we can fend for ourselves, but we're two humans in a world full of gremlins."

"How long could you hold them off if you had to?" Boone asked.

"It depends on how many there are. I don't trust the Path

in this world. If I was well rested and we stuck together, I could keep them off for maybe thirty minutes."

"And after that?" Boone asked.

"I'd be worthless. Actually, I'd be worthless after about twenty. I could keep it going, but I wouldn't be able to move around much and it would take all my concentration."

"And they are Lost," Boone said. "You were right about that. Fighting would be a bad idea."

"I think here, we're the ones that are Lost. If we have to run, though, we do have one option."

"Which option is that?"

"Back to the portal. Toward whatever it is they're afraid of."

Boone didn't look happy about the prospect.

"We should see what they want, and then head back," I said. "As soon as we can."

The gremlins stopped and it was obvious the leader issued orders. Once again, we found gremlins surrounding us, but this time, we at least saw where they had come from. They fanned out as though in formation and surrounded us.

"I'd really love it if they stopped doing that," I muttered.

"They don't look threatening this time," Boone said. "I've seen several of them glancing back the way we came."

"Do you think we were followed?" I asked.

"No, I think they're scared," Boone said.

"Great." I looked behind us, but could only see a long stretch of woods. "How far do you think we are from the portal?"

Boone frowned at me. "You walked it, the same as me."

"So?" I couldn't help the defensiveness. "It's not like there were mile markers."

Boone snorted and I could tell he was trying hard not to laugh at me. Glowering at him, I put my hand on my hips and waited for a real response.

He held up a finger and cleared his throat. "Hmm, ah, we probably went about three and a half miles."

I looked back the way we had come, as though I could see through the trees. "How much water do we have?"

"Not enough. I'm hoping that whatever town they're taking us to has more."

"And food—what are we down to?"

Boone didn't say anything.

"That bad?" I asked.

"We ate the last of what we had last night."

I nodded gloomily. "When Wyna meets back up with us, we'll have to see if there's anything around here that's edible."

"There will be a gralorge." Wyna appeared from seemingly nowhere. "A feast. For your honor."

"Why for us?" Bone asked.

"Not that we're complaining," I added.

"The young ones are what you would call, formal. Things must be done a certain way."

Most of the gremlins I had seen were older and meshing what I knew of gremlins and what Wyna said wasn't working. Looking at Boone, I could see he was struggling with the concept as well.

The lead gremlin started speaking.

Wyna didn't look at him, and instead kept her eyes on us. As he spoke, however, she broke out into a grin. She didn't look amused, which made me feel less apt to trust her than I had our entire time in gremlin world.

What was it about the woman that made me distrust her so? When her grin widened, I decided it didn't matter. I wouldn't want to be stuck alone with her.

The gremlin went silent, so I looked expectantly at Wyna, figuring she would fill us in on what he said.

When she didn't say anything, I pressed her. "Was there something particular he wanted us to know?"

"Yes," Wyna said.

I crossed my arms and waited.

"The words do not translate well. He says your trial starts at sundown."

"What?" Boone steamed.

"When you are convicted, a gralorge will be held in your honor. You will have a night of rest and reflection, and then you go to meet death."

Coldness started to spread through me. "What are you talking about?"

"Those are closest words of translation." Wyna's grin set in place. She looked as though she was thoroughly enjoying herself.

"A trial for what?" Boone asked.

"We haven't done anything," I said, glaring at the woman.

"It is formality and not meant to be fair," Wyna said. "They follow their procedures. It is their nature."

Trial? That didn't sound like a trial, and we weren't being treated like criminals. "So, what happens until then?"

Wyna glanced at the sky. "You will sleep a few hours in torment chamber."

"What?" It came out as part yell and, sadly, part shriek. I felt a pinch in my side, but carried on. "I think you're mixing up your words."

Wyna chuckled and my skin ran cold. "You can hope."

The world began to dim, taking on a shadowed, unreal look. "What the—" Feeling unsteady on my feet, I clutched at Boone's arm to try to stay upright.

"They have seen what you are capable of. This for your safety and theirs," Wyna said.

The dim surroundings started to move. Boone grabbed me

and whirled me around. My body stopped, but the movement of the clearing continued.

He plucked something out of my side and held it up. I tried to focus on it, but that wasn't happening. The ground moved in waves. Sea legs, I thought, feeling giddy. I needed sea legs. Land sea legs?

Boone spoke, but he sounded far away. He stood steady on the land, and I was at sea. The waves didn't take long to lull me to sleep.

"Where am I?" was what I tried to say. It came out more as, "Whem mar a?"

"That was fast." Boone's voice came from nearby.

It took me a moment to realize I couldn't see him because my eyes weren't open. I had to shake off the fogginess and wait until my tongue caught up.

"What. The hell. Just happened?" I wasn't yelling, but I wasn't happy about my predicament.

Boone sat on a wooden bench not far away with our bag at his feet. "Here." He handed the water bottle over, which I felt thrilled to find full. My mouth felt like it was stuffed with cotton.

One thing was missing. He wasn't upset. He wasn't happy, but not mad, either. As I drank, I looked him over. He sported a wrap on one forearm but aside from that, he just looked grumpy.

That's fine, I thought moodily. I can be mad enough for two.

"How are you feeling?" Boone asked.

"Pissed off," I snapped.

A ghost of a grin appeared.

"What happened?" I repeated.

"You were drugged."

I waited for more, but it wasn't coming. "Yeah, I got that part. What happened after that?" I kicked my legs off what had been a fairly comfortable bed, then stood up. The room spun and I immediately sat back down.

"You okay?" Boone said again. "They said there'd be no side effects."

"Yeah, I'm sure they've tried it on loads of humans." I leaned over and put my head in my hands until the room decided to settle down. When I dared to look up again, it was to glare at Boone, who still hadn't shared what had happened.

"You went down and the gremlins closed in and took us here."

"That's it?" Did he think I was dumb? I started looking around the room, but put off standing. "Then what's with your arm?"

Boone shrugged. "I didn't make it easy."

It was my turn to grin.

"I'm not sure if they drugged me or what, but I didn't resist for long." He didn't look happy about having to admit that. "I think that woman did something."

"I'm not convinced Wyna is one." In truth, she seemed like a curse more than anything else.

"What, not a woman?" Boone asked. "You think she's a he?"

I shrugged. "When we say he and she, we have a very particular thought in mind. It's a very human thought. She may be female, but I think she's a step further away from human than I originally thought."

"Well, whatever she is, it's not good," Boone said.

"Where are we?" I asked. The brightly lit room was airy, and there were plenty of windows. They were barred, of course, since we were apparently in some sort of prison. The bed I had been lying on was shoved against a wall. The only other furnishings were the bench Boone sat on and a small table with chairs in the middle of the room.

"We're in the room of torment." His use of sarcasm was impressive. "This is their idea of punishment."

"Is it?" I asked. I took a chance and slowly stood again.

Boone watched me, as though inspecting my actions. "We have food, water, a bed, and something that looks like a game, though I'm not really sure what it is." Boone gestured to the table.

I made my way across the room. The vertigo kicked in about half way, but I made it to the table and fell into a chair. I ended up putting my head down and closing my eyes, waiting for the room to sit still.

"Right," I said under my breath. I picked up a small but solid bar of metal. There was also a metal rod, and a few other pieces of what looked like scraps of metal. All the metals were different colors.

Boone joined me, but didn't sit.

"Are we supposed to do something with this?" I asked.

He shrugged.

"Maybe to a gremlin it is a torment. Are we locked in?" I spotted the closed door, but it didn't exactly look ominous. Nothing in the room appeared bad. It could have been a guest room if not for the bars on the windows. Paying closer attention, I saw they, too, were wooden.

"We are." Now Boone sounded upset.

"Are we okay with waiting here?"

He shrugged. "I'm not sure we'd get very far if we left. Wyna said this was protocol, and they always follow protocol."

"It's no wonder they go crazy when they're older," I muttered while looking around the room.

"You're okay now?" Boone asked.

"No, they drugged me and locked me up. I'm ticked off." The room was more comfortable than anything I'd seen in days, so it didn't bother me to wait for whatever the gremlins were planning for us. But the point was, they hadn't asked nicely.

"You look pale," Boone said. "Maybe we should rest up while we get the chance."

"Sure," I said. "Just a minute." I wanted to make a statement. I didn't have to go anywhere, but I needed them to know how I felt about their actions. Closing my eyes, I reached for the Path.

I faced a small struggle, but my daily meditation paid off. It helped that the Path at this location wasn't running away from me. It still didn't flow in the nice patterns I was accustomed to, but it was something I could work with.

First, I studied the door, and then turned my attention to the windows. I couldn't manage all the windows. With the Path flowing, I once again felt as though I was on a boat. Two windows and one door. Taking a deep breath, I concentrated. Making the Path solid burned through energy and made me feel queasy, but I soldiered on. It took some weaving of the flow, but I wrapped thick threads around the door and bars of the windows, and when I felt as though I pushed myself too far, I tugged.

The door wrenched itself open and the bars flew out, the wood splintered and broke apart. Then I closed my eyes and pushed away the Path.

The door was the last thing to stop moving. When it did, the world hushed for a few moments, then a hurried conversation of screeches and yammering went on outside the room. Before long, a head peeked into the room from around the doorframe.

I waved politely and turned back to Boone. "Yeah, I could use some rest."

Boone's expression was impossible to read. *Was he about to yell at me or laugh?*

Well, it didn't really matter either way. I was sure I had gotten my point across to the gremlins. I yawned and stretched before pulling myself to my feet again.

The room spun faster and I sat back down hard on the chair, gripping the table for support.

"Was that necessary?" Boone asked, watching me.

Blinking the movement away wasn't working, but I gave Boone an incredulous look. "They drugged me and locked me in a room. Yes, it was necessary."

"And now?" Boone asked.

"As soon as the room stops moving, I'm going to take your advice and rest up while I can. You should do the same." I gestured at the windows and the door where gremlins stood, examining the damage. "I'm pretty sure we're well guarded now, and the bed is way more comfortable than it looks."

Boone shook his head and held out his hand. "Come on."

Reluctantly, I took Boone's hand, and with his help, I made it across the room and fell back into the bed.

"I'll take the floor," Boone said.

I looked at him as though he had grown another head. "That's stupid. The bed's not long, but it's big enough for two."

"I don't think—"

I rolled my eyes and interrupted. "You don't think that we should both get some sleep in comfort. This may be the last chance we get for a while."

Boone didn't look convinced.

"I can keep my hands to myself." I moved over to the other side of the bed and turned over on my side, away from him. It wasn't long before he joined me.

I'm not sure how long I slept, but it was the best sleep I could ever remember having. It had to have been because I had been deprived of comfort for so long, but I didn't care why. When I woke up, I felt refreshed for the first time since entering this world.

The ceiling of the room was wooden and I stared at it, following the grain of the wood and letting my thoughts wander while Boone snored next to me.

Everything about the gremlins was backwards. The old people acted like kids and the kids acted like adults, taking charge and following the rules strictly. They probably even sat on their porches and yelled at the old people to get off their lawns.

They were smart, though. Smarter than I had given them credit for. I wondered if anyone back at the agency knew about the younger gremlins.

Maybe, but they wouldn't hear about them from me.

Boone might be a different story. I still had no idea what he would do or say about the gremlins or about what I had told him regarding myself.

It had been a mistake to tell him, I knew it was. Unfortunately, it was a mistake I knew I would repeat.

My thoughts veered toward home to friends and family, but I firmly stamped them back down.

Gremlins, they were interesting. Wyna, she was a puzzle to figure out. Those were things I could focus on that wouldn't threaten to consume my mind.

Getting out of bed without waking Boone turned out to be a chore, but like me, I think he found the bed more comfortable than he had originally thought and he was sound asleep. Taking a quick look out the windows, I saw a guard posted at each one.

The door was shut and I didn't bother trying to open it. At

the table, I puzzled over the pieces of metal for a short time, but it was only a passing idea of filling time. I drank some water, and then when it looked like the sun was starting to hang lower in the sky, I went to wake up Boone.

He had been sleeping easy when I left him, but now his face was contorted.

"Boone," I said. I'm not sure why I whispered it. I was trying to wake him up, after all, but still, I didn't raise my voice.

When I didn't get a response, I shook him.

Boone gripped my arm and launched himself out of bed, trying to pin me to the floor. My response was automatic, having been etched into my brain by what seemed like countless hours of drills. From the ground, using my hip, I leveraged Boone up enough to draw up my feet, which I planted directly on his chest and pushed as hard as I could while still holding one of his arms. When I let go, Boone fell hard and I rolled away, bounced to my feet, and backed away.

Shit, I had made this mistake once before with Rider. He'd been sound asleep, and I had woken him and received an unintentional punch to the chest.

Boone didn't get up and I didn't get closer. The adrenaline burst that I had received had already drained away and I felt tired. I knew I'd recover quickly, but my hands were shaking, and I decided to make my way over to the table and sit down. While I got myself back under control, I watched Boone do the same.

"Are you alright?" he asked, more formally than I had expected.

"I'm fine," I said. "You?"

He sighed. "Yeah." He got to his feet, making no quick movements. I got the feeling he was doing that more for my benefit than because he was sore in any way. "I apologize."

"No big deal." I said.

He raised an eyebrow at me.

I forced a smile. "Have you ever woken up a werewolf from a deep sleep when he was expecting trouble?"

The eyebrow raised farther and the other joined it.

"No harm, no foul," I said.

I grabbed the water bottle for something to do and drank what I could while Boone sat down on the bench and stretched.

"That was unexpected," Boone said, still being careful with his words.

"Huh," was the only response I could give. Yes, it had been unexpected, but it wasn't like he had meant to do it.

"I've studied your file."

"You've mentioned," I said.

"Your training was rushed and rudimentary."

I could feel my face turn red. "So?" I said trying and failing to make it not sound defensive.

"It happens a lot in cases like yours," Boone said dismissively. "What I didn't see on there was anything that would lead me to believe you could defend yourself. Did you use your abilities to help you out?"

"You're asking me if I attacked you using my powers? You're kind of an ass, you know that? I wouldn't have thrown you using my powers. Keep you away, yeah. If someone attacks me on purpose, sure. Believe it or not, I don't need to use the Path for everything."

My voice was heated, but Boone seemed to take no notice of it. He only nodded.

"You taught yourself?" Boone asked.

"Well, no, I take lessons. And a friend from the city teaches me some things when I get the chance to visit him." Taylor knew more about fighting than anyone I had ever met, aside from Logan. "Are we done with the third degree? You're the one that attacked me, remember?"

It wasn't a very nice thing to say, but Boone let it roll over him.

I took a meditative breath to try to unwind my aggravation. "Besides," I said after a few moments, "you didn't put up any resistance. You let me throw you."

"It took me a minute to realize where I was," Boone said.

I knew that feeling well. Nightmares would rear up and when something wakes you up, you think you're still living the nightmare.

"You seemed to have spent a lot of time reading my file," I said, trying to change the subject.

"Your whole team." Boone leaned back against the wall and stared at the ceiling. "At least what my clearance level covers. There are a lot of blanks. Some facts removed, and as I'm learning, some stuff left out of the official records."

"So, you read about us and you came to study us?" My nose curled up in distaste. "That seems strange to me."

Boone shrugged. "I thought it would be the best way to learn."

"You're human, right?"

Boone lifted his head and eyed me quizzically. "Can't you tell by reading me?"

"If you want me to, sure. But I don't automatically read everyone around me."

"Yeah, well, that seems strange to me. The few men I've worked with that have abilities use them to get every edge they can with those around them."

"Huh. You've worked with a lot of idiots, then? Doesn't matter. Look, people's lives are their own business. I don't automatically read my partners, family, or friends when I see them."

"And coworkers?"

"That gets more complicated. It depends on what they're doing, but when I read them, I have my reasons. Why do you want to know all this?"

Boone shrugged. "What else do we have to do?"

"Fine. Let's flip the tables."

THIRTEEN

For once, he didn't look uneasy about the idea.

"Fair enough." He didn't sound enthusiastic.

Now, what did I want to learn about Boone? "Where did you learn survival training?" It seemed the easiest place to start.

"Military."

I rolled my eyes at the one-word answer. "How long have you been in the agency?"

"Officially?"

"That just opens a whole load of other questions, but it's a place to start."

"Two years. Unofficially? For most of my military career I was part of a small group assigned to work with the Lost in other parts of the world."

"I thought other governments had their own agencies that work with the Lost."

"Most of the places I went didn't have what you would call a real government. There were other countries where the government wasn't exactly in control. Or in some cases had too much control."

I had never thought about what must happen to the Lost in war. "What did you do for them?"

Boone leaned forward on his bench and gripped the seat, but his voice remained level. "It depended on the Lost. We did what we could for them."

"I don't know what that means."

"Some needed more help than others. Some refused to leave their homes, and others had lost their homes. We discovered a few were forced into one sort of slavery or another. Usually to fight, but not always."

Slavery. Not always. Most of my questions died away for fear of what answers I might get.

"In a few areas, the Lost fought against us on their own," Boone said. "Like I said, we did what we could."

"That sounds awful. What did you do when you rescued them?"

"Some found a place in nearby countries. Others came here." Boone shook his head. "Came to the US, I mean. The European nations took in some refuges. Many settled in South America. Then there's an island in the Pacific that's almost all Lost. They live openly with humans. We took a few there."

"Vincent mentioned the island once. That would be interesting to see."

"It's something else, but not always easy for them. It's not the only place that's set up like that, but they are few and far between."

"And when you left the military, you came to work for the agency?"

"Something like that."

He didn't seem sad, but I could tell talking about his work for the military put a heavy weight on his shoulders, so I decided to steer the conversation away. "And you've never worked with gremlins?"

"No. When I knew there was a chance of being around them, I looked them up, but this is the first time I've actually seen them. That portal is the only one AIR has on record that comes to this world. The details were sketchy, but it's interesting that it reopens all the time." Boone sighed. "Or at least it did."

"They'll get it open again," I said.

"It's possible. There's a lot of red tape with that sort of thing."

"You don't think they'll be given permission to open it?"

Boone took his time answering. "No," he said at last, "I don't think they will."

"Even with two agents trapped on the other side?"

"The people that put us here are the only ones that can say what happened. The agency may decide it's better we're here."

"There's not a story they could tell my friends to convince them not to come after me."

"Even if—"

The door to our room opened. Glancing out the window, I could see the sun had started to set. The gremlin at the door spoke, but since Wyna wasn't around, I had no idea what the gremlin said. When he stood aside, opening the door wide, we got the hint.

"Do you have any idea of what we might expect here?" I asked.

"Wyna said it was a formality. A protocol of some sort."

"That doesn't tell us much," I said, trying to be cautious as we left the room. "But, we got some sleep and there's a feast later. That's a plus."

"Maybe," Boone said.

We went down a hall and out into the dying light of the

day. It was the first chance I had to look at the village. The entire landscape looked carved out of the woodland area. I had pictured it in one of those strips of field, but now that I saw the houses nestled into the trees, it was hard to imagine a gremlin town being anywhere else. The houses, the paths, the trees, and the little open area where we were headed, fit together like a puzzle.

The whole town looked like it belonged—as though it were a part of the forest as much as the forest was a part of it.

We entered the open area, which was surrounded by gremlins. They stood formally, almost as though they were at attention. No one peeked around anyone else or jostled for a better view of us as we entered the clearing. They stood still, but some watched us, and some watched the line of gremlins we faced.

I noticed no one stood behind those gremlins. It was difficult for me to tell one person from another, since only the old ones had gotten close to us, but I was betting Aghrah was one of the gremlins that was being watched by the crowd.

One of the gremlins to the side spoke and someone up front responded.

"You must move to the center."

I jumped. Wyna was at my elbow. I hadn't seen the woman approach, and I hadn't heard anyone let her through the formal wall of gremlins.

"How do you do that?" I asked out of my own surprise and frustration. It unnerved me the way she kept coming and going without notice.

She grinned, but only gestured to the clearing.

I didn't mean to hesitate, but something about being in the middle of all those gremlins made me nervous. I'm sure it was because I didn't like being the center of attention. It probably had nothing to do with the fact that we were on trial.

Boone walked to the center. It would be worse if someone had to prod me forward, so I followed on my own.

That was all it took for the proceedings to start. The gremlins up front spoke, mostly to the crowd, but sometimes their focus was on us. There was at least one gremlin from each side of the square surrounding us that spoke.

"What are they saying?" I asked Wyna, who stood off to one side.

Apparently, that was the wrong thing to do. Arguments broke out, or maybe it was only that they were yelling at us. It was hard to tell.

"They are speaking charges and debating the action to take," Wyna said. "You should not talk at this point."

"We're not even allowed to know what they are accusing us of?" I asked.

"Accuse is harsh word. More a suggestion of what is possible, what you have done, and what you could do."

"They're blaming us for stuff that hasn't happened?"

"Not blame. They are weighing the possibility. This should be over soon."

"Then what?"

"A feast, rest, and tomorrow they sent you back."

"That's it?" I crossed my arms and glared at the gremlins. "This is crazy."

"Protocol."

"Let's let them get this finished," Boone said. He sounded as testy as I felt.

Glaring at the gremlins, I didn't say anything. When we stopped talking, they stopped yelling at us and went back to their statements, or whatever it was they were doing. I couldn't speak gremlin, and the screeches, howls, and chittering noises they made were completely indistinguishable to me as a language. However, after a while, there was a feeling of monotony to the proceedings. Maybe it was better we didn't know what they were saying, because they sounded quite bored with it.

The sun had fully set and lights were set out. While the gremlins spoke, I studied the lights. It wasn't flame, and it didn't look like electricity, but it glowed steadily and the area shined with a lovely blue tinted light.

Unfortunately, I couldn't get closer to investigate. I took one step away from the center of the square and squabbling broke out again. I rolled my eyes, moved back, and then they began to drone on again.

It's hard to imagine screeches as a droning, but that was definitely what was happening.

Yawning widely, I looked around at the gathered gremlins. They could have been watching a tennis match as their eyes bounced from one speaker to another without moving their heads around.

When they stopped talking, it took me a few moments to realize that they were waiting for something from us. Boone looked at Wyna and waited for her translation.

"Say..." Wyna seemed to search for the right word. "Closed."

I wanted to ask why, but it looked like Boone wanted to be done with the whole affair. He said the word, Wyna translated, and the gremlins broke ranks. Many gremlins disappeared, but others came up and patted our arms. They screeched at us, but it seemed to be in an odd, friendly sort of way.

Gremlins that had left reappeared carrying tables and chairs. After several had been set up, we were guided over to take a seat.

Across from us, Wyna and the gremlins that had run the trial sat down.

Looking at Boone, I saw that the gremlin-sized chair and

tables weren't working well for him. They were small to me, as well, but Boone looked like he was being folded in half.

"I'm so confused," I said as what might have been food was sat before us. My stomach growled at the smell, but I couldn't identify anything. "Why did all that happen?"

"Before the gremlins sentence you," Wyna said, "they must first be convinced of a crime. With no crime, they cannot sentence you."

That idea made me cranky, but before I could talk, Boone broke in. "So they trumped up charges to sentence us to something."

Wyna frowned. "I do not know that word. Trumped."

"They made stuff up," Boone said.

"Young ones have very little ability to make something up, and it's against their beliefs," Wyna said. "You eat while you have chance."

Looking around, I saw that all the gremlins had settled down. They were eating, and I stared at their plates trying to determine what it was. Boone already had a plate full of food. I added small scoops of stuff to mine.

A blue gelatinous substance that had little pockets of steam inside, sat in front of me. Something that had to be a meat of some sort was being passed around. It almost looked like BBQ chicken, but since I had seen no birds, I couldn't hazard a guess as to what it was. A thick, pasty substance, something that looked like crumbly dry stuffing and a thin brown sauce that everyone seemed to pour on top of everything else, rounded out the meal.

Swallowing hard and ignoring my growling stomach, I watched Boone, who ate slowly, but he was eating a bit of everything. I wanted to see what type of reactions he was having to the food, though I may as well have been reading a blank slate.

Cautiously, I poked the blue substance with a wooden utensil that looked like a cross between a shallow spoon and a spatula. Then I tried it. It was tart. Very, very tart. Without noticing, I ate an air bubble. When it popped in my mouth, the hot steam released, leaving a sweet taste in its wake.

I tried bits of other things. The meat was more like chicken than I had expected, but there were little white pieces embedded in each bite. Gristle, maybe? When I chewed, it seemed like gristle. The stuffing was bark. There was no way around it. It was bark, with maybe a few roots or something. I tried a little of the brown substance on top, but the flavor didn't improve, turning more bitter than I was prepared for.

Nevertheless, it was food. When I saw the gremlins take seconds, I added more of the blue stuff and meat to my plate, but passed on the rest.

"You might not want to eat too much," Boone said, keeping his voice low.

"I don't think there's much fear of that."

He grinned, but went on. "My digestive system is used to different types of foods. If yours isn't, you may want to wait a while before you eat anything else."

I hadn't thought of that. At the same time, I was starving. I ate a little more of the blue stuff and meat, but stopped there.

A commotion at one end of the clearing caused heads to turn. I heard the clatter of wooden place settings being shuffled. Then I saw the gremlins and Wyna move their chairs back from the tables.

Then we were overrun with gremlins, the old gremlins, the ones I was used to. They jumped on the tables, the chairs, and even on top of the young ones. The younger gremlins tried to ignore them as best they could, like a rude, uninvited guest, but one they didn't want to offend. It took dedication to ignore a gremlin bouncing up and down on your lap.

One crawled up on me and tugged on my shirt, then clattered up onto the table and ate some of the blue stuff. I had expected the gremlin to eat with their hands or put their faces into bowls. Instead, they snatched up the spatulas and fed themselves.

Some of the younger people were having trouble staying in their chairs as the older ones pulled on their clothing. It then struck me, I wondered if the old ones were their parents. Their parents wanting them to come away from the table to play.

I had to cover my mouth to stifle the giggle. Not a laugh, but a giggle, and I didn't care. It was cute. Another gremlin ended up in my lap and it started to nibble on my arm playfully.

This might work with other gremlins, with their tough looking skin. But the old gremlin's pointed teeth sank straight into my skin. I yelped and slapped a hand over the holes that were starting to bleed. It stung like mad.

The table went quiet. I looked around, worried I had broken some sort of etiquette. Not that it would bother me too much if I did. They had put me on trial and sentenced me to something, after all.

The little gremlin in my lap patted my arm gently.

"You okay?" Boone asked.

"Yeah, I don't think it knew our skin isn't quite as tough as theirs."

"You didn't, did you?" I asked, forcing a smile and looking down at the old one.

Noise broke out again, as though it hadn't stopped. The gremlin jumped off my lap, and before long, the old ones had their fill and started finding spots to lie down.

Hearing things falling and breaking in a nearby house, I guessed not all of them had decided to sleep under the stars.

"Time to go for night," Wyna said.

"What do we do?" Boone asked.

"Go to central house. Room for you there."

"Where's that?" I asked, still holding the stinging bite on my arm.

Wyna spoke to a gremlin before addressing us again. "Aghrah will lead. I will come in morning."

Aghrah stood, and without waiting for a response from us, he walked away. We had to hurry around the table to keep up. He led us to a house, slightly larger than some of the others, and opened a room for us.

"Thank you," I said uncertainly.

Boone ducked and entered the room and I followed, shutting the door behind me. He opened the bag and rummaged around. I went straight for one of the beds. There were four in the room along with one table and two benches.

"I wonder if they have showers or a bath," I said.

"Not that I've seen," Boone said. He tossed the first-aid kit to me. "Clean your arm, though."

"It's okay, it just stings a bit."

"Clean it and wrap it well," Boone said. "If it gets infected in this world there's not much we can do."

My nose curled up at the idea. "I hadn't thought about that."

Once the arm was cleaned up and covered, I stowed the first-aid kit and fell into bed.

"Tomorrow we go back to the portal," I said, staring up at the ceiling.

"We'll need to figure out what we're doing after that."

"What do you mean?" I asked.

Boone shrugged. "How long do we wait? We'll need to decide."

My heart sunk. He didn't think we were going to get back.

It was always a possibility, but one I was prepared to ignore. "We don't have to decide yet."

He didn't say anything, but I heard him get into another bed.

LIGHT STREAMED THROUGH THE WINDOWS, but I wasn't in a hurry to get up. We'd be going back to camp, and while I knew we needed to be there, I also knew I'd miss having other people around. Even if I didn't know the language, it was enough that they were there.

When I heard Boone moving, I finally relented and got up.

"Think they'd let us drag a bed back with us?" I asked.

"They're a lot heavier than they look," Boone said. "They left us breakfast."

My stomach wasn't feeling its best after dinner last night, but food was food at this point. We ate in virtual silence until someone opened the door and poked their head in, making what might have been polite inquiries as to our whereabouts. It could just as easily been a crude joke at our expense, but it sounded all the same to me, so I'd pretend it was polite.

I grabbed our bag and we left the house. Outside, there were gremlins lined up, and we walked between two rows facing one another to Wyna, who stood waiting for us.

Wyna beamed and it looked almost sincere, but there was a hint of darkness beneath the look that still made me not trust the woman.

"So," I said, "we're free to go?"

"Yes," Wyna said. "And they are giving you this." She took a cloth-wrapped package from the gremlin next to her and gave it to Boone. "Food," she added when Boone pulled back a corner and inspected the contents. "And these." She passed over two short spears, each one with a sharp tip that appeared to have been baked out of clay.

"Um, thanks," I said.

"You have water," Wyna said. "And this for you." She handed me a little bottle. "They are sorry about the injury and want you to drink tonight."

"Um, okay," I said.

"It will stimulate healing, but takes several days," Wyna said.

"Well, um, thanks. Tell them thank you," I said. I turned the sturdy little bottle of red glass around in my hand. It was the first time I had seen glass here.

"Now, you face the beast," Wyna said.

"We're going back to our camp, and then going home, I hope," I said.

"Yes," Wyna said. "That is where you will face the creature."

"What?" I tried to keep the accusation out of my voice.

"That is your sentence. To be fair, they are luring the creature to you," Wyna said.

"That's not—"

Boone interrupted me before I had a chance to get a good grip on my anger. "Maybe it's not as bad as we think it is. What is it they want us to do?"

Wyna grinned and looked straight at Boone while speaking to the gremlins. Two ran off. "Fair question. They created a sample of the creature."

While awkwardly holding the spear they had given me, I crossed my arms. "You're asking us to kill something."

"Kill the killer, yes," Wyna said.

"This isn't our world," Boone said. "We don't go to other worlds and kill things."

Wyna cocked her head. "This is not a creature of this world. Like me, like you, it is not from here."

"We only have your word that this thing is causing trouble," I said. "For all we know, you're causing the trouble." It was the wrong thing to say.

Wyna's eyes hardened, but before she could say anything, the two gremlins returned carrying a small statue.

"This is the beast," Wyna said.

I looked at the figure and blinked, not believing what I saw. Large wings spread out from the smaller body. The metal gleamed, but I knew in real life that the creature would be inky black with leathery wings. It had a long beak, even though I knew it could speak in some semblance of our language.

"It looks like a pterodactyl," Boone said.

CHAPTER

FOURTEEN

My heart nearly seized when Boone's words cemented my understanding. "How did it get here?" I demanded.

"We do not know," Wyna said.

"You didn't call it here?" I asked, not wanting my dread to take hold.

"No one I *know* would bring this here," Wyna said with a cruel glint in her eyes.

"Where did it come into this world?"

"We do not know. We know where the killing began," Wyna said.

"What have you done to stop it? What have you tried?"

Wyna shook her head. "Nothing that worked."

"Is it at least injured?" I asked, barely waiting for her whole answer.

"No one has been able to damage the beast," Wyna said.

My heart pounded and I breathed heavily, but I couldn't take in enough air.

"Do you know what this is?" Boone asked.

"You people lured it to our camp?" I asked, hoping I had misunderstood something along the way.

"For you, yes. For easy access," Wyna said. Her grin was back, and this time she showed teeth.

I looked around at all the gremlins, then back to Wyna. "You let it get this close to a village?"

Wyna shrugged. "That is why we are sending you. If you are unable to deal with the creature it will not matter how far away they live."

She was right about that. A creature like this could devastate this world.

"Cassie," Boone said a little louder. "Do you know what this thing is?"

I glanced at him before turning back to Wyna. "How far away is this thing now? Is it going to be there when we get back?"

"Depends on speed it travels. You have more information than we."

I rubbed my forehead and tried to think fast. There had to be a way out of this.

"Agent Heidrich," Boone snapped. "Answer the question."

"Yes!" I yelled. "Okay, yes, I know what it is."

"Is it a dinosaur?" Boone asked.

"No, it looks like a dinosaur, a sordis, I think, but it isn't one." I tried to wrack my brain for everything that Logan, Rider, and I had discussed when we had last faced the monster. "And it's a demon."

"A demon." Boone looked at me blankly, not getting the magnitude of the issue.

"Yes, and if you haven't run across one, count yourself lucky." It couldn't be the same one, could it?

"I've heard of things called demons," Boone said, "but I haven't heard that from anyone in the agency."

"They're not allowed in our world," I said.

"They are not allowed here, but it could not be prevented," Wyna said.

"Have you see one before?" I asked.

She shook her head. "No, in your world, many things are called demon. Including humans."

I nodded and looked blankly at the gremlins. They remained standing in their rigid lines. Turning my attention to the short spear they had given me, I couldn't see how it would be any help in a fight with this thing.

"You need to get the gremlins farther away," I said. "There was mention of a city. Maybe it will avoid something larger."

"You wish them leave their homes?" Wyna asked.

"I want them to survive," I snapped. "This thing will make short work of this place."

"I speak with the leaders, but make no guarantees," Wyna said.

"Try," I pressed.

Wyna nodded, though she looked reluctant. She started screeching at the gremlins, and they broke their formation and moved to the village square.

"Now," Boone said, "it's time you fill me in. If you've fought something like this before, we might have some sort of advantage."

Needing to get a grip on myself, I took a few meditative breaths. "I can't see any sort of advantage, but you know more about fighting than I do. Wyna's right, there are lots of things called demons, even by the agency. This is only one of them, but it's one I've run into before."

"How did you beat it?" Boone asked.

"With Logan, Rider, and I working together, we brought it down, but we... we weren't able to keep hold of it."

"I need to know everything you know," Boone said.

He wasn't wrong, so I told him. The entire story of our previous director and the deal he had made. How we had tracked it, lured it out, and brought it back to the agency. Then, how it had opened a portal directly in the office and made its escape. Everything I could remember, I told Boone.

"Your advantage," I said, wrapping things up, "it will want to kill me above all else."

"They made it sound like an animal," Boone said.

"It's one of the Lost," I said. "It's smart, careful, and calculating."

"And you're saying it can use the Path?" Boone asked.

"It uses energy. The Path in our world doesn't much like the creature, but it steals energy from it." Sadly, I had learned many tricks from the demon, including how to make the Path solid, but Boone didn't need to know that.

"But you can take it down?" Boone asked.

"What? No! Last time it took me, an elf, and a werewolf, and we were still badly injured. And it got away."

"You know more about it now, though. And our goal will be different this time."

"How so?" I asked.

"You were trying to capture it. I don't think we have that option here."

"You want to kill one of the Lost?" I asked.

"Do I want to? No. But they've lured it to the portal and we need that site."

Feeling miserable, I shook my head. "Maybe I can lure it farther away." There was no real hope for that. It was a temporary solution, if anything.

"No. Our only hope at this is going to be to stick together and fight together."

There was no hope for that, but I kept that thought to

myself. We couldn't go into a fight with this thing with a defeatist attitude. Well, at least we both couldn't.

"Do you have an idea?" I asked.

Boone hesitated. "Not yet, but I will. If this is going to work, though, we're going to have to plan and execute as a team."

"You mean we have to trust each other," I said.

"Yes." He didn't look abashed at the question.

I shrugged. "You're the soldier here. I'll trust your judgment. The problem is that I'll see things you won't. Can you trust me if something changes?"

There was another hesitation. "You've had my back so far."

He didn't sound convinced of his own words.

"You know as well as I do, this is different," I said, not pretending I believed him. "As far as the fight goes, I'll follow your lead."

A hint of a grin appeared. "Even if I give an order?"

"In a fight, absolutely," I said. "If you try to make me peel potatoes or whatever, we'll have a problem. But you're not going to have all the facts when you're giving the order. If you say flank left and I see a barrier invisible to you, what are you going to do when I don't go left?"

Boone rolled his shoulders. "Do you know what it means to flank left?"

He was playing for time, so I went with it. "Is it your left or mine? Or someone else's? I never asked."

He grinned again. This time it reached his eyes. "Let's go with your left."

"Your call," I said. "In all seriousness, though, if you use hand signals, I'm going to have to make things up as I go along."

He laughed. "Maybe I can teach you a few."

The laughter helped me catch control of my frantically pounding heart and get a grip on myself. "Outside of agency training, that's the first time someone has offered to teach me the hand signals. How is it everyone automatically knows them?"

"It must be a guy thing," Boone said.

That made me crack a smile. "I think it's more of a 'not Cassie,' thing. While you're at it, you can tell me what you do when you keep watch, especially when there's not a tree to lean against."

"Sure thing," Boone said with a grin. Although he still looked in decent spirits, he turned serious. "We both need to get familiar with each other's strengths and weaknesses in a fight. And we'll need to learn fast."

"Let's get started, then," I said.

Boone nodded at something behind me. "We may need to wait till we're outside of town."

Wyna walked over with a small group of gremlins, each one carrying a spear and wearing wooden slats on their forearms.

"There was some success," Wyna said. She appeared to be in a better mood than she had been earlier. "A few will leave."

"And the others?" Boone asked.

"Some will stay and some will travel with you," Wyna said.

"What? Why?" I asked.

"To understand," Wyna said.

"If they're coming with us they might not get the chance to understand anything." I looked around at the gremlins. The largest was a half foot shorter than I was.

"Not the right words," Wyna said, appearing to think. "If you fail, they will know more."

"They're going to stay out of the way?" Boone asked.

Wyna shrugged. "They will fight if they know they will win. They will not take orders from you."

"That sounds familiar," Boone said, again with a hint of a grin. "Ask them to stay back during the fight until the creature is down."

"I will ask them, but they will do what they do," Wyna said.

"And we can't get them to leave the village?" I asked.

"Not one wishes to leave their homes. Some have hope you will win," Wyna said.

Some, but not all. Not that there was much for me to say about it. I also didn't think we'd succeed.

"Right," Boone said. "Before we go, we need traps."

"Traps?" Wyna asked.

"Yes, we found one next to our camp. We need more of them. As many as you can put together."

Wyna made a few noises and one of the gremlins ran off. "They have a few in town. They will be gathered."

"And whatever they used on me," I said. "To make me sleep. We're going to need that. Lots of it."

"It has been tried with no effect," Wyna said.

"They wouldn't have been able to pierce the demon's skin. I'm not sure we'll be able to, either, but we have to try," I said.

Wyna nodded. "They will bring what you ask for."

"Do they have anything else they think might help?" I asked.

"Nothing," Wyna said. "You will need to leave soon."

"Okay," Boone said. "We'll go."

I took one last look at the peaceful village, sad to see it bristling with so many spears, and we left. Shortly after we had gone beyond the town, the traveling band of gremlins began to follow well behind us.

"Do you know where we're going?" I asked. "I wasn't exactly conscious when we entered town."

"I mostly know the way," Boone said.

Mostly? Well, it was better than me, I guess.

We were well outside of town before Boone began to express what he had apparently been bottling up. "I don't like this," he said.

"That makes two of us," I said.

"I feel like we're being forced into something here. Forced into someone else's fight."

I hesitated, but knew it was a time for honesty. "From your point of view, that's what's happening. I think this may be my fault."

There were a few screeches behind us. Boone glanced back and took the opportunity to give me a surreptitious look.

"I'm going to need more than that," he said.

"This thing can open portals," I said.

"Wait," Boone stopped and looked at me, the surprise evident, "isn't that a good thing?"

"Nothing about this thing is good." I was certain of that one thing.

"How is this your fault?"

"My dream, the one before the storm. I think it really was my grandmother's friend."

Boone looked at me, waiting, so I explained. I gave more details about the dream and the crazy old man that said he was helping.

At some point, Boone started walking again, seemingly lost in thought as I poured out everything I knew. When I finished, Boone only had one thought on his mind.

"Can this thing get us home?" he asked.

"We can't let a demon back into our world," I said. "We can't let it stay here, either." I glanced back at the gremlins, wondering how they would survive with a demon stalking the world.

"You're right," Boone said, giving up the idea faster than I thought he would. "We need to come up with a plan."

"We'll have to before we get to the camp. It travels fast when it wants to. There's no way to know when it might show up."

"It sounds as though this thing likes the night," Boone said.

I shook my head. "I don't think it cares one way or the other. It opened multiple portals all at once, bright and early in the morning. It opened another late in the day, but it was still light out."

Boone seemed to think about that for a few minutes. "Does it sleep?"

"It lived in a cave, which I assume it used for sleeping. It slept when we tranquilized it as well. Sort of, anyway."

"Sort of?" Boone said.

"It kept trying to wake itself up. It drew in energy from its surroundings, even though it was unconscious. I think Dr. Yelton shot it up with tranquilizers used for elephants. That was the only thing that fully knocked it out."

"Let's take a break here," Boone said.

"Already?"

"Yes, I need to see what you can do and you need to know what to expect from me," Boone said.

"If I'm going to use the Path later, I don't think—"

"Not the Path," Boone said. "You took me by surprise this morning. I want to see what else you know."

I glanced around at the blue-green grass, which may as well have been as soft as a training mat back home. "Can't I just tell you?"

"It's better this way."

Wringing my hands, I looked around again. "Here?"

"Best place there is," Boone said.

"And you want me to... what?"

Before the last word had left my mouth, he launched himself at me, going for my throat. In classes, the attackers went slow, ensuring you had plenty of time to move. Boone came at me fast. When he launched himself at me, instead of trying to strangle me, like most humans would experience, he tried to hit me.

Thankfully, Taylor had also taught me a few things and practiced with me. Dr. Taylor knew full well what I might face at work, and he knew there was a good chance it wouldn't be a human attacking.

I crouched down and sidestepped his hand. As I moved past him, I elbowed him hard in the back and moved away, but he didn't let up. He came at me again, faster this time. Blocking his attack with a forearm, I stepped into him, instead of away, and once again used my elbow to strike out and up.

Boone's stance became tighter, less sloppy, and more refined. Next time he punched, I managed to block his arm but missed his knee.

I staggered back, wincing from the blow. He gave me a few seconds and I gladly took them. When he moved in again, I was ready. I was able to block his arm and beat him to the kick, knocking his feet out from under him.

It worked! I hadn't expected him to go down. The elation was short lived.

Back on his feet again, Boone punched out. As I blocked, he grabbed my arm, used my own momentum to yank me forward, and kicked me behind the knee.

Thankfully, it wasn't a hard kick, but it knocked me to the ground all the same.

"Okay," Boone said when I didn't get up, "your turn to attack me."

"What?" I asked. Being wary of a ruse, I watched him carefully when I stood. "Are you sure?" The thought of hurting him never surfaced. The fact that I was going to look like an idiot was taking up all the space. Attacking didn't come naturally to me.

"Come on," Boone said.

There wasn't much choice. I readied myself and could feel my face grow red. Pretending he was a practice dummy, I lashed out. He easily knocked my arm away, not even using his forearms to block. My second attempt wasn't much better.

"You're not trying," Boone said. "Don't you fight with elves?"

By that point, I was hot and sweaty. Since there was still no shower, it wasn't helping that I could smell him as much as he must have been able to smell me.

"Are you kidding me?" I asked, panting. "Who in their right mind would fight with an elf?"

"Logan didn't teach you any of that?" Boone asked.

"No. I've seen Logan train his son. I wouldn't stand a chance. Did you fight with elves?"

"No, but I know you didn't learn all of that stuff in a self-defense class."

"I have a friend who helped out."

"And he didn't teach you to attack?"

"We've been concentrating on what I can do to stay alive." I rolled my eyes. "I know our priorities are completely messed up."

"Again," Boone said, ignoring my sarcasm.

It was no good. I sucked at attacking. I punched, he blocked. I tried to punch and kick and he blocked both.

"Try harder," Boone snapped.

Fine, try harder. How do you just attack someone and mean it?

I took a few steadying breaths. He's a bad guy, I told myself. Not a friend, but a dangerous person that had to be taken down. Hitting with and sort of fist never worked for me.

When I tried to punch, I immediately followed it elbow to his side before jumping back out of his reach.

"Better," he said. "Again."

And I attacked, trying the same combination. This time, he didn't let me back away. He managed to hook my leg and pull it out from underneath me.

I hit the ground hard. Dammit! That hurt!

"You can't back away," Boone said. "Come on, get up."

Breathing hard, I got back to my feet feeling distinctly pissed off.

"Try again," he said.

I hit, he blocked. I kicked, he blocked. It wasn't until he tried to hit back that I had something to work with. I grabbed his arm, and much as I had done that morning, I fell back, dragging him with me, planted my foot on his stomach and kicked out as hard as I could. He didn't quite get thrown straight over me, like he had previously. This time, he fought the throw, so it ended up being more to the side and back. Still, he hit the ground with a satisfying thump.

"Time out," I called, panting from the ground.

"Thank goodness for that," Boone said.

I noticed he wasn't in a hurry to get up either.

Trying to catch my breath I said, "You could have called it yourself."

Boone shrugged and got up, going back to where he had dropped our bag. "We should get some rest, and then we'll move on." He took out the water bottle. He had already caught his breath and didn't look too much worse for the wear. He was sweaty, but he moved easily.

Where I was sore as hell.

"You okay?" he asked.

It was enough to force myself to my feet. "I'm fine."

We heard a screech behind us and turned. The group of

gremlins following us had paired up and were fighting. Silently, Boone handed me the water bottle and we watched as gremlin attacked gremlin. The attacker would get thrown down and the other would patiently wait for his partner to get up, then they'd start again.

"They're copying what we did," I said, stating the obvious.

"And learning it," Boone said.

"I'm not sure that's a good thing." I was uncomfortable with the idea of teaching the gremlins how to fight. Although, I guess we hadn't taught them so much as they had decided to learn.

Boone shrugged. "Today, it can only help them. At least if the demon finds them."

I shivered thinking of the demon ripping through the little creatures much as it had the troll back home.

"We'll need to refill the water," Boone said.

"Did you notice a place on the way?" I asked.

"No, but maybe they can tell us where to find one."

"Maybe." I watched the gremlins throw each other around a little longer. "They don't speak the language, but I don't think we'll have too much of a problem communicating. At least not for water."

"Hey," Boone called out.

The gremlins stopped, or rather some of them did. The distraction caused a few eager gremlins to get their attacks through, and more than one screeching squabble broke out.

Two of the gremlins approached, but they looked uneasy and didn't get too close.

Boone shook the water bottle and pointed to it. There wasn't much more than a few drinks left. "Do you know where there is water?"

The two gremlins looked at each other. Then they turned and ran into the woods next to the field.

"Huh. Do we follow them?" I asked.

One came back into sight, screeched at us, then disappeared again. Boone grabbed the bag, and the gremlin appeared again with what clearly sounded like a screech that would be translated as 'come on,' then left again.

"Is this out of our way?" I asked.

"We have to go through these woods to get back to our camp," Boone said. "But we didn't come this way."

"Close enough, I guess."

We followed the two gremlins into the woods, and a little while later we heard the others following behind us.

Boone looked behind us. "We have our own armed escort."

"I think *we're* supposed to be the armed escort." The words broke up in a yawn at the end.

Boone echoed the sentiment. "We'll take a break when we stop for water. Maybe eat something. I don't think we'll get much rest later."

"Definitely not. Even knowing it's in the same world makes my skin crawl."

"Your director called this thing to our world?" Boone asked.

"Yep." I looked around as though taking in the sights.

"And he tried to have you killed?"

"He wanted me out of the way. I guess killing me seemed the easiest course of action."

Boone shook his head. "It's no wonder you read the Path of your coworkers."

"Everything I told you is classified," I reminded him. "I don't think the agency will appreciate it if they see it show up in reports again."

"I'm sure they wouldn't," Boone said under his breath.

The sound of running water distracted me. Since it was a conversation I wanted to leave, I changed the subject. "The water you found before, was it a stream?"

"No, it wasn't much larger than a puddle."

The sound grew louder and a small waterfall came into view. The gremlins were standing under letting the water cascade over them.

The noise escaped me before I realized it. It was a wistful groaning sound at the thought of a shower.

Boone chuckled, but I ignored him.

The two gremlins looked at us, chatted for a moment, and then jumped into the little pool of water. It was crystal clear with a rocky bottom. In a few strokes, they were climbing out the other side. They made noises in our direction and disappeared into the woods, skirting wide around us.

"Come on," Boone said. "We can fill the water bottle and we may as well get clean while we have the chance."

He dropped the bag and peeled off his shirt.

"Do you think they'll mind?" Not waiting for an answer, I was already sitting down and taking off my shoes and socks.

"I think it was a hint," Boone said.

I laughed. "Maybe so."

CHAPTER

FIFTEEN

Boone's shoes, having been ruined in his effort to remove the metal, practically slid off.

I was hesitant for a moment, but it didn't last long. The thought of getting clean overpowered most of my embarrassment at getting almost naked in front of a stranger. Although, I guess Boone was hardly a stranger now.

Still, we both left our underclothes on, and after refilling our water bottle from the waterfall, we copied the gremlins and stood underneath the water.

It was cold, but not freezing. More importantly, it was clean. I closed my eyes and let the water pour over me. When I heard a splash, I looked around. Boone surfaced in the pool below and swam a few strokes away. I combed my fingers through my hair in a vain effort to dislodge as much of the grime as possible, and then started scrubbing my skin. Boone floated—his eyes were focused on the sky and he looked like his thoughts were hundreds of miles away.

Or perhaps a dimension away.

Looking over the edge, the water didn't seem too far away.

Even so, it took me a few heartbeats to convince myself to jump. Once I plunged in, I finished scrubbing in the water.

"We're probably contaminating this pool for years to come," I said.

Boone chuckled. "I'm sure it'll bounce back." He sounded far away.

I didn't want to bring him out of whatever reverie he was in, but I wasn't about to sink into my own. If I set my mind to other things, it would be bad. I just had to focus on the next thing we'd face, then the next, and the next. Eventually, I'd be back at home and worried about visiting the Sanctuary and if Logan was going to suggest the horses again.

He would, of course.

I grinned at the thought and shook my head before swimming to the edge of the pool and leveraging myself onto a rock and out of the water. Walking carefully across the rocks, I went back to my clothes.

"Use your shirt to dry off," Boone said from the water. "You'll probably want to make sure your feet aren't wet when you put on your socks and shoes."

It felt refreshing to be clean for the first time in days. I dried off as best I could, then threw my shirt over a branch to dry out some. The last thing I wanted to do was sit on the ground now that I was clean, so I found a large slab of rock and laid back against it, waiting to dry out the rest of the way.

I heard Boone get out of the water a little later, but I didn't look up. It wasn't sleep, but resting my eyes and lying quietly was the best I was going to get.

"I should have let you use my shirt," Boone said. "Sorry about that. I wasn't thinking."

"It'll dry," I said, still not getting up.

"I haven't worked in the field with many women," Boone said.

"Huh. From what I've seen of the agency, not many have."

"True enough. If we get back, though, the experience will be put to good use."

"*When* we get back," I corrected. "And how so?"

"When we get back." Boone stressed the when, even if it was only for my benefit. "My new team has two men and one woman."

"Will you all be in the field? They all have abilities, right?" I asked.

"Yes," Boone said.

"That's good to hear," I said.

"We should eat something before we're on the go again."

Sighing, I got up, slipped my socks and shoes onto my now dry feet, and then joined Boone. "I'm not sure what it is they gave us."

"I'm going to guess and hope it's sort of jerky," Boone said.

He handed me a piece of dried food about the size of notebook paper, but rigid like bark.

"Do you think you'll still monitor our team when we get back?"

Boone looked uncertain, but his concentration seemed to be on the food, which definitely worried me as well. "If I get the chance."

I took a tentative bite, but it turned more aggressive when the food refused to break apart.

Boone cleared his throat. "Like I said, though, it's been a big help working with you. Seeing a team of four in action would still be useful."

"Glad I could help," I said before attacking the stiff dry sheet and finally prying a small piece apart from the rest.

"The new team is pretty unique, though. It's all confidential, of course," Boone said.

"It usually is," I said, trying to grind down my food.

"When you're working with your partners, do you tell them everything?"

"They know everything that affects our work."

"Only your active work?"

"Mostly active work is all there is. We're friends, though, so we do sometimes talk about other things. I'm not sure what you're getting at."

"If I tell you about my work, will it get back to them?"

I shrugged. "If your team works with ours, it likely will."

"I don't see that happening anytime soon."

"Then no, if you don't want me to say anything, they wouldn't know."

Boone nodded. "Good to know."

"Do you want to tell me about your work?" I asked when he didn't say anything for a while.

"You've told me a lot."

"I've told you what you need to know."

"Nothing you've said has been an issue."

"I'm getting better at control," I said feeling uncomfortable. "It's not like I try to be weird."

"It's good you told me, especially with what we're facing." Boone sounded like he chose his words carefully.

"We should start to come up with a plan of action," I said with no real conviction.

"Yeah, we should," Boone said.

I could feel my face turn red, but I wanted to get my thoughts out in the open. "And if you want to tell me about your team, it'll stay with me, but don't feel like you have to tell me because I told you something."

Boone looked at me as though calculating his next words. Maybe I had been off base with what I was thinking. I should have kept my mouth shut.

"I'll keep that in mind," Boone said at last. "When we get back, I'll stick with the facts in our report. Nothing personal."

"What's said in gremlin world stays in gremlin world?"

Boone laughed. "Something like that."

"Same here," I said.

"Let's go," Boone said. "We can walk and plan at the same time."

"We should remember how to get here," I said. "We'll want to come back."

"Sure thing," Boone said.

"And by that, I mean you should remember how to get here."

Boone frowned and looked sideways at me while he put on the backpack. "Not you?"

"I have a terrible sense of direction."

His face split into a smile. "Aren't you kind of a tracker with your powers?"

"If I'm reading, sure. Although with the Paths this world makes, I might end up walking in circles."

He chuckled. "We'll put up some sort of markers or signs."

By the time we got back to the camp, the sun had begun to sink. We had spent far too long getting clean, but it had been worth it. If I was going to die, at least I wouldn't be stinky.

I'm not sure if you could say we had a real plan. As soon as Boone dropped our bag, he called out to the gremlins. Even though they were out of sight, we knew they were behind us somewhere.

By the time one arrived, Boone had taken out the trap we found on our first day and he waved it at a gremlin. The gremlin ran off and returned a while later with a few friends.

They had sacks with a few traps and a few glass bottles of what had to be the stuff they had used to knock me out.

One of them noticed Boone examining the trap, and so they demonstrated how to use it. Before they left, they patted us each on the arm and disappeared.

"I get the feeling they were saying goodbye," Boone said, watching them go.

"I'd prefer to think they were saying 'good luck' or 'go get 'em '," I said.

"Go get 'em?" Boone appeared amused by the notion.

"It's better than goodbye."

"Right. Well, let's go get 'em, then."

"You're making fun of me?"

"I wouldn't do that," Boone said.

"And you're lying to me, too," I said, trying to keep the grin from my face.

"Maybe," Boone said. He grinned at me, and then turned to the woods.

Any sense of jest fell from the atmosphere.

"I'm going to set some traps," Boone said.

"I'll go with you. I want to see where they're at."

"It'll be fully dark soon. I don't want you to accidentally step on one."

"Me either. That's why I need to know where they're at." I tried to keep my sarcasm reined in and I followed Boone into the woods.

"Let's keep them away from the portal," I said when Boone moved toward it.

"We can do that." Boone walked to the left of where the portal had scored through the ground and moved deeper into the woods. He set traps, working his way back to the portal. Then he did the same on the opposite side.

When he finished, I had an idea of where they were placed.

Boone stood in front of our would-be portal and stared at the empty space.

"You know," he said. "I can't believe I made it so easy for them to send us into this world."

"How were we to know?" I asked. "Even when you went through, I hadn't realized they were responsible. I thought it was an accident."

"I'm sorry you got caught up in this."

"Do you know what this is?" I asked. "Why they wanted us out of the way, I mean?"

"They sent you here because you were a witness. It's hard to say why they sent me. It might have something to do with the project involving my new team. Not everyone is happy about it."

"Won't it still go on without you?" I asked.

"It depends on what the agency thinks I've done."

"Well, soon we'll get back and set them straight. I'd love to see Dempsey in jail."

Boone sat quiet for a minute. "I shouldn't ask this, but I'm going to anyway. Is it still there?"

Sensing how badly he wanted to know, I closed my eyes, breathed deeply, and made the jump into the Path, preparing to stamp back the flow in an effort to preserve energy.

"It hasn't faded any further." The surprise I felt showed in my voice. I had avoided looking, assuming the Path would have swallowed it up.

Boone let out a breath.

"Do you think Dempsey didn't close it all the way on purpose?" I asked.

"I think that would be giving him too much credit. He put us here—I think he would do what he could to make sure we couldn't return."

"You're probably right," I said. "Maybe he's just not good at what he does."

Boone shrugged. "Maybe it always looks like this from the other side. Save your energy."

Ignoring the hint, I reached out to touch one of the beads of light, knowing it needed to move—and quickly at that—to bore our way into our home dimension.

"Cassie?" Boone said.

"Got it." I closed my eyes to push the Path away. The trickle of power I had allowed free didn't want to leave, but I forced it back. After a short struggle, I extracted myself from the Path.

He looked at me expectantly.

"It's frustrating is all," I said. "I see how it works. Well, I get the gist. Get it open and home is a step away."

"We'll figure it out. For now, though, we should save our energy. Where's the knockout drug?" Boone asked.

"Here." I pulled three thick glass vials from my pocket. "Wait, that's mine." I kept hold of the red bottle and passed Boone the two clear ones.

"Didn't Wyna say to drink that tonight?" Boone said.

"Yeah." I looked through the bottle and shook the liquid around inside. "But I don't really know what it is."

"It's not likely to hurt you. She knows you're the best hope they have at killing this thing."

My face started to heat up, and I was thankful it was dark. "Even if we manage it, it won't be from me alone." I thought about what we were about to do and decided I may as well voice my biggest concern. "I'm not comfortable killing one of the Lost."

"You couldn't kill it? Even a demon?" Boone asked.

I shrugged and popped the top off the vial, drinking the small amount of liquid. "It is what it is. It doesn't belong here, but maybe we can... I don't know, convince it to go home?"

"You said it's intelligent," Boone said. "You want to make a deal with it?"

"I'm not Faust or my old director. I get the impression it sticks to its agreements, though."

"Could we be certain of that? Certain it wouldn't return?"

I sighed. "I doubt it."

"Do we even have anything to offer it?" Boone asked.

I shook my head. "It'll want me, but that won't help us much. It will just want to kill me."

A screech in the forest interrupted our discussion. Over the hill, where our gremlin friends hid, came answering howls.

"That doesn't sound good," I said.

Another loud voice, screaming this time, sounded much closer.

"Did they say how they were luring this thing to us?" I asked.

"They didn't mention. Let's get back to the camp." Boone ran the short distance to our camp and I followed. He handed me a spear. "You're good with the plan?"

"Yeah," I said.

"Even if it means killing it."

A scream tore through the darkness and I steeled myself. "Let's do this."

"Take this dose of knockout liquid. If I don't get through, you've got to."

"I've got it," I said.

"Okay," Boone looked me over, "get its attention."

I closed my eyes and once again reached for the Path. The jump was smooth, and power crashed over me.

The change in the atmosphere was slight but notable. Like fingers of fog creeping in, an oily residue began drifting over the Path.

"It's close." I hadn't notice I was trembling until I spoke. "I'm going to let it know we're here."

Just like the last time I faced this type of Lost, it didn't feel right to call out. Yells and screeches broke out in the woods— there was no use adding to the din. Intent on our goal, I sent strands of power in the most likely direction of the creature. When the inky blackness of Path grew stronger, I stopped.

Why was I so scared of this thing? No. That was a stupid question. Any sane person would be afraid of a demon. The issue was I allowed it to affect me too much. If fear lived in the forefront of my mind there was no way we would win.

This whole situation sucked, and more than anything, I wanted to go home. To do that, we had to live through the fight. Thinking of what Logan, Rider, and Vincent would do in my place, I rolled my shoulders and shoved all that fear into a tiny corner.

With a clearer head, I pulled my power away from the creature and urged the energy over a new route. This time, if the thing followed, it would walk straight over the traps. Once I found an impenetrable wall of filth over the Path, I sent a channel of power down, making sure it was enough for the demon to know there were bigger fish to play with.

The noise in the forest stopped. Sounds of scurrying feet continued, but the rest of the noise in the forest had died away. Gremlins, old gremlins, running, using their knuckles on the ground to propel them away faster, ran past us and into the clearing. They went straight over the hill and out of sight.

"It knows we're here," I whispered.

We stood, tension rising, watching the shadows in the woods, wondering which direction the dark shape would move from. I could still feel it out there, analyzing the situation. The ropes of energy I had been using to detect the demon jerked away and I didn't hesitate in dropping the lines of power.

My muscles tightened to the point that, I was surprised they continued to move.

A flurry of movement announced the creature. The motion was followed by snapping traps, though it sounded like they caught nothing but air. I knew it was fast, but fast enough to set off the traps and not be caught?

I readied the energy around us. If I created a sort of shield now, the creature would see it too quickly and the shield would become useless to us.

A hissing noise began to reverberate through the air and a shadow grew into the shape of our monster. It had the same sharp beak, but the wings stayed close to its body. A glossy sheen to the leathery flesh made it look as though it had polished itself.

It limped with one clawed foot wrapped around a shape. When my brain made sense of the figure, I almost lost every recent meal I had eaten. My skin turned cool and clammy. The gremlin it clutched was dead. There was no chance it could be that broken and still breathing.

Please let it be dead and not suffering.

I swallowed hard and ignored the last thought. I broke out into goosebumps as the cold I felt began to be burned away by fury.

"Go," I snapped at Boone.

Boone ran away. The plan called for him to circle around to the side of the thing and drug it, which was strange since Logan, Rider, and I had the same plan the last time we fought a demon.

"Gooo..." the creature hissed, trying to mimic my words

"You're not the one I faced before, are you?" I asked.

"Fassssed," it mimicked.

"Yeah, I didn't think so. How did you get here? Into this world?"

The beak swung up and opened. A hissing screech, sounding almost like a gremlin, rang out.

"You're out of luck," I said. "I don't speak that language."

Wouldn't it be nice if I could, though? Maybe there was a way to talk to this thing. To use it in some way.

The creature kicked out, throwing the dead gremlin in my direction. It missed me, but the following flow of power didn't. Thick bands of blackness struck against me, knocking me back off my feet.

I landed hard on my back. The demon slowly wrapped the power around me and squeezed. It tried crushing me slowly, allowing me time to think about what was coming.

Well, screw that. Instead, I cut off the flow of energy and the bindings fell away before any damage was done.

"Too slow," I said, getting to my feet. "Your friend was a lot faster than you."

The creature stepped out of the woods. It was time. Boone had to have been in place. With barb-liked whips of power, I lashed out at the creature, testing its defense. It cut through the solid Path and began to reel in the energy, straight from me.

It threw me off balance. I dropped the lines and instantly made the Path around the beast solid. The bubble of energy was something the creature could brush away with ease, but before it had the chance to try, I flipped the Path.

My fingers were mentally crossed, knowing this had worked with the previous beast. This one scrambled with its power, and then it physically scratched at the enclosure.

"Now Boone!" I called.

Boone appeared a few moments later beside the creature, his face a mask of grim determination.

The beast screeched again and beat its wings against the

glassy smoothness of the bubble inside. Each time it struck the edges, my power wavered, but I managed to keep hold.

This part worried me. Boone had to get into the cage without the creature getting out. And without getting killed.

Boone didn't have a moment of hesitation. He ran at the bubble, which was invisible to him. The creature lifted its head to shriek and I dropped the wall just long enough for Boone to get inside.

It was the only moment the creature needed. Energy shot out of the prison and sank into the exterior. At the same time, the thing's wings shot out and caught Boone in the chest. He bounced off the inside of the cage. Dropping the protection around the creature, I wrapped bands around it, as it had me, and tried to crush its wings down. It worked, but only for a moment.

Boone rose unsteadily to his feet and the beast ripped away its bonds. "Its mouth," I hollered to Boone.

As the creature won its way free, it poured power into a solid ball. I took that moment to wrench its beak open.

The ball of power rushed at me, but I held steadily onto its beak, prying it open. The beak cracked, which churned my stomach. Boone was on the creature, but I missed what happened next. My world erupted in a ball of black energy. Oily residue poured over me. My stomach tried to heave.

I could hear nothing and saw only darkness. Panic welled up as I started suffocating. I didn't want to die here. Not in some strange dimension. Boone needed me. I was sure of that.

And we had to get home.

The slick tarry trap had to go. Instead of making the Path solid or moving the Path, I called to it. It wanted to flow and it wanted all remnants of this creature scrubbed away. Using as much strength as I could muster, I dragged it, not to me, but through me.

As though taking a wave to the face, the Path surged through me.

The inky pool surrounding me vanished, but the scene around me had changed. Things weren't quite right. It took me a few moments and many deep, steady breaths, to figure out why. In pulling on the Path, I had caused the future of the Path to play out before me. The creature stood, wings outstretched. Boone was somehow on its back, gremlins swarming in from all sides. But the bright light behind it all held my attention.

My power dwindled with the Path, and I knew things continued around me in the present. I hadn't moved in time, only the Path had. I closed my eyes to the world around me and concentrated hard, trying to force the flow of the Path to slow its frantic movements and show me the present.

I'm not sure what hit me, but a tight pressure on my chest knocked me back. Once again, I slammed into the ground. This time, Boone was on top of me, blood smeared across his face.

Fear pulsed through me. I couldn't see around the man, but I slammed down raw power around us. Boone rolled off me and, wavering slightly, made his way to his feet. Catching sight of the demon, I jumped up as well.

"What's it doing?" Boone's voice was tight and he looked ready to spring.

"It's getting something ready to attack. I don't know what it's using." My ribcage ached. I had no idea if the Path I saw was the future or only a possible future, but I didn't care. I needed to set the stage. "Move around behind him, I have you covered."

CHAPTER

SIXTEEN

Pressing my hand down tight on my ribs, I circled to one side of the beast with Boone on the other. My power declined, but I was ready to use whatever was needed to keep Boone on target.

My own strength couldn't open the portal. Even if I was well rested and I hadn't read the Path in days, I just didn't have the energy to open it.

This creature did, though.

"You need to leave this world," I yelled at the demon.

Talking distracted it, but only a little. As it watched me, it continued to pool power.

I could take power from it. Its tar-like energy would latch itself to me as it had before, but maybe it would work.

With its power, could I open the portal?

Could I even use the power?

I didn't think so, and I didn't want to experiment with it unless forced. There were too many risk factors; too many things could go wrong. No, I needed the creature to open the portal.

First, it had to know our world was nearby.

"That world," I said, motioning to the air where the portal should stand. "You aren't allowed in."

Its gaze never left mine. It followed my movements as I circled.

"Your friend went there." I pointed to the closed portal again and hoped like crazy it would take the hint even if it didn't understand the words. "He couldn't hack it."

Where's an English-to-gremlin dictionary when you need one?

"Promises were made there and broken."

"Promisessss," the demon hissed. For the first time, it took notice of the empty air where the portal had stood.

It was also distracted, which, thankfully, Boone noticed and used to his advantage.

There was no way for me to know if Boone had been able to put the poison into the demon's mouth earlier. Now, as Boone jumped on the demon's back, it further distracted the demon and I used the opportunity to run forward. Once again, I used my power to wrench the creature's jaw open. In one movement, I uncorked the glass bottle and threw it down the demon's gullet.

It tore itself away from me before I could get out of range. A wing slammed into me and I crumpled onto the ground.

Fighting for breath, I rolled away, groaning involuntarily when I put pressure on my chest.

I saw the demon shove all the power it had been collecting into the portal. At the same time, it reached around with its beak and snapped at Boone.

The creature's beak struck the shield I had thrown up using the tiny amount of energy I could gather in time.

Gremlins poured out of the woods. Boone used his plastic-bladed knife and plunged it into the creature's neck.

Light from the portal lit up the dark night.

I had hoped the entrance of our world was coming, but it still took me by surprise. Boone and I were both distracted. The demon slammed its body back into a tree.

Stunned, Boone fell to the ground and the gremlins rushed at the creature.

The demon's power continued to pour into the portal, but it slowed. The portal was almost open, and I could feel the pressure in the air compressing me from all sides. The little beads of power spun.

The demon cried out, and the power stopped.

"No, no, no!" I yelled.

The gremlins were taking a beating, but the demon moved sluggishly. Could they handle the demon alone?

They could if I subdued the demon more than the knockout liquid had. Taking its strength away would help. Looking from the creature to the portal, I made the decision.

The demon's power lashed out at the gremlins—I grabbed everything I could and drew it in. Oily residue instantly stuck to me. It clung to my skin and found its way into my mouth as I breathed heavily with the effort.

"Damnit," Boone yelled. He stared at the portal, keeping one eye on the fight. At least he was back on his feet, which was a relief.

The portal's stunning glow faded.

Closing my eyes and trying to ignore the thick film which worked its way down my throat, I slammed the power into the portal.

Boone turned back to the fight, ready to reenter the fray, a grim expression displayed across his face. He didn't get far before a gremlin jumped in front of him, screeching and blocking his way.

I couldn't take a distraction, so I tuned it out. Sitting on the ground, staring intently at the bright light, I put more and more energy into spinning balls of light. From the beast, from the ground, from myself.

I could feel sweat and tears roll down my face and neck. My head began to swim, but still the power surged.

Our way home opened.

Screeches sounded out around me, but I didn't look. I couldn't look away, couldn't risk slowing the energy I poured into the portal.

"Come on!" Boone yelled.

"Go, you idiot," I tried to yell at him, but it came out as a whisper, lost in the noise the gremlins made.

Boone cursed and ran over to me. "Hold it. Don't you dare let go."

Was he yelling at me? Being lightheaded, I couldn't tell, but I had no intentions of letting go. I felt myself rise from the ground and bright light filled my world. My lungs froze, causing my chest to hurt worse than before, but still I concentrated.

The pressure released, but the bright light remained. Yells erupted all around us, but in my intense concentration, I couldn't make them out.

"Let it go," Boone said.

The words didn't quite sink in.

"Let it go!" Boone barked out the order like a drill sergeant. It broke through, and the power from the portal snapped back. The bright light winked out.

"Did you just yell at me?" My voice came out as a croak.

He didn't look at me. "I'm surprised you could even hear me."

The bright light of the portal died away, but the noise didn't. It took me a few moments to figure out there were more lights. Flashlights pointed at my face. It wasn't lost on me that the shadows around the lights were guns, carefully trained on us.

Luckily, the Path was still at hand, though no more than a dying cinder remained. I'm not sure I would come back from what I had used. If I did anything else with the Path, I'm fairly certain there would be no coming back.

Still, there was no way I traveled across dimensions just to make it home, just for me be killed.

Words started coming into sharper focus. "... down. Hands..."

The voice was Logan. I closed my eyes and let out a sigh of relief.

"No time to sleep just yet," Boone said. "You want to say something here?"

He shifted, trying to keep me up. I had forgotten he held me.

"If you all shoot either of us, I'm going to be pissed." It only came out as a whisper, but the yells stopped.

Only one steely voice remained. "Put Agent Heidrich down and step away."

Vincent.

I smiled. We were definitely home.

"Hold off!" Logan yelled.

My partners. My friends. We were home.

"I'm not sure what's going on." The words were barely audible to myself, but I knew Logan would hear. If Rider was around, he would as well.

I didn't get the rest out. Boone wavered, and we both fell to the ground. I sucked in a sharp breath when pain spasmed through me.

When I opened my eyes again, Rider's face swam into focus. "You should let go of the Path. You are home."

My thoughts floated. Blinking slowly, I tried to smile, but I don't think it worked. "I'm not sure what happens when I let go." If this was a dream, it was a good one, and I didn't want to let it leave.

"But you know what will happen if you keep reading."

I sighed. "This is going to suck. Make sure Boone's okay."

There was almost nothing left to push away, but when I managed it, darkness took me again.

※

INKY BLACK WATERS SURROUNDED ME. I'd been swimming for a while. Was I swimming away from the shore or toward it? For that matter, was there a shore?

Setting off in the direction that felt right, I began to hear sounds and the darkness grew lighter. Then noise faded. Time and again, a current dragged me back out into the darker water.

So I stayed there for a while. Mentally, I wandered to Gran and Mom, to Logan, Rider, and Vincent. Thoughts of Ethan drifted past, and even Boone came into focus for a short time before floating away.

Had I really gone into another world?

While drifting, I stared up. It took me a while to distinguish the sky from the water, but I relaxed and watched until stars popped out. My thoughts fanned out further and I thought about my life, pondering the future.

It was Vincent's voice I had heard, right? As soon as his voice, cold as it was, rang out, I had clung to it as a fact. He was there. Somewhere. But when Vincent came to the forefront of my brain the rest went foggy.

Maybe I should find out if it was real, any of it, all of it? Serenely I drifted, saved my strength, and when I felt light creeping back in, I surged forward breaking the surface.

The room was lit, but dim artificial light shone from somewhere behind me. It left a soft glow on the ceiling. Little black dots on the tiles jostled each other and I blinked. Before they came into focus, the beeping did. The soft noise pinged from beside me. Looking around, I saw the IV bag.

Hospital? Clinic, maybe? I took my time looking around the room. When I moved too fast, my stomach felt like revolting.

No. It was the clinic at work. I'd been there enough times to know.

On the other side of my bed, I saw a chair pulled up next to me, but it was empty. Frowning, I looked closer around the room and tensed. Was I in the right place?

A noise broke through the beeps. Shoes on the floor. Someone was there, but pacing. I wasn't alone. A sigh of relief escaped me and I relaxed.

"Cass?"

Vincent appeared at the side of my bed as though from nowhere. I blinked in surprise, and then tried to talk. I sounded like I had been chewing gravel, so I stopped and tried to clear my throat.

"Here." Vincent snatched up a cup.

I watched him while I drank, afraid he might disappear if I looked away. I'd never admit it, but the fear I had lost him would have been overwhelming if I had thought about it too deeply.

He watched me with the same intensity, but I wondered if he had the same concern.

Sadly, my eyes were heavy and I felt... detached.

"I'll get the doctor," Vincent said when I passed the cup back.

I wanted to say, 'don't go.' I'm pretty sure I tried to say it, but when Vincent turned away, I blinked one time too many and fell back asleep.

Opening my eyes the next time was a million times easier. Unfortunately, it was a million times brighter. I scrunched up face and used my arm to shield as much glow as possible. I had forgotten about the IV, which distracted me enough that I adjusted to the light before I tried to move again.

"You are awake." From the chair next to me, Rider jumped up.

"Am I?" I asked. My thoughts felt like they were still catching up.

Rider's face crinkled up in confusion. "You appear to be." He looked me over more closely. "Yes, I will get the doctor."

"Wait," I said.

Rider waited, but I wasn't sure what I wanted to say. What I did know was I didn't want to deal with people hovering over me until I could think more clearly.

"I need a minute," I said.

Rider looked at the clock and watched it tick down the seconds.

"Is there water?" I asked.

He found the cup. While I drank, he went back to watching the clock.

I smiled. "I didn't mean an exact minute. How long have I been here?"

Rider took an uncertain glance at the door. "I should get the doctor while you are awake. He was very specific."

"Fine." My smile faded fast. "Whatever."

"That never means what I think it should mean," Rider said.

"No." I stared at the ceiling. "It probably doesn't."

"It has been over thirty hours since we brought you here."

"Almost two days? That can't be right."

Rider glanced at the clock again. "It is correct."

I rubbed my head and tried to remember coming back. "How's Boone?"

"Agent Boone is injured, but recovering."

Closing my eyes, I nodded.

"You must stay awake to see the doctor," Rider said.

"Okay. Go get him," I said, resigned.

While I lay there, I realized my reappearance was not what I had expected. I hadn't let myself dwell on it while I had been stuck in another world but I had expected to be on my feet with my friends and family. Where was everyone? I felt empty. Cheated, even. Was everyone used to me being back? How could I miss my own homecoming?

"Good afternoon, Agent Heidrich." Dr. Yelton walked into the room holding a tablet in his hands which he then unceremoniously dumped onto the bedside table. "It's good to see you awake. Tell me how you feel."

He pulled a penlight out of his pocket and I waited until he finished waving it around.

"Tired," I said, "but it sounds like I've slept more than enough."

"Take the rest you need." He took out the stethoscope and listened to my heart. He asked me to breathe deep.

Dull pain greeted the deep breaths.

"You came back to us severely dehydrated and with cracked ribs as well as a few cuts and bruises, but from Agent Boone's description, it sounds like you ended up lucky."

"How is Boone?" I asked. "Can I see him?"

"He's on the mend. As to seeing him, it's not my decision. Now, I'll need a little more detail about how you're feeling."

"Tired, sore, hungry. Oh, and I'd kill for a shower."

He asked more pointed questions about the pain and had me describe the tiredness, but all in all, I didn't feel bad.

"You've had a rough first week back to the office," Dr.

Yelton said. "I'm going to draw some blood, and there's also a few people who want to see you."

Pixies started dancing a rumba in my stomach. It was bad enough being in the hospital. I hated the idea of people standing around the bed watching me.

"Unless you'd rather me ask them to wait?" Dr. Yelton said.

I'm not sure if he saw the anxiety in my face or saw it in the machines attached to me. "No, it's fine. That's it though? Dehydration and sore ribs?"

"Well, things were a bit unsteady when you came in. Your blood pressure was low, dangerously low, for the first day, but you rallied back. You ran a low-grade fever for a while. You've lost some weight in a hurry, but we've put a stop to that. You were deficient in a few nutrients, but everything is coming back in line. As for the rest, it's a little harder to determine some of the issues."

"How so?" I asked.

"Well, for starters, you've slept longer than we expected, but we're chalking it up to use of your gifts. Or overuse, if you will."

That part made sense at least. I'd never been that tired.

"You've had some interesting blood work, but everything is settling back to normal. We don't know if it's diet related, atmospheric issues, or dimensional problems that caused it, so we'll keep an eye on it. You had several blood vessels rupture. Again, we're putting it down to dimensional issues. Boone said the same thing happened when you first left here. So, if we believe his story, it could have been caused by crossing dimensions."

How could I not have known so many dimensional difficulties were possible? "Is that normal?"

Dr. Yelton laughed. "I'm not sure anything can sound quite

normal when you're talking about interdimensional travel, but different people have different reactions."

I nodded, but not enthusiastically.

"Now, are you ready to see some people?" Dr. Yelton asked.

"Yeah," I forced a smile on my face, "I can't wait to see everyone."

CHAPTER

SEVENTEEN

Logan entered wearing a big grin. As tired as I was, I couldn't help but smile back. For some reason, seeing the elf made me feel lighter. Somehow, I had forgotten the cowboy hat. He now held it instead of wearing it.

"Howdy, partner," Logan said.

Rider and Vincent weren't far behind him, although neither smiled. It didn't take long for Logan's good mood to infect Rider.

"We hear you've been on quite the pony ride," Logan said, pulling the chair over to the bed.

I raised an eyebrow. "You know, that's the best comparison to riding a horse I've heard. You should keep that one."

Logan laughed—the music filled the room and my tension melted away.

"Well, we're glad to have you back," Logan said.

Rider stood next to Logan and he looked around the room. He had to have the place memorized by now, so I wasn't sure what he was looking for. Vincent stood on the other side of the bed. He picked up the doctor's dropped tablet and avoided looking at me.

"How's Gran?" I asked. "She knows I'm back, right? I'm surprised she's not here."

Rider winced, but answered. "Margaret knows you are back."

"That's good—where is she?" I asked.

"Well, we have a problem there," Logan said. "The Farm is closed to all visitors at the moment."

Vincent dropped the tablet back on the bedside table where it clattered and walked over to the window. He cracked the blinds and looked out.

I looked worriedly at Vincent, but didn't get the chance to say anything.

"There are still no leads about Clancy," Logan said quickly. "And after your incident, no one comes or goes without clearance."

"I'll bet Gran's not happy." My voice trailed off into a yawn.

"Margaret is very unhappy," Rider said.

The way he said it made me worry. "But she's alright, isn't she?"

Vincent finally wandered over to the bed.

"She sent us to get you," Logan said. "At the portal, I mean."

I beamed. "She knew I was coming back? Leave it to Gran."

Logan shook his head. "She only knew we needed to be there. Once you were gone, you were gone. She couldn't see you."

There was nothing I could say to that. Poor Gran—not knowing must have driven her crazy. She seemed to feel it was her responsibility to see things ahead of time.

"She asked us to bring you home after we found you at the portal," Rider said. "We called her immediately."

"Ordered," Vincent said. "She ordered us to bring you home."

I bit my lip, but couldn't hide my grin. That sounded like Gran. Vincent saw the look, and I received a weak smile in response. It was the first time I had seen it since I returned.

"Yeah, she's steaming since we brought you here," Logan said. He looked unsettled about the idea, but nothing compared to the anxiety Rider displayed.

"I'm surprised you didn't take me home," I said, trying to inject humor into my voice.

No one said anything for a while. Logan twirled his hat on his finger, apparently all his concentration fixed on that, Rider wrung his hands and Vincent's blank mask dropped onto his face.

"What did I miss?" I asked.

"Well, it wasn't as easy as driving you home," Logan said. "You didn't look so well and—"

"It did not look like you would survive," Rider said.

Logan frowned at Rider and went on. "We wanted to have the doctor take a look at you, and with Boone in custody, we thought it best—"

"What do you mean, in custody?" I couldn't tell if I was scared, worried, or angry, but I sure as heck wasn't happy at the phrasing.

"Maybe this should wait," Vincent said.

"No," I snapped. "What do you mean in custody? Did you arrest him?" I tried to sit up straighter, but I didn't have any luck and no one looked willing to help me out.

"We did," Rider said.

"He's only in custody," Logan said. "He's not arrested, and he's hasn't been charged with anything."

"Then why—where is he?" I asked. I tried hard not to glare at my partners, but I'm not sure I managed.

"He's still here in the clinic," Logan said. He tried to smile. "I think the doc's done with him, but keeping him here so he isn't put in a holding cell."

I closed my eyes and rubbed my head. "Where at? I want to go see him." None of it made sense.

"No can do," Logan said.

This time I did glare, but he put his hands up. "Slow down now, partner. That decision is above our pay grade."

"What's that supposed to mean?" I asked.

"Once the doc gives the go ahead, Agent Paulson will come in and get your side of the story."

That didn't sound good. None of it did. "I'm missing something." Pressure began building in my head, and I rubbed the sides of my head again as though to ward off an impending headache.

"Rest is what you're missing," Vincent said. "This can wait."

"I've rested too much." I said the words, but I knew he was right. The entire situation started to get muddled in my head.

"You should call Margaret," Logan said.

Gran was something I could focus on, at least. "She *is* okay, right? I mean, this had to be hard..." Thinking about what Gran must have gone through made my eyes start to burn. I swallowed hard. "And Mom. Does she know what happened?"

"Your mother knows. She's been keeping an eye on Margaret. We all have," Logan said. "She stayed with your mother a few nights and we even visited over there."

"At my mother's?"

"I can't say she was happy about it," Logan said. "Your mom stayed at Margaret's a few nights as well."

"A few nights in each place?" I tried to concentrate on the number of days. "I thought I was only gone for a few days."

"Your mom's been at your place since you've been back,"

Logan said. "Margaret wanted to make sure she was there when you get home."

"Margaret is more comfortable at home," Rider said.

I nodded and closed my eyes for a few moments. Why was this so difficult?

"We should give you a break," Logan said. I could hear him stand.

"Phone," I said, opening my eyes. "I need a phone to call her."

Rider started to say something, but Vincent got there first. "We'll bring you one."

Nodding, I closed my eyes again and heard them leave. The noise of someone settling into a chair made me realize not everyone had left. Vincent had taken Logan's place in the chair.

"I thought you were getting me a phone," I said.

"Rider will bring one," Vincent said. "I think he's looking for yours."

Sighing, I nodded. "And Mom and Gran are okay?" I asked again.

"They're fine," Vincent said. "They sent flowers." He scooted the chair closer to my bed, and faced me so I could see around to where the flowers were lined up. "There's some from us, the office, your mother and grandmother, and Ethan."

I blinked at him. "Ethan?"

"He wanted to get in to see you, but couldn't. You may want to call him as well."

I shook my head in confusion. "You told Ethan?"

Vincent nodded, but I could see hints of unease around his eyes. "I asked Logan to call, but I've spoken with him a few times."

Well, it was too late now. I closed my eyes and settled back into bed. "It would have been better if he hadn't been told," I said.

"He might have noticed you gone for a few days. He stopped in to check on Margaret a few times, too."

I felt run down, but I opened my eyes long enough to look at Vincent, trying to get a sense of why he would have had Logan call Ethan.

"Was there a card?" Had I imagined Ethan and me breaking up the night before I got lost in another dimension?

Stony faced, Vincent went and retrieved the card. After a moment's hesitation, he plucked the cards off the rest and brought them to me.

I gave a weak grin. "Hope you remember which card goes with which."

He nodded, still not a hint of emotion played across his face. Usually I could read him, but being tired must have been putting me off my game.

I read the first one from Gran and Mom. "Hope to see you back at home soon. Love, Mom and Gran."

Then came the one from the office. "Welcome back."

Ethan's note came next. "Thinking of you. Your friend, Ethan."

"That makes sense, at least," I said. There was another from Neil. The note had been printed and only said, "Dude, call me." I chuckled. Taylor also sent some, which was a nice gesture, but he had only signed his name.

Shuffling to the next, I saw the one from Logan, Rider, and Vincent. Written in Logan's tidy, scrawling cursive it read, "It's good to see you back. Don't do it again."

I smiled. "Thank you." I handed back the cards. "Which flowers are from you all?"

"The one on the end," Vincent said. "Rider picked them out."

The flowers were an array of vivid colors Mother Nature never made on her own.

"No roots?" I asked.

Vincent's face broke, allowing a hint of amusement through. "No roots." He placed the little signature cards back on each set of flowers.

"So, Rider," I said, not knowing how to ask, "is he..."

"It can wait." Vincent said. "Get some rest."

Since I was exhausted, I didn't argue. "The phone?" I asked, closing my eyes.

"Rider will bring it."

SWIRLING nightmares popped up and melted away, only to return stronger. Black, leathery wings wrapped themselves around me, a broken gremlin landed on me, and I couldn't get up. Wyna disappeared and reappeared throughout. Luckily, the rest of the dreams were lost. I had a feeling darker images lurked not far away.

When I woke up, the room was bright again. Logan and Hank were talking by the door. I watched for a short time, but Logan must have sensed my eyes on him.

"Morning, partner!" His cheerful voice was welcome after the night I'd have.

"Morning." I pushed myself up farther on the bed and was thrilled when I realized I could push myself up. My ribs ached, but the lingering fatigue had evaporated. I was still tired, but it was the regular, 'I've just woken up,' kind of tired.

"How are you feeling this morning?" Logan asked.

"Better," I said. "Much better."

"Glad to hear it. Hank, do you want to grab the doc?" Logan asked.

Hank nodded. "It's good to see you back, Cassie." He gave Logan a smile, for him alone, and left the room.

"Boy, it's good to see you up and about," Logan said. "There's a lot of people worried about you."

"It's good they can stop worrying, then. As soon as I get a shower, I'm sure I'll be as good as new." My statement was somewhat diminished when it ended in a yawn. "What have I missed?"

"Missed?"

"Yeah, while I've been gone and while I was asleep. What have I missed?"

"Slow down there, partner. The doc will have my ears if I don't let you rest up more. We'll see what he says."

I rolled my eyes. "At least tell me how everyone's been."

"We're good. Better now you're back, although Margaret has threatened to cut off our sugar supply if we don't get you home soon."

I laughed. "You'll have to make your own cookies? Sounds like the world may come to an end."

"Store-bought isn't the same."

"How's Boone doing? I still haven't seen him."

"I'll be stopping by his room later. I'll let you know."

"Thanks, I wanted to get the chance to talk to him."

"You sound good today," Dr. Yelton said, coming into the room.

"Feeling much better," I said.

"Logan, can you wait for us outside?" Dr. Yelton asked.

"Sure thing, Doc." Logan left, shutting the door behind him.

Dr. Yelton, poked, prodded, and did a thorough examination. Along the way, he told me my blood work was almost back to normal and that he would take some more x-rays tomorrow.

"Tomorrow?" I asked. "I'm feeling so much better. I was hoping I could get out of here today."

"Not a chance for today I'm afraid," Dr. Yelton said. "We'll see how things go tomorrow."

My shoulders fell and I sighed. I didn't want to hear I'd be stuck here another night.

"You're going to have a busy day today, though. I'm going to let the director know you're up for answering a few questions."

"I was wondering why no one has asked me anything yet," I said.

"We needed to make sure you were up to it first. Kyrian will have lots of questions, but we're still not certain we've seen all the reactions you might have. If you start feeling bad or need a break, click your call button."

"I'm sure the director will love that," I said.

"She'll understand. Any of us will right now. Don't push yourself. And those are orders." He stared at me until I nodded in response. "I'll let Kyrian know she can see you."

As soon as the doctor left, I itched to talk to Boone. Most of the time before turning in a report, I had the chance to talk to the people that were with me. It bothered me that I still hadn't been able to see him. It had been, what, three days? Four? After going through so much with the man, it felt wrong that I hadn't seen him yet.

I didn't have time to dwell on it. Kyrian must have stopped whatever she was doing and had come straight to the room. And she wasn't alone. Agent Paulson walked in behind her.

Kyrian wore a smile, which didn't look right on her. I wasn't sure if she was faking the smile, or if I was used to not seeing one there.

"Agent Heidrich, it's good to see you," Kyrian said.

"Thank you," I said. I pushed myself up straighter and placed my hands on my lap. It was close to a real sitting position, which was good. I'd hate to lying down while they were in the room. "It's good to be back."

Paulson's smile looked real. "You're looking much better."

"Thank you," I said.

"We have a few questions for you." Kyrian still had the smile, but at least she had the direct tone I knew well.

"Sure," I said.

"We want you to provide as much detail as you can, starting from the point where you left the office," Kyrian said. "As much as you can remember."

And so, it started. Naturally, they needed to know what had happened, but I started to see a trend after a while. Kyrian and Paulson both asked questions and many of them focused around Boone.

I played down many areas. Anything I did which involved my powers, I altered slightly. When I gave the gremlins the metal, I didn't mention the shield, I left out doing anything in the gremlin house, and when we came back, it was the demon that had opened the portal—I merely directed the power, which is what almost killed me.

They seemed to buy it all, or at least they didn't dwell on it. However, they were interested in what Boone had said and done the entire time we were gone. Naturally, I left out our conversations. Before they were done, a headache had begun to form and I started to grow agitated.

When they started to go over everything again from the beginning for the third time, I'd had enough. "Look, it doesn't matter how you phrase the questions, the answers are the same." That didn't look like it went over well, so I rushed to continue. "What happened to the two agents we were with? Walden and Dempsey?"

Paulson looked at Kyrian, who surveyed me as though she had x-ray vision. She took her time, but in the end, she nodded.

"Agents Walden and Dempsey left about a day after you disappeared."

My mouth dropped open. "You let them leave? Why?"

"There was no reason to disbelieve their statements," Kyrian said. "Their records are exemplary, and there was no reason to doubt what they said."

"What exactly did they say?" I asked.

Kyrian tapped her fingers on the arm of the chair, which she wore like a throne. "I'll let Paulson explain. There are some things I need to attend to." Kyrian got up and started to leave the room. It wasn't until she reached the door that she seemed to remember something. "Go through things one last time with Paulson. I want to be sure we have all the facts before we release Agent Boone. Hope you feel better soon."

She shut the door behind her when she left.

The moment the door clicked shut behind her, I turned on Paulson. "I thought they didn't arrest Boone."

"Agent Boone was not arrested. No charges were filed—he's being held for questioning."

"That might as well be the same thing. I can't believe you arrested him. What were you thinking?"

Paulson shook his head. "Your team took him into custody. Neatly I might add, which I hadn't expected."

"Neatly?" I asked.

"They showed restraint. For a few days, your team had been thinking Agent Boone killed you."

EIGHTEEN

An icy tingle started in my arms. "What? Why would they think that? What exactly did Dempsey and Walden say?" My distress must have been evident, because Paulson held up a hand to try to stem my response, which only ticked me off more. "Don't wave your arms at me. Would you wave your arms at Logan?"

Paulson put down his hands. "Not if I wanted to keep them," he muttered. Louder, he added, "I'd like to think I would if he had been sitting in a hospital bed for a few days."

I closed my eyes and rubbed my forehead. "Just tell me."

"Agents Dempsey and Walden phoned in as soon as they got back to the truck," Paulson started.

"Is that what they told you, or do you know?"

"Both. The portal readings showed it open, then close. Not long after it closed, Hank had the satellite up."

"It wasn't on us before then?"

"Apparently, things went ahead of schedule. We saw the two of them at the portal together for about twenty minutes before they went back to the truck."

"Fine," I said. "What did they say happened?"

Paulson cleared his throat and looked uncomfortable. "They said the portal fully opened while they were in the process of closing it permanently. They said it appeared as though Boone had a device that must have caused it to open." Paulson swiped through what must have been pages of notes on his tablet. "They stated Boone took you hostage, opened the portal, then as he pulled you through, they thought they saw Boone cut your throat."

I didn't say anything for a few moments, stunned by the enormity of the lie. "And you all believed that? You weren't even going to try to reopen the portal?"

"Well, yes and no. Seeing Boone's record, it was easier to believe he might do something drastic, than it would be to think Dempsey and Walden were lying. But, we didn't take their statements at face value. After twenty-four hours, we let them go, but we continued our investigation at the site. Agent Dempsey and Walden were adamant the portal was completely closed and could not be reopened by them.

"At the site, Rider was convinced you had left this world uninjured. A werewolf's nose doesn't lie, so we assumed he was right. We started to search for another way through to find you or Agent Boone—or with luck, both."

"This is so bad," I moaned, more to myself than to Paulson.

"There's more, I'm afraid."

"What else?"

"We've recalled Dempsey and Walden. Agent Walden should be on a plane now, but we haven't been able to reach Agent Dempsey."

"Why did it take so long to recall them?"

"Bureaucracy. They were on assignment between when they left here and yesterday. We still aren't sure if Dempsey is on assignment or if he has disappeared."

"You're going to release Boone now, though, right?"

"Technically, Dr. Yelton has to release him from care first. But, with the details you've given us, he can go. He'll have to stay local for a while, though."

"Didn't Boone tell you what happened when we got back?"

"He was injured, but we managed to get a few details from him the night your team brought him in. The next day, we got the full story, but we had nothing to compare it to. Now that you've corroborated his statements we won't hold him."

"This sucks," I said. "I should have woken up."

"You weren't faring so well when you got back. No one's blaming you for anything. Even Boone."

"Did my team... I mean, for the days I was gone, did they think I was—"

"I can't be sure," Paulson said. "Outwardly, at least, they assumed you were alive. Once they saw the site, they didn't appear to consider an alternative. It's hard to say what they were thinking though."

That was good, at least. "This is such a mess."

"Don't worry about it. It's my mess for now. You're back, and that's what's important."

"Why is it yours?"

"It might not be for long. We've been working on the assumption that this is related to Clancy's murder. With your statement, there's a good chance the two aren't connected."

"Are you sure?" I asked.

"It's unlikely Agent Boone killed Clancy, and now we know he didn't kidnap or kill you. Agent Dempsey and Agent Walden got into town late the day Clancy was killed, many hours after he died, and they didn't access the Farm until the following day."

I wasn't convinced, but I kept my mouth shut. "Is there

anything else I should know? I feel, I don't know... behind, I guess."

"I'm sure your team will fill you in on anything I missed. It's good to see you back. I know I already said that, but I can't imagine getting trapped in another dimension. I've thought about going to one on purpose, one we have a nice stable portal for, but to get into one and blocked off? To be honest, the thought is scary as hell."

"Before this, I had never thought about it." Now it would plague my thoughts, but I kept that to myself.

"Well, I'm going to get back to Kyrian so we can give Agent Boone the good news."

"Thanks," I said. "Let me know if you need anything else from me."

He left the room, and I felt relieved when he shut the door behind him. Once again, I felt the need to take a few minutes to myself, before people came in and I'd have to deal with them again.

On the plus side, I felt better. The interrogation had worn me down a little. Finding out everyone had thought I died hadn't helped matters, but in all, I was antsy to get to my feet. Before I could do that, I needed to convince someone to bring me clothes.

I didn't get long to think about it. Dr. Yelton came back in to check up on me since my interview was over.

"I'm fine," I said. "Better than I thought I'd be."

"That's good to hear," Dr. Yelton said. He didn't take my word alone, though. He checked me over again. "I'm going to ask a nurse to remove everything except the IV fluids. We'll keep you on those until tomorrow."

"I don't suppose I have any clothes lying around here, do I?" I asked.

"Logan brought a bag in for you. Once the nurse is done,

she can help you into your clothes, but that doesn't mean you get to start running around. Stay in bed."

"Can I get a tablet?" I asked.

"No working."

I sighed, but at least I could get dressed. The nurse took Dr. Yelton's spot a few minutes later. After she disconnected me from various machines, she hovered while I changed. Once I climbed back in bed, she left. Checking everything within easy reach of the bed, I looked for a phone, any phone, I didn't care whose, but I didn't find anything. Had I been in a real hospital, one would be in my room, but I had no such luck in the clinic.

Outside the room, coming from down the hall, I heard whistling. The enchanting whistle that could only come from an elf. Even though the song probably talked about cowboys, I couldn't help but smile.

Logan came into the room, his cowboy boots clicking when they struck the floor. "Howdy, partner."

"I'm glad to see you," I said. "I need your phone, any phone, I want to call Gran and Mom."

"Sure thing." Logan dropped his hat on the bedside table and dug around his pockets for his phone. "Rider will bring yours later today."

"Wasn't he supposed to bring it last night?"

"Doc asked us to hold off. Today though, even after your busy morning, you're looking better."

"Thanks. I'm feeling loads better. I'm crossing my fingers he'll let me out of here tomorrow."

Logan handed over the phone.

"Have they released Boone yet?" I asked.

Logan shook his head. "Haven't heard they were going to."

"Oh." I couldn't help but feel disappointed.

"We have a meeting in a few minutes. Maybe they'll fill us in there."

"We, as in the agency?"

"No, it'll be Hank, Vincent, Rider, and me. I think Paulson and one of his crew will be there, along with the director."

"I take it I'm not invited." It sucked to think I couldn't be at the meeting. It wasn't that I enjoyed the meetings, but I hated feeling left out.

"Not this one. Don't be in a hurry to rush to your feet." His light tone had a kernel of seriousness tucked in it.

My partners had spent days worrying I died, then I came back, they thought they were watching me die. I could see his point of view about not wanting to see me rushing back to work.

Clasping my fingers together, I twiddled them around in my lap. "Paulson filled me in on what happened while I was gone."

"Did he now?" Logan asked.

I couldn't tell if Logan was upset about that, but I moved on. "I'm really sorry if you all thought..." My eyes started to burn. "I mean—"

Logan chuckled. "You're apologizing for being dragged into another dimension by a madman?"

"Pushed in," I said, wanting to set the record straight. "I was pushed in."

Logan raised an eyebrow, but didn't ask what I meant. "We figured you'd give Boone a run for his money."

"Did you?" I asked, trying to smile.

"We were worried, but after the first day, we went at it assuming you'd be waiting for us to get the portal back open."

"After the first day?"

Logan dropped some of his smile. "Well, they tried to keep us off site for a while. We only heard what happened."

"I can't even imagine." I tried to shake the thought out of my head, but it lodged in tight. Sniffing, I knew I'd break down if I followed that train of thought. "So, they tried to keep you out."

"Well, there wasn't much they could do to us to keep us away. Agent Paulson was the only one even to try to block Vincent's way. No one likes the idea of standing between a black-eyed Walker and his intended destination. Especially when he's adamant he's going to be there."

"I imagine they'd be pretty hard pressed to stop a werewolf or an elf." I grinned, imagining the picture.

"Well, they do know what we can do. Mind you, I thought all bets would be off when Vincent grabbed Paulson's arm."

"What? He didn't try—"

"No," Logan said. "He just pulled the man closer for a private chat. No idea what he said, but Paulson thought it over, then let us through. He watched us, naturally. Once Rider was convinced you hadn't shed a drop of blood on this side, we had hope. Vincent thought your soul was still kicking, so we figured we'd better get the portal open."

"We waited there on the other side." My eyes burned and I knew I had to change the subject. "Speaking of which, we need to rethink our gear bags."

Logan stood. "Funny, we were thinking the same thing. We'll do that when you get back to work."

I grabbed his hand and gripped it. "I knew you all were coming to get me."

He gently squeezed my hand and let go before picking up his hat. "You went and beat us to it. It's good to see you back."

"It's good to be back." I settled against the bed, but didn't lay it flat and remained propped up. "Will you close the door behind you?"

"Sure thing."

When the door clicked shut, I looked at Logan's phone for a

minute and took a few meditative breaths before typing in Logan's code and calling.

As soon as I heard Gran's voice, I realized I should have meditated longer. "Gran, it's me."

"Darlin', it's so good to hear your voice." Gran's voice cracked.

After that, there were a lot of tears. Being at work, I tried to restrain mine, but someone would have had to be made of granite not to tear up when Gran cried. After a few minutes, Gran passed the phone to Mom. There were more tears. Mom was the first to recover, and then she turned all business.

"When are they letting you out of that wretched place?" Mom asked.

"I'm hoping tomorrow." I tried to reign back in my emotions and get myself under control.

"Well, if not, I'm calling the police. They can't keep you locked up for no reason."

I chuckled. "I assure you, Mom, I'm not locked up. It's basically a hospital, but the doctor only has a few patients. Trust me, I'm getting better care here than anywhere else."

"Well, your grandmother insists you come home as soon as you can. She can't see anything about you in the building. Too much interference, she says."

"Yeah, that's usually the case."

"I heard Logan and the others stopped by," I said.

"When they weren't at work, one or more of them would stop by to check on us. They kept us filled in on their progress, and Vincent made sure your rabbit was fed. There seems to be something wrong with the thing, but your grandmother wouldn't let me take it to the vet."

"Frank's okay, and he has a doctor," I said, thinking about Taylor. I'm pretty sure Taylor could count as Frank's doctor. He takes blood samples, anyway.

"Well, that's good to hear, at least."

"I should let you all go," I said.

"But you might be home tomorrow?" Mom asked.

"I hope so, but it's up to the doctor."

"Well, be sure to let me know when you are on your way home and I'll stop by. I can stay for a while if you need me."

"You don't have to do that, Mom." Mom was fine in short doses, but I didn't think a few days of her would work.

"I don't want any extra stress on your grandmother right now. I can take care of you."

It had to have been a hard time for them, those past few days. Or had it been a week? "I'll be fine when they send me home. Actually, I'm fine now, but they want to monitor me for a while."

"Do you not want me here?" Mom asked. I could hear the hurt in her voice, but there was a hint of warning there as well.

"Of course I want you there, Mom. It'll be great to have you around," I lied. "You and Gran, you're okay, right?"

"We are now that we've heard from you. Get some rest and come home."

"I will."

The talk with Gran and Mom had done what the doctor, visitors, and interrogation hadn't been able to do. It had worn me down. It didn't help that my head pounded. I put Logan's phone on the table by the bed and used the controls on the bed to lie down a little more. I had intended on only resting my eyes, but I fell asleep.

When I woke up, it was quiet and outside the window, it looked as though the sun had given up on the day. The door clicking shut had been what woke me.

Seeing Vincent, I couldn't help but smile again, although if he kept sleeping here, he would never get any real rest.

"Hi," I said. "How did the meeting go?"

He smiled at me. "It went well. Boring stuff." He walked over to the tall table that stood beside the bed.

My smile fell. "What's wrong?" Something felt off. Vincent didn't smile like that. At least he rarely did. Not for the whole world to see.

"Nothing's wrong," Vincent said. He looked nervous.

Vincent didn't do nervous. Maybe I was mistaken and he was just really happy. "Okay," I said, unconvinced. The smile looked manic and creepy, but I didn't say anything. "Did anything happen today?"

"The usual." He dumped something onto the table and wouldn't look at me. At least the weird smile began to fade.

"Did they let Boone out?"

"Don't worry about Boone. I'll be seeing him next."

"Listen," I said, reaching out and touching Vincent's arm, "I wanted to talk to you..."

Vincent looked down at my hand, and then went back to whatever he was doing.

No fire sprang between us. No energy. No connection.

This wasn't Vincent.

Swallowing hard, I took my hand away and tried to ease myself to the other side of the bed, away from the man.

My stomach felt like a stone had landed in it and I knew talking would give me away. I reached my hand over to the call button.

He snatched the button away. "The doctor is busy at the moment. You don't want to go bother him."

"Right," I said. "Listen, I was going to go down the hall and..." I swung my legs over the edge of the bed.

The man gripped my arm, hard, and yanked me back toward him.

When I looked back at him, his eyes were flat black. A clone of Vincent's face—even the thin scar that ran across his temple, but this wasn't the black-eyed Walker people feared. The features were the same, but the face contorted with emotions.

Then I saw the needle. Swinging my leg up, I kicked the man in the chest. He let go, looking stunned that I had kicked him. I scrambled off the side of the bed, pulling off the IV tube on the way. The man rounded the bed faster than I had anticipated.

"Cassie, what's wrong?" he asked.

"Who are you?" I hated that my voice quavered. I glanced at the door, but I was on the wrong side of the room and I wasn't sure I could get past him.

"You've had a hard few days. You need to relax. That's all I'm trying to do."

My head pounded, but I felt steady on my feet. He moved toward me and I moved back. When I realized I was retreating, I stopped and reached for the Path.

Through the pounding in my head, I had expected there to be resistance, but I jumped smoothly into the Path. A light, rippling overlay flowed around the room. Drawing in more energy, I tried to let it build when he moved toward me, but not much power came to my aid. When he got close, I threw what little I had at him.

His hair ruffled as though the room had a draft.

I'm not sure what crossed my face, but he used my distraction to his advantage. He shoved me into the wall and had the needle in my arm before I managed to land a kick right where it counted. He stumbled back, clutching at his groin. Somehow, the needle managed to stay in my arm.

I'm pretty sure I screamed at that point, but all logic had left, and I yanked the needle out and threw it across the room.

"What is happening?" Rider came into the room, but I barely registered it.

My eyes were glued to the needle until the fake Vincent answered.

"Something's wrong. She's not herself. I'm going to get the doctor." He hurried to move out of the room and I launched myself at him.

I only managed one sharp hit before Rider had me. It wasn't the best time to panic, but I did. Could I even trust this was Rider?

"What are you doing?" I yelled, struggling to get out of his grip.

The man rushed out of the room.

"Why aren't you stopping him?" I yelled.

With Rider's strength, he could easily crush me. Strong arms wrapped firmly around me, but only firm enough to keep me from breaking free. That had to mean he was the real Rider, right?

NINETEEN

Still, Rider and I hadn't been on the best of terms.

I continued to struggle and berate the werewolf. "You're seriously going to let him walk out of here?"

"What's going on?" Boone entered. He moved slowly and looked leery, but I knew he would be no match for a werewolf.

"Use your nose, you stupid werewolf. That's what it's there for, isn't it?"

Rider held tight.

"I think you need to step away," Boone said. He looked as though he were steeling himself for a fight.

"Rider, if you don't let me go, I'm going to..." In my frustration, I couldn't even think of what I could do to him. "I'm going to be pissed."

His grip loosened, and I rammed my elbow back and into his stomach as hard as I could. Rider let go, but I don't think my hit caused it.

"Cassie, I think—" Boone said, approaching cautiously.

"Stay out of this," I snapped at Boone, moving away from Rider. "Rider?"

Rider didn't look at me. He began to move around the room, looking thoughtful.

Boone stepped back when Rider came his way, but didn't say anything. Boone didn't look happy about it, though.

Finally seeing Rider doing what I expected, I started to calm down my breathing. My friend—and I was convinced by now he was my Rider—found the needle and his nose scrunched up and his lip curled back.

Seeing the thing, I once again took a step back and hit the wall. Memories of being trapped in a basement and being injected welled up and I started to shake. Those memories were hard to push down once they were out.

Rider threw the needle on the table. "It was not Vincent."

"No shit. Go find him!"

Rider nodded and strode to the door.

Vincent chose that moment to walk in.

Rider picked Vincent a foot off the floor and pushed him into the wall. Blank faced, Vincent looked at his partner. It was Vincent. I could sense it the moment Rider picked him up. It was the real Vincent.

Slowly, almost hesitantly, Vincent's green eyes began to cloud over.

Once again, I tried to work with the Path, but met a rivulet instead of the heavy torrent I had been used to.

"Rider. Put me down. Now." The words came out clipped, but didn't contain the cold undercurrents I expected.

"That is Vincent." I tried not to get angry. "Smell him already and go."

Rider gently set Vincent down. He looked around the room, but not at us. Rider's eyes focused on something else—the trail, maybe? Then he left the room.

Vincent watched him leave and adjusted his shirt. His eyes were back to normal when he turned to me.

"What was that?" Vincent asked. His voice held no emotion, but I could see Rider's actions troubled him.

"Rider had her arms pinned down," Boone said.

I rubbed my head and looked around the room. The Path barely made an impression. Nothing I could work with remained, so I leaned back against the wall and pushed the useless energy away.

Vincent spared a cursory, but not too friendly glance at Boone before he came over to me.

"Why would Rider do that?" He aimed the question at me.

Behind him, Boone moved to the table.

My hands shook and the ordeal made me tired. I was also more than a little confused. When I looked at Vincent again, I tensed. It was him, right? Rider would have been able to tell. He looked like my Vincent.

He sensed the apprehension and kept his distance. "I need you to fill me in when you can."

"Someone came in," I said. "And... things got confusing from there."

"And Rider?"

I let out a shaky breath. "Got confused."

"He's not the only one," Boone muttered.

Vincent ignored him. "Come on. You can sit down and let me know what happened."

I nodded, but when I looked over Vincent's shoulder, I saw Boone holding the needle. Those memories hadn't been pushed down far enough. Before they took over, I closed my eyes and wrestled with them again. The basement had happened months ago. The clinic looked nothing like it.

I was fine. Vincent was fine.

"Put it away, Boone." The harshness in Vincent's voice made me jump.

The moment my eyes opened, they strayed immediately back to Boone. "I'm fine," I lied.

Vincent moved into my line of sight. He looked pale and practically vibrated with anger.

"The person that came in," Vincent's eyes roved over me. He took one arm and started to turn it over. "Was it someone familiar? Did he—were you injected?"

"I don't know."

Vincent glared at me and my eyes darted over his shoulder again. "Boone, if that isn't out of sight..." He turned and saw a little black folio that looked oh-so-familiar.

Boone saw us watching him, and he dropped the folio and rolled the table out of sight.

A muffled clatter could be heard in the distance and a soft alarm rang out. Steel doors started to close over the window. It was much quieter in the clinic, but I knew the rest of the building would hear a blaring alarm as the building went into lockdown.

Vincent turned to me again. "Boone, get the doctor. Now." He started moving his hands over my arms in a panicked way, but he kept his touch extremely gentle.

"It's not the same person." I knew what he was thinking because I was trapped in the same nightmare.

"How can you not know if you were injected?" He didn't say it cruelly, but it stung all the same.

"The needle went in here," I tugged up my sleeve, "but I think I kicked him away before—"

"Does any of this hurt?" Vincent asked, pushing the skin around the injection site.

"No." I said. "I'm okay. It's over. I'm fine."

He didn't believe me, and I couldn't blame him. I couldn't even convince myself. Everything had moved too fast for me to know how I felt.

I sighed and pushed away from the wall. "I'd like to sit down, though."

I didn't have time to hate having to say the words. Vincent picked me up and dropped me unceremoniously on the bed. He frowned and started prodding my arms again.

"A little warning might be nice," I mumbled.

He put the back of his hand against my face and I pushed his arm away.

"Stop," I said. "Just stop."

He ignored me, which worked out well. I could concentrate on being mad at him instead of freaking out.

Dr. Yelton ran in, followed by two nurses and Boone.

"You were injected with something?" Dr. Yelton asked.

"No," I said.

"Yes," Vincent said at the same time.

"Where is it, and what symptoms does she have?"

"Over here," Boone said, drawing the doctor over.

"Any trouble breathing?" Dr. Yelton asked from behind the curtain.

While Boone showed Dr. Yelton the needle, the nurses were attaching the heart rate thing, the blood pressure cuff, and adjusting the bed to make me lie down again.

"All this just came off," I said. "And he didn't inject me. The needle went in, but he couldn't do anything after that beyond clutch his groin."

Dr. Yelton appeared at my side again. "Nurse, take this and get started. I'll join you shortly."

Seeing the nurses rushing around ratcheted up my anxiety, but the doctor stayed calm and quick.

"Open your mouth, wide." He inspected my mouth, ears, and nose before moving to the injection site. He checked blood pressure, temperature, heart rate, something about oxygen levels, and had the nurse take blood.

He kept asking me questions until I started to get aggravated answering the same ones over and over. After listening to my lungs and checking my throat for a final time, he spoke to the nurse while she removed the IV. The flurry of activity in the room died down, but a lot of people remained. Many more than I had realized. Vincent spoke with another agent, and someone in gloves wheeled out the table.

If this guy had looked like Vincent, he could look like anyone, right?

"Where's Rider?" I asked. Vincent appeared to be the only one paying me any attention which, somehow, made me feel better.

"He's in the hall," Vincent said, raising his voice enough for me to hear him without coming closer to me.

I nodded. Was he watching who was coming and going? Closing my eyes, I took a meditative breath.

When I opened them again, the doctor stood next to me drawing a shot. I stared at it, unsettled. Thankfully, I wasn't the only one who wasn't comfortable with the sight.

"Dr. Yelton, what are you giving her?" Vincent left the agent that was still talking to him. Still, the man didn't hurry to follow Vincent or stop him.

"This is something to help her sleep," Dr. Yelton said.

Vincent nodded. I glared at him when he asked nothing else, and instead, talked with the agent again.

"I don't want to sleep," I said.

"I'm going to run a few tests," Dr. Yelton said, seeming to ignore my comment, "and see what we're dealing with. They're going to ask you a few questions, but only a few." Dr. Yelton aimed the last half of his last statement at someone nearby. "Then get some rest."

Agent Paulson took Dr. Yelton's place. "I wish we could wait on this," he said, pulling the chair over. "But we can't."

"I get it." What I didn't get was why there were so many people here. I kept glancing around, anxious to keep everyone in view.

"Walk me through what happened," Paulson said.

Vincent moved over, intent on hearing the story. It made me feel better to have him close by.

The story went fast, since there were no interruptions. I could tell Paulson wanted to get the details before I drifted into la la land and couldn't give him anything else.

I didn't need to look at Vincent to feel his anger building, though it wasn't buffeting me from side to side, as it once did. Instead, it swirled through the room enough for me to sense it, but not be affected.

"How did you know it wasn't Vincent?" Paulson asked.

"He looked off, somehow. It was as though he didn't get things quite right when pretending to be him." It's not like I could tell him Vincent still had a piece of my soul, or I had a part of his. I'm pretty sure something like that would add to the paperwork.

"Anything else?" Paulson asked.

"Well, he usually doesn't go around attacking me with a needle. That was a big clue." Then I giggled at the idea and slapped a hand over my mouth, surprised the sound came out.

"There's going to be a guard on your door," Paulson said, knowing our interview was coming to an end.

"And Boone's?" I asked.

"If the doctor keeps him around, there will be," Paulson assured me. "Once we clear out, there will be limited access."

"Thank goodness," I said, feeling relieved. Then I bit my lip, realizing I had said it out loud.

"Do you need anything before we go?"

It crossed my mind to say a shower, but I remained lucid enough to hold my tongue. "No, I'm good."

"Let's go," Paulson called.

Everyone started to file out of the room, including Vincent.

"Where are you going?" I blurted out.

"He's going to take a look at some video footage," Paulson said.

"Oh, yeah," I said, my thoughts swirly and light. "That doesn't work for me."

Paulson started to answer, but closed his mouth. He looked at a complete loss for words, but Vincent's mouth twitched in amusement.

"I'll meet you outside," Vincent said.

Paulson hesitated, but nodded.

Paulson left the room and I hollered after him. "And close the door." After it snapped shut I muttered, "Raised in a barn," which is exactly what Gran would have said.

"You needed me?" Vincent said.

"Always," I said, my tongue feeling looser than it ever had. "Come here."

When he got to me, he started to protest when I sat up.

"Shut up," I said.

He raised an eyebrow, but didn't say anything, which was good. I grabbed his arm, pulled him in, and hugged him.

Warmth spread over me and I shut my eyes and sighed. He patted me awkwardly on the back a few times, sort of returning the hug, but when I didn't let go, he relented and embraced me.

His muscles were tense and stressed, but the longer I held on, the more relaxed he became. In the end, he was holding on to me as much as I was clinging to him.

"That wasn't so hard, right?" I asked after a short time.

It was his turn to sigh. "You're killing me, Cass."

"Good. It's about time I tried to kill someone and not the other way around." Then I giggled.

"That's not funny." Vincent pulled away, but sat down on the bed and held onto my hand, as if he never wanted to let go.

It felt right. Exactly as it should be.

"You're right." I smothered the laughter and I put my hand on his, content with the contact.

As though he had just realized that he still held on, he let go and stood up. "Sorry. I shouldn't..."

Depression welled up. "Right." Thankfully, a floaty feeling kept the emotion at bay.

"Rider has you covered outside." Vincent said, changing the subject. "No one's getting in here without him knowing who it is."

"Is he going to stay outside? He can come in here."

"He's more comfortable in the hall for now."

"Of course." I swallowed hard. This homecoming sucked. Rider should be over whatever had caused him not to talk to me, but he was still distant. Then there was Vincent. He and I were... what?

"Cass, don't." Vincent stood there looking lost.

"Don't what?" Then I sniffed. Wiping my face, I realized I had teared up. "No, I'm fine. It's been a long day, and the medicine and all..." It's amazing my nose didn't grow longer. I yawned, hoping to emphasize the statement.

"Do you want someone in here with you?"

"No." It killed me to say those words. "I'm just going to be asleep. And there's been so many people around..."

"If you're sure," Vincent said.

"I am. I could use my phone, though. I'd like to call Gran in the morning."

"No one's given you your phone?"

I laughed weakly, with no humor to hold it up. "No, but I'd like it back if I can."

"I'll check on it." He looked troubled, but I only shrugged.

"Can I get you anything before I go?" Vincent asked.

"No."

He didn't move anywhere and appeared to be thinking hard about something. I'm not sure where his thoughts had wandered, but I wanted to know. Whatever it was, he didn't share it with me.

"Goodnight," Vincent said.

"Night."

Vincent quietly shut the door behind him. The room felt lonely, but at the same time, it was nice to be rid of everyone. I needed sleep, but it wasn't coming. It's hard to sleep when you're silently berating yourself. Who cries at work?

I scrubbed my face with my hands to make sure no evidence remained, and then I sat in the quiet room, trying to get my brain to shut down.

At some point, the medicine must have kicked in to put me to sleep, but when I woke up, I still didn't feel rested. Looking at the clock, I saw why. I'd only been asleep for a few hours.

A noise in the hall caught my attention, and I could see the flickering shadows of feet standing in front of the door. Farther away, someone dropped something metal and it clanged on the floor.

Why had no one left me a gun? I swung my feet off the side of the bed. The knockout drugs were still in my system, making me unsteady, but I could manage. Another crash came, louder this time, and I started to look around the room for anything I could use as a weapon, but came up with nothing.

No phone, no gun, what was a girl to do?

Gunshots rang out down the hall. I jumped and felt my heart begin to pound.

Even if I had had a weapon, it wasn't as if it would shield me from gunshots. My door quickly opened and Rider came in, snapping the door shut behind him and bolting it. He started toward me.

"Don't," I warned him. How could I tell if it was Rider? My Rider could be somewhere bleeding out.

Looking all business, he ignored me, and as he moved forward, I moved back against the wall. When he reached a few feet in front of me, he turned and waited.

Another shot punched through the air and Rider backed up into me.

"What are you doing?" I tried to push him off me, which felt like trying to move a boulder.

"Guarding," he said.

"Do you have to stand on top of me to do it?" I pushed again.

"I would not stand on you." However, he took the hint and moved a few inches away.

"At least I know you're my Rider," I muttered. "What's going on?"

"I have only a small idea of what has occurred. The shots came from Boone's room."

"What?" I ducked around Rider and went straight for the door.

Rider wrapped one arm around my waist and easily picked me up.

"What are you doing? We need to see if he's okay."

"We will stay in the room until it is clear."

I tried to pry his arm off me, but we might as well have been welded together.

"Put me down," I snapped.

"Our orders are to stay here," Rider said, seemingly unconcerned.

"Orders from who? Vincent? Of course he's going to say that."

"From Logan."

That doused some of the fire that had been building. "Did he say why?"

"Any more people would add to the confusion, and there would be two targets instead of one."

It made sense, but I didn't have to like it. "Fine."

Rider made no move to put me down.

People were rushing down the hall outside.

"There were guards on Boone's room, right? Why is he still in the clinic?"

"Guards, yes. I do not know why."

Rider's phone rang and he answered it, one arm still holding me in the air. "It is me."

He listened, and I tried to pry his arm off again.

"Yes," Rider said.

"You can put me down, you behemoth," I snapped.

Rider looked down at me confused. "I do not know what that is."

I couldn't make out words from the other end of the phone, but the chuckle was clear, then whoever it was started talking again.

"Yes," Rider said. After a longer pause, he said, "I will tell her."

TWENTY

Rider didn't seem inclined to put me down while on the phone, so I reached for the Path. Once again, there was an eerily smooth transition when I closed my eyes and slid into the Path.

"Logan has asked us to stay here," Rider said. "He said Boone is uninjured."

"That's a relief. Did he say what's going on? Did they catch whoever is doing this?"

"They did not catch the person responsible."

"You can put me down now, you know," I said. The Path had me distracted. The gentle, rippling overlay of our world held no strength.

Lying to myself was something I was fairly good at. The first time using the Path after my return showed me the same lazy flow. Since then, I'd been telling myself the Path would be back, that I would get over whatever had caused the issue.

Now I was beginning to realize that wasn't the case.

"Rider, you can put me down," I repeated.

Still he didn't move.

"Rider?" I tried to crane my neck to look back at him.

"Logan asked us to remain here," Rider said.

"Not remain right in this spot. He meant in the room. Put me down."

Rider appeared to consider this. "That sounds reasonable."

He set me on my feet and I started to look around at the slow, glittery flow of stunted Path around me. Rider looked nervous when I walked around the room.

"You will stay in the room, right?" Rider asked.

"I'm not going anywhere," I said. What I didn't say was that it would be no use to go anywhere. The Path looked weaker than it had when I had first joined the agency. Could I do my job now?

I tried to find the flows of my attacker earlier in the evening, but in my limited state, it wasn't visible. It hadn't been long ago—I should at least be able to see that Path.

"What is wrong?" Rider asked.

I sniffed, realizing it as I did so. "Nothing." I stopped and tried to focus my brain toward solving the problem, not dwelling in it.

Had I used too much power and burned myself out? I'd never heard of that happening, at least not with the Reader surviving at the end.

"Those stupid gremlins," I muttered. And that woman, Wyna. They had to be the cause of my loss of power.

"Are the gremlins stupid?" Rider asked.

"What? Oh, no, not really." I went to the door, but Rider appeared content on letting me wander. His Path, always the easiest to see, was still there from when he had entered the room. He had been scared, nervous, and upset. The twisting Path of greens and browns still showed his Path switch from someone running on instinct to someone thinking things through, as though they were giving and taking from one another.

"Why do you suggest they are dumb if they are not?" Rider asked.

"It's nothing," I said.

Rider nodded, looking morose. He sat down on the floor while I followed small, individual little flows of Path, trying to make them move faster or slower, shift them forward or trace them back, anything that would indicate I had some sort of ability left.

"You will not tell me what is bothering you?" I'm not sure if Rider had meant it as a question, but it sounded like one.

Did I want to tell anyone about my loss of power? "No," I sighed. It wasn't like I was actively working. Maybe I could figure this out before I needed to tell anyone.

"I have broken our friendship," Rider said. He didn't sound sad; it was more matter of fact.

"What?" I stopped and looked at Rider. He was almost as blank faced as Vincent could get.

The Path would wait. When I pushed it away, I wavered. How could I be tired? I hadn't done anything. That would be something to figure out later.

"I am torn as to whether I should stay or go," Rider said.

"What? Why would you go?" I moved over to him and sat on the floor, leaning back against the wall to hide my unsteadiness.

"This world is wrong in so many ways," Rider said. "I have made mistakes and do not understand."

"That doesn't mean you have to leave. And you haven't broken our friendship." I thought about that and figured now was the time for honesty. "Actually, I'm not sure where we stand. I don't know what happened."

"Vincent said the same. I did not believe him, but I should have."

"Tell me what happened," I said.

"You challenged me."

That didn't make any sense at all. "Challenged you? For what? How?"

"Your wolf challenged mine. I could keep our friendship while I made my decision to accept the challenge, but I did not do that well."

"I don't understand." I rubbed my head as another headache started to form. I had no idea if it had come from the conversation or my use of the Path, but either way, the timing was bad.

"I came to this world because I would not accept a challenge from my brother. He had already killed one of our sisters, and I had no interest in taking his position, so I left."

I put my hand over my mouth. "Your brother killed your sister?"

"Half-brother and half-sister, but yes. He wanted to maintain his status and knew we could be a threat. I could either fight or leave. I chose to try this world."

"I am so sorry, Rider. I had no idea."

"This is the only area of this world I care about. I did not wish to leave, but I did not wish to fight."

"I don't want to fight," I said. "I don't understand why you thought I would want to fight."

"You challenged me the morning after Einar came to your house. I thought it was because of Vincent, but I did not understand. I still do not understand."

"I don't know what happened that morning," I said. "And I don't understand it any more than you do."

"Vincent has suggested you have been imprinted with the memories of others. Something in you made the challenge."

"But it wasn't me, and I don't know how to fix it. Can we forget it ever happened?"

Rider hesitated. "There have been other mistakes."

"Whatever it is, tell me and I'll try to stop."

He shook his head. "The ones you have made I am not concerned with. You do not always know."

"Huh, that's putting it mildly."

"These are the ones I have made. Decisions which were not right. Friends in my world and friends in yours do not do these things."

I frowned and looked at him. "I don't remember anything you've done."

He stayed silent for a moment as though lining things up in his head. "When we came back from the city. After we got Vincent back, I told Ethan what happened. Not everything, but more than I should have. I asked Logan about it afterward and he thought it was a mistake. He told me to tell you about what I said, but I did not."

"That's what you're worried about? I knew that."

Rider's brow furrowed. "Ethan told you?"

"There were some things he said which made me assume you told him. I was going to ask you about it, but finding Frank made me forget."

He nodded. "As I struggled to make my decision about the challenge, I was not happy with you."

"Yeah, I could tell." I tried to keep any bitterness out of my voice, but I still remember him kicking me out of the hospital room after he'd been shot.

"I tried to make it easier for me to decide."

The conversation was becoming uncomfortable and I had no idea what to say.

"In the mountains, after you were injured by the wolf, I told Ethan about you and Vincent."

"About our souls? I know that. It doesn't matter."

"It has made it so you two may never truly become friends."

"It's not that big of a deal. Ethan and I weren't right for each other anyway."

Rider scooted back and leaned against the wall next to me. "I do not understand why you are with him if you are not right for each other."

"I'm not. We broke up."

"Because of what I said." It was a statement more than a question.

"No, I messed that relationship up on my own. I kept things from him. You shouldn't do that with someone you want to stay with. You shouldn't feel the need to hide things. At least not with anything that would be important to them."

"Does Vincent know you are no longer with Ethan?"

I shrugged. "I guess so—he said he's talked with Ethan a few times."

Rider nodded, and then sighed. "I told him about you and Vincent on purpose. It was not an accident and it was not for a good reason."

My brow furrowed. "What reason?" I never thought of Rider as someone who could do something mean, so I couldn't imagine why he would say anything.

He was quiet for a moment. "I had hoped it would change our situation."

"You thought it would fix it?"

"I thought it would make it easier to leave. It did not."

Things weren't connecting for me. "How would that have made it easier?"

Once again, he took his time in answering. "I knew it would make Vincent upset. And it did."

"But I didn't want you to leave. I still don't want you to leave."

"I did not know that until after you were gone." For the first time in our conversation, Rider looked strained. Whatever hold he had on himself began to break down.

"Well, okay. You know now. I'm sure we can get over it and still be friends."

"I did not know until the day we found you."

"So? I was gone. Now that I'm back, we can fix this."

"When you left, I realized I might not have to make my decision. I could stay."

"You can still stay now. No decision needs to be made."

Rider leaned his head back against the wall and didn't say anything.

"It doesn't, does it?" I asked.

When he closed his eyes and didn't answer, I thought over what he had said. Realization came slow.

I looked down at my hands and leaned forward so I wouldn't look at him. "You didn't want me back."

"That is not what I meant," Rider said. "We all wanted you back. There was one moment, after we knew you were alive, that I thought if you did not come back, I could stay."

My head slumped forward and I concentrated hard on my hands. "Why are you telling me this?"

"Because I am ashamed. It is not the thought a friend should have, and you deserved to know."

Worst homecoming ever. "Why didn't you talk to me... before I was gone, I mean? I tried so many times to talk to you, to see what I did wrong, and you wouldn't let me."

"I did not understand. I thought you wanted a decision and I would have to leave."

"How could you think I wanted you to leave?" I was raising my voice, though I didn't care.

"There is nothing else I can say," Rider said. "There is no good reason."

It was time to get a grip on myself. My brain was cluttered with things I worked to ignore. This, too, I could sweep away and bury under a corner. "It was a thought." My voice sounded dull, even to myself. "One passing thought. People think stupid stuff all the time."

Rider didn't say anything.

"It was one passing thought, right?" It was a stupid question to ask, but I had to know it was no worse.

"One I am ashamed of," Rider said.

That was something, at least. I leaned back against the wall and stretched out. "I'm sure there are several people who have had the fleeting thought something might be easier if I were gone." Had Vincent thought the same thing?

"I do not believe so."

"It would have let Vincent off the hook. I'm sure there are several others here in the office that—"

"Vincent did not take your absence well."

I shrugged. "You never know what someone is thinking." I couldn't help but add, "Unless they tell you openly."

"Telling is better than keeping it in. I should have spoken to you. Now it is too late."

A jolt of fear shot through me. "What do you mean too late? You're not leaving." I was adamant about that last part. Sure, I may have been upset and more than a little hurt, but there was no way I was going to let him go.

"I have broken things." Rider sniffed and my heart felt squeezed.

What to do here? I didn't want Rider to leave. Our relationship had felt like it was crumbling around me for ages, but that didn't mean I didn't want to get it fixed. Maybe not today, with my heart so heavy, but tomorrow was always a possibility.

I took a deep breath. "I'm going to be honest with you, Rider. You were honest with me, so you deserve to hear the truth. There were times when I needed you in the past month or so and it sucked you weren't there. I'm upset, and I don't think that's going to change right away."

Rider nodded sadly.

I hurried on. "But it will change. It may take us some time, but just because we've messed things up, doesn't mean it can't be fixed again."

For some reason, this didn't look like it cheered Rider up any.

"Look," I said frankly, "you're not allowed to leave, and that's that."

Still, not much of a reaction.

"What?" I asked, feeling apprehensive about what I was missing. Silently, I crossed my fingers and hoped it didn't get any worse.

"Vincent does not know," Rider said.

"Vincent doesn't know what?"

"That I thought it might be better for me if you did not return."

Hearing the words again stung, but I could tell he was twisted up about it. "Why does Vincent need to know?"

"I do not want to make another mistake."

"A, it doesn't have anything to do with him, and b, even if you tell him, he's not going to be that upset."

Rider shook his head miserably.

Why can't I just be sad about this and then have it go away? "Ugh. It was a flicker of an idea, Rider. We all have them. Have you seen the expressions Vincent has on his face sometimes? I'm sure his mind throws up all sorts of weird stuff. Sometimes, we can't control it. It's like when you have a dream. Sometimes, it just pops in our head and then it goes away again."

Finally, a spark of hope showed up. "Do you really think this is something which can be mended?"

"Of course it can, but don't tell him now. Wait until all this mess is over."

"Why should this wait?"

My lips drew up, though I tried to force them down. "It's my turn to be upset. Once I get over it, he can have his turn."

Rider's face fell again.

"No," I cried, pushing myself closer to him. "That was supposed to be a joke." I leaned into him, feeling better knowing my best friend would stay in my life.

"It was not funny," Rider said.

"No, it was a bad joke. But you should wait." I nudged him. "It'll be okay. I promise."

Rider leaned in to me as much as I did in to him.

"How are you feeling?" Rider asked.

"Useless," I said without thinking.

"How so?" Rider asked.

There was a knock on the door. Rider hesitated, but rose to answer it.

He didn't say anything when he reached the door, but waited. For what, I didn't know.

The muffled voice came from behind the door. "It's Vincent."

"You will wait until I am certain," Rider said.

Vincent didn't say anything, but waited.

"What are you doing?" I asked.

"There are many smells."

I nodded and crossed my legs again.

Rider opened the door and stood aside to let Vincent enter. Once the door opened, I could tell Rider checked Vincent's scent again, to be sure. He wasn't obvious about it, but I knew him well enough to notice when he sniffed the air.

"Is everyone okay? Vincent asked after waiting for a few seconds, possibly knowing Rider was double-checking to make sure it was him.

"We are not injured," Rider said, being more exact.

Vincent walked in and gave me an odd look when he saw me on the floor.

Rider locked the door once again.

"Is Boone okay?" I asked.

Vincent tensed, but nodded. "He walked away unscathed."

"That's good," I said. "Where is he?"

"We're getting ready to meet downstairs," Vincent said.

"We as in who?" I asked.

"Boone, Logan, Hank, Kyrian, and myself," Vincent said.

My brow furrowed. "But not us?"

"It could be we are dealing with a changeling," Vincent said.

"Seriously?" All the other changelings I knew were nice people. Sure, they could turn nasty if they wanted to, but I had never thought we might be put up against one. "If that's what this is, aren't we going to need Rider out there?" If I had been up to strength, I would have included the fact that they'd need me. Since I wasn't prepared to tell anyone, I left myself out of the equation.

"Rider's busy," Vincent said.

Looking at the werewolf, who remained fixed to the wall and watching us, I could see exactly how busy he was. "Yeah, he's breaking under the strain."

"Rider is where he needs to be," Vincent said.

"He would be of more use out there," I said.

"He's the only one that can make sure the people around you are safe to be around you," Vincent said.

"Which I will do," Rider said.

Lines of worry were etched across Vincent's face. He looked tired, and Rider seemed dead on his feet as well.

"Fine," I said. "What do you want us to do?"

Vincent looked surprised at the turn in direction. "You two have to stick together. Rider, no one approaches Cass without your say so."

Rider nodded.

"Even me," Vincent said. "Especially me."

I turned a weak smile in his direction. "I know if it's you or not."

"Don't rely on that. It's Rider's approval, or rely on the Path if pushed. Nothing else."

I rolled my eyes. "Fine, okay, we stick together. Are we going room by room or something?"

"What? Why?" Vincent said.

I looked at him like he was an idiot, but mostly because he'd been behaving like one. "To find who's doing this."

"You're not going after him," Vincent said. "We don't know what we're dealing with yet. We're meeting so we can come up with a plan."

I stood and crossed my arms. "Why wouldn't we track him down? Rider and I may be the best shot we have at finding this thing." It wasn't my intention to add myself to the mix, but to stick with Rider, I had to actually be with him. Besides, I could still read the Path. Finding the person's Path may work as well as Rider sniffing him out, even without my former strength.

"Maybe, but you're safer here. They'll have to find another way," Vincent said.

I narrowed my eyes at Vincent. "That sounds like they agree Rider and I should be a part of this."

"If you two can track this thing, we have to assume you both will be targeted," Vincent said.

"Since when has that stopped us?" I asked.

A ghost of a grin appeared on Rider's face.

"Since someone forced you into another world," Vincent's voice wasn't able to hold the steel he might have intended.

I gave Vincent a sad smile. "But then I found my way back. And if I hadn't, I know you all would have found me."

Vincent looked torn. "Rider, do you mind if I talk with Cass alone?"

TWENTY-ONE

"I will never mind you two talking. I will be in the hall," Rider said.

After Rider closed the door behind him, I turned to Vincent. "They want us down there, don't they?"

Vincent sighed. "They do, but I'm asking you to stay here."

"But if we can help, we should. Before someone else gets hurt."

"You've barely been back. You should be at home, but since you can't be, I am going to keep you safe."

I bit my lip, trying not to say all the things I wanted to say to him and stick with the issue in front of us. "You know that's not your call, right?"

Vincent's stony mask frayed around the edges. Even a stranger could probably read his weary frustration.

"Hey," I said, walking over to him. "What's wrong?" I put my hand on his arm. Instantly, warmth spread up my arm, and the air between us became charged.

He removed my hand, held it for a moment, and then put

some distance between himself and me. It aggravated me, but it looked like it pained him almost as much.

"Rider said you weren't well while I was gone," I said.

"I'll have a chat with him," Vincent said.

"You look tired now. When was the last time you slept?"

"Sleep can wait."

"Why don't we go down to the meeting, and afterward, you and Rider can get some rest?"

"Is there anything I can do to keep you here?" Vincent asked.

"I'm sure there's loads of things you could do." Some of the things he could have done to keep me there, with him, made my heart race and my cheeks color. "But I don't think you're willing to do any of them."

"You're not released by the doctor yet," Vincent said.

"Like that would stop me." I grinned at him.

He smiled back and my heart skipped a beat. Dropping his guard enough for a genuine smile was rare and I cherished the look. "I knew you wouldn't stay, but I had to try."

"I get that. Especially after what happened earlier."

"Will you stick with Rider, at least?"

"Or you. The two of you are the only ones I can be sure of."

"Only Rider, Cass." I heard an edge to his voice that surprised me.

"Like I said, I can tell if it's you or not."

Vincent shook his head and moved closer. "I saw the doubt in your eyes when you looked at me earlier." He took my hand again.

"I was momentarily confused. That's all."

I wanted to close my eyes and relish in the feeling, but I could only stare at Vincent, who watched me intently. Caught up in his gaze, I didn't want to look away.

"I don't want to see that doubt again," Vincent said. "Stick with Rider."

My voice couldn't be trusted, so I nodded. For a moment, a split moment, I thought he might kiss me. Instead, he closed his eyes and tore himself away.

"We still have ten minutes or so." He drew himself back in, trying to get back to business. "You should give home a call. And maybe Ethan."

"You said Ethan knew I was back and okay. I'm sure that's all he needs. I'll call when I get home." Vincent looked like he wanted to say something, so I hurried on. "Besides, I still don't have my phone."

Vincent frowned. "No one's given it to you yet?"

"No," I said.

"I'll check on it." He drew back to his normal, everyday self, as though nothing had occurred between us.

"Can you tell Rider to get me in a few minutes?"

"When I said you need to stick with him, I meant by your side. If this is a changeling, it can get in about anywhere."

I grinned. "Nothing is standing between me and a shower. And while I know it wouldn't bother Rider, I'd rather be alone."

Vincent let out a small chuckle. "I see your point. Have him check the bathroom before he leaves you."

Did he think a towel would jump out at me? "Sure thing."

Wait, could a towel jump out at me? I mean, if it is a changeling, surely it would stick to people, right?

"You okay?" Vincent asked.

"What?" I came out of my reverie about killer soap. "Oh, yeah. I'm okay."

He didn't look convinced, but nodded all the same. "I'll see you downstairs soon."

Rider did, in fact, check the bathroom. To make sure

Vincent was happy, I even had Rider check the shower stall and everything.

It had nothing to do with me imagining the shower curtain attacking.

Once he left me alone, I didn't waste any time getting into the warm shower. The water poured over me while I thought only of the warmth for a while, then I turned to meditation.

The Path was almost non-existent now. It was possible keeping the portal open, or maybe going through it, might have burned me out.

If that were the case, though, I'm sure I would have started to recover by now.

No. This had been the gremlins. Wyna had handed me the innocent little bottle, said they apologized and the liquid would heal me up. She had implied the cut would heal, but even at the time, that hadn't made sense. I needed to see if the contents had healed my soul.

Fearing what I would find, I didn't rush the process. With the bathroom steaming up around me, I stood under the shower and let my attention slowly come together and focus. My thoughts almost drifted to the edge of my understanding of the world ended and a black chasm spread out.

When I reached that spot, I took a few deep breaths and concentrated on the abyss. At first, I saw nothing, but that wasn't surprising. It sometimes took a while for my soul to come into focus.

Careful not to force it, I watched, looking for sparkling shards, hoping that was what filled the void between the Path and me. Intent on finding the jagged edges of my soul, I almost missed the gauzy wave. Once it came into focus, I was mesmerized. Like never-ending waves on an ocean, my soul lay stretched out before me. A glimmer stood out in a few places.

Careful not to probe too deeply, I glided above the smooth surface, inspecting it before moving to the next. Each shining piece rose above its surroundings, but also moved with it. It took me a while to realize the bulges in my soul were not originally mine. They were fragments that had belonged to other Lost.

At least they had been. Now, they were very much a part of me, entwined in my own soul. There were no breaks and no jagged edges. My power no longer bounced between different pieces of my soul, amplifying the energy.

My power was weak. The thought broke my meditation. I shut off the water and stood for a moment, feeling lost. Then I shook my head and grabbed a towel.

Vigorously, I dried myself. I would still be useful. I had to be. The Path was still there. This monster could still be tracked, as long as I didn't have to go too far into the past to see it. No one needed to know that I'd be nearly useless at defending myself.

Almost no one.

"Rider," I said softly, knowing he would be able to hear everything, "I need you to know something before we go downstairs."

As I put on fresh clothes, I told Rider everything. Once I was dressed, I opened the door, checking the expression on his face, and continued my story.

"So your soul is no longer broken?" Rider asked.

"It doesn't appear to be." I dragged a brush through my wet hair, thinking my friend had missed the point.

When I looked over, Rider wore an expression I hadn't expected. He beamed at me.

"What?" I asked. "This means I won't be able to do as much. I can help you find whoever is doing this, but I don't think I'll be useful when he's found."

"This means Vincent will no longer need to carry the guilt he has somehow harmed you."

A thought stole over me. "Do you think he'll leave?"

"Why would he leave?" Rider asked, looking confused.

"He said he would stay until he fixed what he broke." Looking down, my hands were gripped together, but I didn't really see them. I was trying not to stare into a life without Vincent around.

"Vincent will not leave."

"I wish I could be as sure of that as you sound."

"It is not easy to leave those you love. If I must go away, you will have each other."

I narrowed my eyes at him. "You are not leaving." I put as much emphasis into the words as I could. "And I only told this to you now because you need to know. I don't want the others to find out yet."

"You do not think they need to know?" Rider asked.

"You and I are a team today. Besides, if they know, then it's possible the guy who tried to kill me will find out."

"You should at least let Vincent know," Rider said.

"If Vincent thought I couldn't defend myself with the Path, he would try to lock me up in a room until I died of old age."

Rider looked shocked and offended on behalf of his friend. "Vincent would not do that."

I grinned. "Not really, but he certainly wouldn't let me help, and he would ask you to stay with me. We need to be out there."

"I think that is true," Rider said without looking thoroughly convinced.

"I promise I'll tell him after this mess is sorted out, but it should come from me."

"There is a lot we are hiding from him right now."

"Not hiding. We're postponing it, but it's for his own good.

He doesn't need the distraction of thinking he could somehow keep me safer."

"This is true," Rider conceded reluctantly. "We will tell him after."

"Thank you, Rider. Let's get downstairs."

HANK, Logan, and Boone were in the conference room when we entered. For a minute, I worried Rider would go around and sniff everyone, but when I sat, he sat down next to me.

"You didn't have that last night, did you?" I asked Boone, indicating a cut across his cheek.

"That's new," Boone said. "Courtesy of the man who is trying to kill us."

"Was anyone else hurt?" I asked. "I heard the gunshots."

"We dangled Boone in front of him, hoping we'd be able to catch him," Logan said.

"They used you as bait?" I asked Boone, not feeling comfortable with the idea.

"I used me as bait," Boone said.

Logan grinned at me. "Not unlike you yourself have done on occasion."

I shrugged off the comment. "So no one was hurt, then?"

"The bad guy had a gun as well," Logan said. "Agent Mackey caught a bullet in the arm, but he'll be okay. The doc already stitched him up."

"Did the man who came after you look like Vincent?" I asked.

"He looked like Dr. Yelton," Boone said.

"So we *are* dealing with a changeling," I said.

"That's our best guess," Logan said. "There's other Lost that can shapeshift, but this guy is fast."

Vincent came into the room, nodded at us, and then sat down across from Rider.

"So, how do we know the people around Boone are who they say they are?" I asked, trying to keep my mind off the exchange Vincent and I had had upstairs.

"He stays with two people at a time," Logan said. "Hank and I have been with him."

"I don't know of anything that can become two people," Boone said.

"And with two people watching him, it's less likely one of us could kill him and get away with it," Hank said. "It was Vincent's idea."

"Three is ideal," Vincent said.

"Hank and I know each other better than most." Logan sounded happy about the fact. Hank, on the other hand, while not looking upset, still didn't look comfortable. "I suspect we'll notice something is off with the other if someone catches us off guard."

Logan smiled at Hank, but Hank somehow stayed resistant to Logan's happy nature. I tried to give Hank a reassuring look, but it didn't help.

"We have confirmation," Kyrian said, entering the room, "Agent Walden did not exit the plane when it landed. His office has people checking his house." She dropped her tablet on the table and sat down.

"You said he didn't exit the plane," I said. "Did he get on in the first place?"

"The airline has record of him boarding, but we are checking the surveillance video to confirm," Kyrian said.

"It does sound like a changeling," Vincent said.

"What about Agent Dempsey?" Boone asked. "Is it possible there are two of them?"

"Agent Dempsey is dead," Kyrian said. She looked uncomfortable and turned to her tablet as though reading off it. "He was found murdered, along with his family. I'm afraid his family, a wife and son, died more than a week ago."

I sucked in a breath, remembering Agent Dempsey being nervous and distracted. Had he known his family was already dead?

"Do we know if the changeling killed Clancy?" Vincent asked.

"Why would it kill him?" Rider asked.

"There could be several reasons," Paulson said. "The big one being that anything the changeling touched would give him away if Clancy touched it as well."

Clancy had been killed because of his powers. The thought struck me hard and I couldn't help but look at Vincent. Many people would probably want to see a Walker dead because of his powers or even rumored powers. I'd already been targeted as well. The idea was unsettling.

"We are doing a thorough search of the building now," Kyrian said, shifting the subject, "but I don't think that's going to do us much good."

"We could try to lure it out again," Boone said.

"It's a possibility, but if we can find the changeling before it finds you, that would be ideal," Kyrian said. "Agents Wolfe and Heidrich, if we lined everyone up, could you root out the one responsible?"

"I don't know the Paths of all my coworkers," I said. "I'm not sure I could tell his from theirs."

Logan frowned, but didn't say anything.

"Agent Wolfe," Kyrian prompted.

Rider looked like he was thinking it over. "I do not know much about changelings."

"What do you need to know to pinpoint who it is?" Kyrian asked.

"When I saw the person earlier," Rider said, "he appeared like Vincent. I did not recognize the difference immediately because his smell had a few similarities. The strongest scent was that of my friend."

I could see the muscles in Vincent's jaw tighten.

"You're saying if the changeling takes on someone's appearance, they take on their smell?" I asked. Maybe I shouldn't have been so hard on Rider when he had believed the fake Vincent over me.

"I am saying I do not know," Rider said. "There was a difference, but is it a coincidence he smelled similar?"

"I'm not sure we'd have much in the way of how a changeling might smell on file," Logan said.

"There should be a base smell," Rider explained. "A smell that is the changeling. One he cannot change."

"Once you know what part never changes, then you'd be able to track him?" I asked.

"Yes," Rider said.

"Can you compare the person we lured into my room to the person that attacked Cassie?" Boone asked.

"I can try," Rider said.

"I'm going to pull everyone we can into the central office," Kyrian said. "Agent Boone, your message has been sent. If you're right, once the news spreads through the office, he should no longer have reason to kill you."

"What news?" Vincent asked.

I swallowed hard and looked at Boone. He didn't seem to notice that Vincent radiated fury, or if he did, he didn't care. Only Rider appeared to notice.

"This person is trying to discredit me in some way. The only reason I can think of for doing this would be to slow or stop the project I'm working on. The director has sent a message from her and myself to my superiors. The project should go on regardless of what happens to me."

"It will know Rider and Cass can still track it while the building is on lockdown," Vincent said.

"Which means two targets instead of three," Kyrian said. "It will either narrow its focus or it will try to find a way out. Agent Paulson has put together a few teams to try to block any exit that may be easier to get out of than others."

"We're on lockdown," Logan said. "Shouldn't be many exits to block."

"After our last lockdown, Agent Paulson found a few spots which were weaker than the others. Ones we wouldn't normally think of as exits. Hank, I want you to get some people together and start going through video footage. See if we can spot any patterns of movement and anything else we can find about this person."

"I'll pull together people in the control room," Hank said, standing up. "We'll stay in the same spot to avoid any confusion." Hank left the room, intent on getting started.

"Agents Seale and Pironis, I want you to start searching the building. Anyone you find gets escorted back to the control room. Use whatever force you deem necessary. Agents Wolfe, Heidrich, and Boone will clear the clinic and start to track this person."

"Should all three work together?" Vincent asked.

"If the message doesn't work," Kyrian said, "it will keep the focus narrowed on them. Agent Seale, I need a word with you. Agent Pironis can wait in the hall. The rest of you get started."

Logan leaned back with his hands behind his head, looking content while we filed out of the room.

TWENTY-TWO

Vincent walked with us a short way before pulling Rider aside. He didn't make an attempt to get far enough away for me not to overhear, but I at least pretended not to listen.

"I'm not doubting you here," Vincent said, "but I am counting on you. You're certain you can tell this thing from another person, right?"

"I will keep her safe," Rider said, patting Vincent's back.

I could see Vincent color slightly, but he nodded at Rider, spared a moment to glare at Boone, and then walked back to wait for Logan by the conference room. Before we rounded the corner, I looked back and watched Vincent leaning against the wall and staring at the floor.

It was harder than I had expected to leave him behind.

"I get the feeling your partner doesn't like me," Boone said on our way to the clinic. "We were getting along fine before I left."

"He spent many days worried about what might be happening to Cassie by your hand," Rider said. "Once he is convinced you have done nothing, he will go back to normal."

I could feel the blush creeping in.

"He has to know by now I didn't harm her in any way," Boone said.

Rider shrugged. "I did not say good or bad by your hand."

Boone grinned. "I get it now."

I wasn't sure my face could get any redder. I hadn't even thought about that. Since I hadn't called Ethan, did Vincent think Boone and I had gotten together?

"And you're not worried about that?" Boone asked Rider.

I shot Boone a glare, but his grin remained and his eyes danced.

"Cassie chooses who she wants to be with," Rider said. "But she and Vincent have endured much together."

"Enough," I said.

Boone's mirth faded and he looked more thoughtful. "Yeah, after Cassie was attacked, I think I saw a piece of something they went through."

We walked in the clinic and Rider looked questioningly down at Boone. "Because someone tried to kill her?"

"Someone tried to inject her," Boone corrected.

"I said enough," I snapped, then pushed past the two. "We have work to do."

"That explains a lot," Rider said.

"It's hard working with people you care about," Boone said. "The job isn't exactly easy on relationships."

"That is true," Rider said.

"Which room are we going to?" I asked. I tried to put my annoyance into the simple statement. When they pointed it out, I stalked straight toward the room.

They didn't rush to catch up, but I went in and took the few moments I could to put their words out of my head. What I needed to do was focus. When I heard them come in, I didn't look up, but instead took a deep breath and shifted smoothly into the Path.

"Tell us where everyone stood," Rider said.

The rippling overlay in the room held ghosted whispers of Paths, but not enough for me to work with.

Boone relayed everything he could, and although I could see nothing, Rider picked up a scent.

"Have either of you fought a changeling?" Boone asked.

"Fought? No," I said, following Rider out of the room. "There are a few Logan and I check on from time to time. Why would we fight a changeling?"

"You never know what you might face in the line of duty," Boone said. "You know that as well as I do."

"Have you ever fought one?" I asked.

"No, but I've heard stories from someone who did." Boone seemed to be trying to check every direction at once while we walked the hall. "They can be really nasty, especially the old ones."

"They mentioned this guy is changing fast. I'm betting he's pretty old," I said.

"Stay on your toes then," Boone said.

Which reminded me Boone needed to know about my power. I plunged straight in, not wanting to avoid the inevitable. As I told him, I wondered how disappointed he would be. The fact he merely shrugged it off came as a shock.

Maybe I hadn't made myself clear enough. "What I did with the demon, back in the other world, I can't do that now."

"Good to know," Boone said. "You catch that side and the front. I'll concentrate on my side and the back."

"You're not bothered by the fact I can't use the Path?" I asked.

Boone shrugged. "I can't use it."

Rider snickered, but didn't turn around.

"Besides, I've sparred with you," Boone said. "I know you can handle yourself in a fight."

"What is sparring?" Rider asked as we left the clinic and headed upstairs.

"It's fighting each other," Boone said.

This time, Rider stopped and turned around. "You two fought one another?" He looked shocked.

"Not a real fight," I said. "More like Logan and Jonathan training together."

Rider's eyes grew wide.

"Bad example," I said quickly. "It was practice fighting. Seeing what the other person was capable of."

He still didn't look happy, but he started up the stairs again and onto another floor. Not a sound was on the floor besides the noise we were making. The floor even felt empty.

"Did sparring help you learn what the other can do?" Rider asked.

"Yeah," I said.

"It makes me sad that we could not be there," Rider said. "But it is good to know my friend had someone else when needed."

Boone glanced at Rider before moving his ever-roving gaze to his side of the hall. "How did you two get to be friends?"

The way he said it made me think he knew what it meant to be friends with a werewolf.

"It started after she shot me," Rider said.

I nodded. "Then I yelled at you some."

Rider nodded. "We spent that entire evening together and I saw who she was."

"And I got to know him," I added, craning my neck to get a better look into the room beside me.

"Without sparring," Rider said, sounding like he wanted to make that clear.

"And then we went for a walk the next day or the day after," I said. "And we talked quite a bit."

"Then we killed a fiend and she died," Rider said. "I was very sad when that happened."

I vaguely remembered that as well, but kept my mouth shut.

"But she pulled herself together and came back to life." Rider stopped and looked thoughtfully to me. "Yes, I think after that, we were friends."

"You also joined AIR soon after," I said.

"And I was no longer bored," Rider said.

"Yeah," Boone said. "I could see how being friends with Cassie wouldn't be boring."

I rolled my eyes. "I'm happy I can entertain you both. How close do you think we are, Rider?"

He stopped and looked at the space between us. "Five feet."

"Huh," Boone chuckled.

"I mean to who we're tracking," I said patiently.

"Oh, we are hours behind," Rider said, moving on. "Are you able to see traces of his passing?"

"Not yet." I tried very hard not to sound depressed over this fact. "I think I suck pretty bad at this now. A few hours is too long ago for me to see anything."

Rider nodded and entered an office. He walked around in a circle before exiting again.

"Was he using that office?" I asked.

"Yes." Rider quickened his pace. "He had a new smell, so he changed again."

"So you know which smell is his now?" I asked.

"I do," Rider said.

"Then we can pick him out of a group of others," I said.

"We will definitely be able to spot him. I think he will look like me," Rider said.

"He wouldn't go after anyone else, though, would he?" The thought of a fake Rider tricking Vincent or Logan made my stomach clench. "I mean, we're all here. There's no reason for him to attack anyone else. Right?"

"I think it depends on what his goal is now," Boone said.

"What do you mean?" I asked.

"If his goal is to get out, I would think he would turn himself into Kyrian and order the lockdown over," Boone said. "Did he turn into Rider to get closer to the director to take her out of the picture?"

"I guess that's feasible," I said.

"Or, would he turn into Rider to get closer to Vincent or Logan," Boone continued, "in the hopes that one of us would turn ourselves over in exchange for your friends."

Rider began to jog when we entered the next stairwell.

"There's no way he would be able to take Logan or Vincent," I said. "He'd have to knock them out before he touched them." That was something I was fairly certain of. There was a reason Kyrian had sent Vincent and Logan to clear the building. They could take care of themselves.

Rider dashed up the stairs, his long legs propelling him up much faster than I could.

"Maybe him turning into Rider would confuse people enough to get an advantage," Boone said.

"Maybe," I conceded.

Above us, Rider crashed his way out of the staircase and into the top floor of the building.

"If a changeling turns into someone, they can't clone their powers, can they?" I tried to get my legs to move faster to catch up. "I mean, when he changed into Vincent he couldn't steal souls. If he could have, he wouldn't have resorted to other methods."

"No." Boone held out his arm when we reached the landing. "It's only a physical change."

"But a werewolf's power is physical, isn't it?" I asked, thinking it through. "Logan's too. Their strength is physical."

Boone gestured for me to wait while he peeked into the hallway. Apparently satisfied, he motioned me forward. Since Rider had been there moments before, I had no problem following his Path. As I did, another one began to take shape.

"That's true," Boone said. "A changeling turning into a Walker only gives him the advantage of the fear others have in Walkers. As a werewolf or an elf, he'd have their strength."

I dashed around the corner, and before I could react, Rider slammed into me and we both fell to the floor. My ribs protested, but I tried to ignore the pain. When I looked up Rider, a second Rider ran toward us.

The Rider, which had fallen over me jumped to his feet. He charged and the two clashed a few feet away. I had to scramble back against a wall to avoid the fight.

"Which is which?" Boone called from the other side of the dueling pair.

I stared at the two fighting werewolves for a short time. Their Paths sold them out. "The one closest to you is Rider."

A growl issued from Rider, my Rider, and an eerie hush fell over the hallway. The noise was one which could cause any warrior to fear the darkness. Shadows crept up and the changeling hesitated.

That gave Rider the upper hand. Not taking any chances, or any extra time, Rider drove the changeling to the ground.

Unfortunately, it wasn't enough. The changeling started to change shape, and in moments, something that looked only vaguely like Rider was there, but what Rider would be if he had been pumping up on steroids. He issued a growl of his own. Nothing like the noise that brought instinctual fear out from everyone in the room, but one of frustration. He shoved Rider off him and jumped to his feet.

He looked up and went for the softest target.

Me.

Rider grabbed his foot and tripped him up, and the changeling fell to the ground.

I scrambled farther away. My heart raced and I struggled to bring more of the Path to my aid. The changeling kicked Rider squarely in the face, but Rider didn't let loose.

Behind Boone, Logan and Vincent came running around the corner, guns in hand—rifles this time. It didn't take long to see who was who in this mess, but to hit the changeling might mean hitting Rider.

"Back up," Vincent yelled.

The fake Rider tried to make another lunge and I ran further away.

The Path wasn't getting any stronger. My soul was the issue. I knew that calm smoothness held back the tide of the Path. When I pushed into my soul, it felt like a sponge. It moved and rippled where I tried to shove it out of the way.

Rider was on his feet now. In fact, both Riders were. My Rider had the changeling slammed against the wall, but once again, that put him in the way. Vincent and Logan were training their aim, but neither took a shot.

The hulking fake twisted Rider's arm. The crunching snap made me cringe. My hand flew to my mouth and internally I started to beat frantically against my own soul.

Rider wasn't done, but he should have been. He should have fallen back, but he gave one last dark growl and tried to push the beast to the floor once again.

It didn't take much. The changeling only had to grab Rider

where the break had been. Rider cried out, then managed to get one more hit before crumpling to the ground.

Logan wasted no time in firing. The shot wasn't as loud as I had anticipated, and when the fake Rider turned to me, I could see why. He had been darted, but he didn't look ready to go down.

Panic welled up, and I heard several more shots go off. Mentally, I stretched out my soul, trying to break through. With a damaged soul, I could stop this thing.

He bore down on me. Another shot came. This time loud. Catching a glimpse behind the creature, I saw Vincent had fired a gun, a real one.

The fake Rider cried out when he was hit, but he didn't stop.

He held out an arm, ready to grab me. I wasn't sure if he planned on using me as a shield, or if he wanted to kill me as he passed. Either way, he wasn't slowing down.

There wasn't much I could do, but he gave me an opening that would be easy to take.

Did this monster seriously think I would stand here and let him get hold of me?

Since the creature didn't slow down, I moved to the side subtly and gripped his wrist. I planted my foot in his stomach and fell back.

The falling back was planned, which was a good thing, because it was happening whether I wanted it to or not. Using the monster's momentum, I tossed him behind me and rolled out of the way. Several more shots rang out. The changeling hit a door at the end of the hall and took it off its hinges. Logan and Boone immediately charged after him.

Some yells came from the staircase and a scream that was cut off. Gunshots filled the air.

From my position, still panting and lying on the floor, I

watched the empty hallway. There was a crash and another scream. Metal crunched and more shots were fired. Then there was silence. I'm not sure what had happened, but whatever it was, it was over.

I dropped my head, resting my forehead on the carpet, and tried to catch my breath. It was over. A few yells made me jerk my head up, and through the fading adrenaline, I realized I had no idea who had made the screams. I shoved myself to my feet intent on running to help.

"Cass!" Vincent yelled.

I turned and saw him squatting down next to Rider.

Oh, crap, Rider. He was still on the floor. I forgot about the others and ran back. When I saw Rider was still breathing a shuddering relief wracked through me.

Rider's eyes opened and he looked panicked for a moment, but he reined himself back. A low groan escaped him when he tried to move.

"I need to check on Logan and Boone," I said to Vincent. "Do you have Rider?"

"No, I don't." Vincent looked like he held a lot back. When he stood and turned on me, I thought he was going to yell, but instead, he grabbed my arm and started turning it in his hands.

Rider groaned again from the floor, catching my attention. He was trying to get to his feet.

"What are you doing?" I snapped at Rider. "Wait until the doctor gets here. We need to check on Boone and Logan."

Vincent shook his head and looked around, putting pressure on my arm at the same time. The pain started to register about the same time I noticed the blood.

"Damn it," I said. I tried to pull my arm away from Vincent, but he didn't let go. Where he applied pressure, the tingling feeling which spread between us was overpowered by pain. "I'll hold this and make sure Rider stays put."

Vincent hadn't said anything, but he still didn't let go.

"It's not as bad as it looks," I said. In fact, it didn't look bad at all. The changeling must have clawed me, trying to keep hold of me when I threw it over me.

There was a noise at the end of the hall and Logan came in. Boone wasn't with him, but Logan didn't look too upset, so I figured Boone must be okay. Logan was ticked off, though.

"He got away," Logan said.

"Where's Boone?" I asked.

Vincent's hand twitched, but didn't let go. Remembering what Rider had said about Vincent's concern with Boone and me, I put my hand over Vincent's and I could sense some of his tension fade.

"That changeling tore through two of our men guarding the door to the roof. Boone and a few others are helping with the injured and someone's run for the doc."

Rider had his arm clutched to his stomach, but he moved to his feet.

"That arm doesn't look too good," Logan said. "Let's get you down to the clinic before it starts to heal and they have to re-break it," Logan said.

I put a hand to my mouth in horror. That didn't sound pleasant at all. Vincent rubbed my shoulder with his free arm.

"You two need to head down there as well," Logan said. "How bad did he get you?"

"It's not bad," I said.

"She'll need stitches," Vincent countered.

"Well, keep pressure on it and let's go," Logan said.

By the time we made our way to the clinic, Dr. Yelton was already in surgery with an agent, but others were around and helping out.

Seeing the chaos, Logan stepped aside to call to Hank, asking Hank to reach out to Taylor, hoping he was in the area.

He wasn't, but he started our way. It would take two hours for him to get to the office, but who knew how long surgery would take.

Rider was taken off for x-rays, and many of the patients were starting to get lined up and sorted out by two nurses. A nurse practitioner started with the worst and did everything they could while they waited for the doctor. What they could do turned out to be far more than I had imagined.

Logan disappeared and lockdown came to an end not long after. We weren't trying to keep anything inside anymore, so the building was opened.

My arm was a low priority, which wasn't a surprise. It was only a cut, after all. Vincent lifted his hand to check on the cut now and again. The bleeding had slowed, but he kept pressure on it. Since I wasn't in a hurry for him to let go, I said nothing. We sat side by side and watched others as they moved through the clinic.

Vincent was mostly quiet. Paulson joined us for a while. He didn't seem inclined to say much, but he asked about Rider and about how we were doing. We hadn't seen Rider since he had been taken for x-rays, so there wasn't much to report.

By the time Taylor arrived—much sooner than I would have expected—the flurry of activity had died down. Some of the patients were merely stable though, and needed a lot more help.

Six agents besides Rider and myself had been injured. Four were badly injured and Dr. Yelton had one in surgery.

Taylor whisked by us with no more than a nod before he disappeared into a room, listening to one of the nurse's litany of descriptions on where everyone stood.

A nurse pried Vincent off my arm almost a half-hour later. His name was Paul, and while he looked really tired, he was friendly and took me into a room with three other mildly injured patients. He inspected my arm and started to treat it. Another nurse poked her head into the room every few minutes to check on things.

When I came back out, bearing ten fresh stitches, Rider was waiting with Vincent. He wore a cast and a dazed look.

We left the clinic and met Logan downstairs.

"Did you all get released?" Logan asked.

I shrugged. "I'm not sure they're doing much in the way of releasing people. It was more like we were encouraged to leave as opposed to being released."

Logan nodded. "I'm meeting with Kyrian again in five minutes. If you'd like to join me, you're welcome to."

"I'll pass," I said. "I just want to go home."

"Let Hank talk with you. You two can walk him through everything and I'll talk with Kyrian."

CHAPTER
TWENTY-THREE

I found a desk near Hank and pulled a chair over to him. The room started to clear out now that lockdown was over. There were many people, agents and staff, that had been holed up in the building for ages. Not everyone had a hospital room to bed down in like I did. There were rooms on one of the floors, but with so many people in the office, they would have had to rotate people in and out of them.

"You look like hell," Hank said.

I gave him a weak smile. "I'm not feeling too bad. Tired, but not bad."

"And him," Hank asked, nodding to Rider.

"They got to him before they had to re-break the arm," Vincent said. "Whatever shot they gave him is starting to wear off though. Again."

Rider was sprawled out in a chair. His lean, six-and-a-half-foot frame never fit in a chair on the best days. Right now, he didn't seem to bother trying.

"He doesn't look very comfortable," Hank said. "You might want to see if there's anything else they can give him."

"He burns through it too quickly," I said. "We'll take him home soon though. With some rest, I'm sure he'll be as good as new."

"Well, let's go over everything and maybe we can get you all home sooner rather than later."

There wasn't much to tell. We had done exactly what we had been sent to do. We had tracked the changeling, found him, and tried to stop him.

Vincent filled in his part of the story, which gave me a few surprises. Apparently, he and Logan hadn't been clearing the building. Instead, they were following us around, well out of eyesight and well out of earshot for Vincent.

His voice remained even when he spoke of his approach to the changeling. He had fired several shots, but like us, he had done what he had been sent to do. When the tranquilizers hadn't worked, he took the measures he had needed to take.

He had planned on following the changeling to stop his escape, but Logan asked him to hold back and Boone had taken his spot. We knew almost nothing about the chaos that went on after the changeling had left Rider lying broken on the ground.

Hank told us there were four agents guarding the roof exit and two agents on every other staircase landing on the way down the building. We knew six agents had been injured, but the surgery was going well and everyone else was out of danger.

Logan and Boone chatted at the edge of the control room. Hank nodded in their direction when he was done with us, and Logan and Boone came over.

"Well, partner, you look tuckered out," Logan said.

"You could say that," I said.

"Let's get you home before Margaret tries to break into the Farm," Logan said.

"Sounds good to me." *It did, didn't it?* I'd been wanting to go home for days, what felt like weeks, but the moment Logan said the words, my stomach started to twist.

Still, there was no way I was staying here for another night. I stood and stretched, and tried not to show my trepidation.

"I should grab my flowers," I said, despite the fact I didn't want to go back to the clinic. I knew I was stalling for time.

"We'll get them another time," Logan said.

"Does Gran know I'm coming home?" I asked.

"She does," Logan said. "Agent Boone, she's invited you along. And you may as well grab your bag because she said you needed to get out of this place as much as Cassie."

"Tell her thanks," Boone said, "but I'll be fine here."

Logan grinned. "That might be true, but she'll have my ears if I don't bring you along."

Rider looked more awake and less drug-addled, but I could tell he was uncomfortable. I took one last look around the room before moving toward the exit.

"It's strange," I said. "I don't even know what time it is."

"It's around six in the evening," Logan said.

"What day?" I asked.

"Don't worry about it," Hank said. "We're not expecting to see you in here for a few days unless Dr. Yelton calls you back in."

"Sounds good to me," I muttered. Then I saw Vincent hadn't moved and I stopped. "You're coming over, right?"

Vincent looked at the retreating backs of the others. "I don't think so."

"Oh." I didn't try to hide my disappointment. "Okay." Then I thought about the long day he'd had. The long days everyone had lately. "Do you have a ride home?"

He hesitated. "I'm sure I can get a ride."

"Is my car still around? Maybe you could take it and drop it off for me tomorrow?"

"Thanks, I'll do that," he said.

At least it meant he couldn't avoid me. "Then I'll see you tomorrow?"

His lips curled up in the smallest amount. "I'll be there."

"The keys are... Actually, I don't know where my keys are. In my purse, maybe? They're probably wherever my phone is."

"I think we left most of your stuff in the clinic. I'll bring it over tomorrow."

The thought of going up to the clinic again had no appeal, so I gave Vincent a warm smile. "You're the best. Thank you."

"You should go. I'll see you tomorrow."

Rider waited for me outside by the door. "Logan is bringing the truck."

I only nodded.

"Are you concerned about the changeling?" Rider asked.

"No, not really," I said.

"I am concerned," Rider said.

"Whatever project Boone is working on is going to move forward with or without him. I think once it knew, it stopped caring much about us."

"That could be correct."

Our large SWAT-style truck pulled up and Boone jumped out and held the door open for me.

"Thanks, I'll sit in the back with Rider, though," I said.

"Are you sure?" Boone asked, opening the back door for me.

"Yeah, honestly, I probably won't stay awake for the trip home," I said.

Earlier, I had been tired enough to sleep on the way home and through the night. Now, my stomach felt twisted and nerves were stretched, though I had no idea why. The whole trip home I stared out the window and tried not to think about it.

It could have been because my mother waited for me. She hated everything about my job, so it was a possibility, but not likely. It probably had more to do with the fact that I had been gone for a week. People worried and got upset about my absence. Falling into another world hadn't been my fault, but I had control over where I worked. Maybe that's why I was nervous.

The others being there would help deflect some of the attention—and hopefully some of my guilt with it. Still, I would have felt better if Vincent were there as well.

The truck pulled to a stop at the house and I hesitated. Once Rider and Logan got out, I forced myself to open the door. Mom and Gran were at the front door waiting.

Mom ran up and gave me a hug, then she started crying. Actually crying. Gran ushered the others into the house where I knew they'd find themselves around the kitchen table.

"I'm okay, Mom," I said, patting her awkwardly on the back.

"Of course you are." Mom didn't let it go. "But you scared the life out of me. And your grandmother." She pulled away and gave me a critical look, her eyes catching everything from the too-loose clothes to the bandage wrapped around my arm. "You are far too thin. Well, I guess Mom will take care of that in no time."

"They mentioned Gran stayed with you a few nights," I said.

"She did. And Bob went out of town, so I stayed here a few nights as well."

"How is he?" I asked, remembering Gran saying he was sick.

"Never mind that now. He's at work and he's fine. You gave

your grandmother quite a scare, young lady." The tears were gone and she sounded more like herself. "And, from what we've been told, you nearly killed yourself getting back. From using your gifts, of all things. Now I know we taught you better. You know your limits."

"Yeah." I grew wistful thinking of those last moments of power. "It was my limit, but it got us back."

"You have partners, Cassandra. You should have trusted them to get you back. You didn't have to try to kill yourself to get home."

I tried hard not to sigh, knowing a little over a week ago she hadn't wanted anything to do with my partners. "I knew they'd get me back, but I was in a hurry."

Mom stilled. "Was it awful over there?"

I gave her a weak smile. "With Agent Boone there, it was basically camping without a tent."

"Oh my." She pulled me into another hug. "You poor thing. Was the weather bad? Your father took me camping once and it rained. He was happy as can be, but then again, he always was."

I almost held my breath. Mom never ever mentioned Dad. I knew almost nothing about the man. There were never stories, and he had died when I was so young I couldn't remember him.

"It wasn't terrible," Mom admitted, looking lost in thought for a moment. "But we had a tent at least. Well, let's get you inside so you can eat. You are dreadfully thin. Couldn't you find food?"

I curled up my nose. "I ate something blue, and what might have been roots or dirt or something."

"Dirt isn't food," Mom said, leading me inside. "Your grandmother has dinner for you and your friends. I imagine

Agent Boone needs something good to eat almost as much as you do. Where's the other young man, Vincent?"

A lot of noise came from the kitchen. When we walked in, plates were being passed around and my mouth immediately watered from the smell of baked sugar in the air.

"Vincent? He couldn't stop by tonight. He's bringing me my car tomorrow, though."

"That man is a treasure. You need to keep a tight hold on him."

I blushed profusely.

Gran gave me a big hug. "It's good to have you back, but oh my, you are so thin. Sit down and get yourself a plate."

The others chatted, but Boone and I were fairly quiet. After Gran brought out the welcome back cake, Boone started to look a little overwhelmed.

Mom passed on the cake and announced she was going home to get the house ready for Bob coming back into town.

Gran and I both walked her out, and Mom gave me another hug and welcomed me back. For a moment, I thought she would break down into tears again.

We watched Mom drive away, and then Gran looked me over. "Your mother is thrilled to have you back. We all are. After you've rested up for a few days—real rest, not that wretched sleep you got at the office—if you feel like talkin' about it, I'll be here."

"Thanks, Gran," I said. "It sounds like I missed a lot while I was gone."

"You didn't miss a thing," Gran said. "Logan was here every morning, same as usual. Rider came over a few times. I think he's got something on his mind he wants to talk with you about. Ethan stopped by to check on us. And, of course, Vincent was here every evenin'."

"It's nice they came over," I said. "I'm really glad they were here." My eyes started to burn.

Gran hugged me again. "Don't you go worryin' about it."

"And thanks for inviting Boone over."

"Your new friend needed out of that place as much as you did."

I followed Gran back into the kitchen.

"Logan," Gran said, "if you and Rider leave in the next ten minutes, you'll miss the accident on the highway."

Logan wiped his mouth and stood. "Sounds like it's time for us to mosey on out of here."

"Thank you for bringing back my granddaughter," Gran said, patting Logan's arm. "Both of you," she said.

Gran saw the others out, and Boone and I sat in rather comfortable silence.

"I know you must be exhausted," Gran said when she returned. "The guest room has been made up. You need to know you can help yourself to anything in the house."

"Thank you, ma'am."

"You can call me Margaret. Now, when you wake up at two thirty, you're not going to disturb anyone. You come right on down here and I'll leave you something in the fridge."

Boone blinked and looked like he couldn't figure out a reply.

"And don't feel the need to get up when you hear me downstairs in the morning. Logan won't be over until seven," Gran said. "Cassie, dear, why don't you help Boone get settled in? Frank's been missing you, too. Give him this."

"Thanks, Gran," I said, taking the lettuce leaf.

In the living room, I started to grab Boone's bag, but he smoothly stepped in and took it.

It was his, so I didn't complain.

"You get the nickel tour tonight," I said on our way

upstairs. "Your room is here, and the bathroom is next to it. It's all yours."

"Thank you," Boone said. "So, who's Frank?"

I smiled. "He's my rabbit. If you can handle something else off the record, I'll show him to you."

"Off the record? I'm intrigued," Boone said. He dropped his bag inside the spare room and crossed the hall to mine.

The second I turned on the light, an excited squeak rose from my desk and I could hear Frank half bouncing and half lurching around.

"This is Frank," I said.

"Two cages in one? Does he get out a lot?" Boone asked.

I stuffed some lettuce through the wires while Boone watched. "He's never tried, as far as I know. I tried to let him out once to get some exercise, but he wasn't interested."

"Poor rabbit, what's wrong with his leg?"

Poor rabbit? I hadn't expected to hear those words come from Boone. "We think he was hit by something. A car, maybe."

"He survived getting hit by a car?"

"No, he didn't."

For the second time that night, Boone was at a loss for words.

I held out the leaf. "Want to feed him?"

Boone looked from the leaf to the rabbit and didn't say anything.

"Wow, I think that's the first time I've seen you unsure of something," I said.

"Why is it I feel like I've been dropped into the Twilight Zone?" Boone asked.

"I couldn't say."

"And considering where we work, that's saying a lot."

"True."

"The rabbit is alive, right?"

I shrugged. "Define alive."

"There's never been actual recorded evidence of a zombie," Boone said.

"Ouch, don't say the Z word in front of the bunny," I said. I knew the answer, but figured I should ask the question anyway. "There won't be any records of a zombie, will there?"

Boone half grinned, but didn't stop looking at Frank. "Who'd believe me?"

"Where we work? It's hard to say."

"Frank's secret is safe with me. Is there anything else I should know about while here?"

"Yes. In all seriousness, listen to Gran. If she says something, you can count on it happening."

"She's that sure of herself?"

"I come from a family of psychics. Gran is the best of the best. She's never wrong."

"Interesting, and good to know."

"Yeah, there's a reason I'm so good at what I do." The statement left my mouth before I thought about it. I sighed heavily. "Or the reason I used to be so good at what I do."

"You're still good."

I couldn't even force a grin. Remembering my powers were gone, or at least almost gone, made me feel lost, so I couldn't say anything.

"Seeing you and your partners in action today was something else." Boone either didn't notice the change in my mood or was nice enough to ignore it. "I couldn't believe you sent that thing flying. Your partners may not have known you lost your power, except for Rider, but they weren't surprised you could handle yourself."

"We didn't catch the bad guy," I said.

"You can't catch everyone. The fact that this thing took several tranquilizers and a few bullets, and still wasn't stopped tells us we are dealing with an old changeling. I'm not sure anyone could catch one of those."

"Maybe," I said without any real feeling. "Your project is safe though, right?"

Boone shrugged. "It's not really my project. I'm only overseeing part of it, but yes, it's in motion and there's nothing that will stop it now."

"You don't sound too happy about it."

"I've never been on good terms with the project. The fact it almost got me killed makes me more uncertain. But, I've been pointed in this direction, so I'm going to see it out."

"Well, I'm not as much use as I was when we first met, but if I can help you with anything, let me know."

"I'll do that. For now, I'm going to excuse myself and get cleaned up."

"Aren't showers wonderful?" I asked.

"The waterfall was pretty nice, but you can't go wrong with temperature control."

He started to leave, and I figured it was the best time to say what needed to be said. "Before you go, I wanted to thank you."

Boone looked back, eyebrow raised, waiting for more.

"I'm pretty sure I wouldn't have survived out there without you." I cleared my throat and tried not to get emotional. "We never had a chance to talk when we got back and I... I just wanted to say thanks for keeping me alive."

"You're welcome. Working with you wasn't what I had expected, and you made things interesting. More importantly, you got us back."

"Luckily before the gremlins' concoction took effect."

"Even if it had, you would have gotten us back. Your partners would have found a way through. And believe me when I say not everyone can count themselves that lucky."

"They are pretty great, aren't they?"

"I also appreciate the fact you stopped them from killing me when we came through the portal."

I laughed. "They wouldn't have killed you."

"You may want to rethink that. Know the people you work with and know what they're capable of. I'm not saying it's a bad thing, having someone that's ready to pull the trigger when needed, but you should know your partners *will* pull that trigger."

"Yeah, I've seen them at work. Although, I can assure you that they'd have good reason if they hurt anyone."

Boone looked like he was weighing me up. "Make sure you know what it would take. I know Walkers get a bad rap, especially after working with Vincent, but know what he's capable of."

"I think I do. I mean, I hope I do."

"Well, he definitely has your back." Boone got a mischievous look on his face. "And maybe more."

"Cute." I blushed, but laughed at the same time.

Once Boone left, I closed my door, sat on my bed, and looked around. I was home. There had been times when I hadn't been sure I would get back, but I was sitting in my bed in my own room.

Somehow, it felt hollow.

Frank squeaked and I checked up on him. I was tempted to pull the little fluffer out of his cage and hug him. Taylor had said the rabbit couldn't turn anyone into a zombie. Still, the idea freaked me out, so I patted the cage instead.

After checking the time, I decided to get the call to Ethan over. I have to admit, I was relieved when I got his voicemail and had to leave a message. Nevertheless, I let him know I was home and thanked him for checking on Gran, which was the important thing.

After taking a shower—a long one because Boone was right, temperature control was a wonderful invention—I wandered around my room and poked my head in my closet. Everything hung just as I had left it. It was almost like coming home after going away to college. The room was mine, and it was my stuff, but something about the whole thing didn't feel the same anymore.

Maybe it wasn't supposed to. I'm pretty sure I only needed time to readjust to being home. Then I'd have to readjust to not having the Path to rely on. The thought was depressing, so I tried not to dwell on it. After my third circuit around the room, I settled down into my bed.

It took far longer than I had anticipated to fall asleep.

CHAPTER
TWENTY-FOUR

The next morning, I woke up and stared at the ceiling. Whatever this melancholy feeling was, it needed to go away. For some reason, though, I couldn't force myself to be cheerful.

Which was crazy. I was back home. I was alive. My friends and family were around me.

Then I thought about the previous night with Boone. I had mentioned the bad guy getting away. Even more than my powers failing, it sucked that we hadn't caught the changeling. We hadn't caught the man that had tried to kill Boone and me. The man that had injured Rider. We'd let him get away.

I spent a little time while getting ready trying to think if we could have done more, but it was no use. Boone had been right. We'd fought it, tranquilized it, and even shot the changeling more than once. He had hardly been fazed as far as we could tell.

I guess you couldn't win them all.

Once I got ready, I looked myself over in the bathroom mirror. For once, I had ended a case without a ton of bruises.

There were some, but this time, my biggest injuries were meta-physical instead of physical.

At least people don't stare at those.

Someone knocked on my bedroom door.

"Come in," I called from the bathroom. I ran the brush through my hair a few more times. Frank started squeaking excitedly, so I went in to see what the fuss was about.

Vincent stood next to his cage.

Seeing him watch over Frank helped soothe something inside me. Maybe things weren't as bad as I thought they were.

"Thank you for taking care of him while I was gone. He seems to have become attached."

"There wasn't much for me to do," Vincent said.

"I appreciate it anyway." I moved to the corner of my bed and sat down, watching him. "And I know Gran appreciated you coming by."

"I'm not sure your mother liked me being around."

"Actually, you have quite the fan in my mother," I said.

Had anyone else seen him, they wouldn't have been able to notice the incredulity in the look, but I could read him well.

"I mean it," I said. "She told me I was lucky to have you. She even called you a nice young man."

A hint of a grin appeared and he shook his head. "I brought your car back."

"Changing the subject. Smooth."

This time he did grin, but only briefly. "There was some-thing I wanted to talk to you about."

"Sure." I gestured to the chair.

Vincent took a seat, but he didn't say anything right away.

"To talk you need to use your words," I said.

"Maybe this was a bad idea," he said, standing up.

"No! Come on, I was kidding. Talk to me."

"Rider called me last night."

My heart sunk, and I'm pretty sure it showed on my face. "What did he say?"

"A lot, really. More than I had expected."

"He told you about what he thought when I was gone?"

Vincent shook his head. "We all had a lot of thoughts going on while you were gone. He didn't mention it, though."

"Oh. I asked him not to yet, so he's probably waiting for me to tell him it's okay. What did he say last night?"

"Is this something I should worry about?" Vincent said, looking like he already was.

"He had a stupid thought and he's worried you won't forgive him. I told him we all think stupid thoughts from time to time and you'd understand."

"I'll keep that in mind when I talk with him next."

I nodded. "So what did he say?"

"He's been upset over this challenge thing—"

"You know I didn't—"

Vincent held up his hand. "I know. He knows now, as well. He's on this kick about talking. He's determined that everyone should—"

"Cassie," Gran called up from downstairs, "you have a visitor. Ethan has stopped and he will be at the door shortly."

I blew out a frustrated sigh and stood.

"I shouldn't be here," Vincent said. I wasn't sure if he was upset with himself or me, but he sounded aggravated. "I'll go. Give you all some time."

"No." The last thing I wanted was for Vincent to go. "This will only take a minute. I'm sure he just wants to see for himself that I made it back."

"You two should spend some time together," Vincent said. "With me out of the way."

"Why? Just please wait here. For me?"

Vincent looked angry, but there was no heat in his voice.

"No. You all need time to catch up. I'm not getting in the middle of this."

"In the middle of what? Ethan and I broke up. I thought you knew."

The look Vincent gave me was pure confusion.

"Wait here," I said again.

I didn't give him time to say no another time. I ran down the stairs and plastered a smile on my face. Ethan stood by the door looking anxious.

"Hi," I said.

"I wasn't sure if I should stop by," Ethan said, "but I got your message last night."

"It's no problem," I said. A part of me thought I should offer him a seat and coffee or something, but most of me wanted to run back upstairs.

"This is awkward, isn't it?" Ethan said.

I grinned. "A little bit."

"I wanted to check in, is all, as a friend, and to see if you needed anything."

"That's nice of you. And it was great of you to stop by and visit Gran while I was gone."

"You look better than I expected."

I wasn't sure how to take that, and it must have shown on my face.

Ethan chuckled. "I've seen you at a normal day at work and it's pretty obvious when it's been a rough day at the office. You just went to another world and back, and here you are, looking like new except for your arm."

"Which happened at the office. After I got back."

Ethan laughed. "That sounds about right." He looked at me for a few moments and the silence started to draw out. "I should go. Work calls."

"Thanks again for stopping by. It was good to see you."

"It was good to see you, too. Tell everyone I said hi."

"You bet," I said.

I watched him go from the door and Gran popped her head in from the kitchen.

"It was nice of him to stop by. Bad timin', but nice all the same."

I felt myself blush. "Where is everyone?"

"Out." Gran winked at me. "Get on up there before he leaves."

Not knowing if Gran was giving me a prediction or making a passing comment, I rushed back upstairs.

"Sorry about that," I said as I pushed my door open.

Vincent paced the floor and he didn't look in good temper.

"What's wrong?" I felt defensive even though he hadn't said anything.

"When did you two break up?" Vincent asked.

"Before—" I waved my arm around, not knowing how to say before I had left this world. "Before everything. Before I left."

"Because I was here that night?"

"No, I told you before I left that Ethan didn't have anything against you. It was his choice."

"This is why Rider wanted us to talk, isn't it?" Vincent asked.

"No, at least I don't think so. Why are you so upset?"

"I'm not."

I crossed my arms and glared at him.

"Not with you. With myself. For getting between the two of you. I should have done things... differently."

"I told you this wasn't your fault. I'm not saying it again," I said.

A ghost of a smile appeared and vanished in an instant.

He stopped pacing and looked like he was getting hold of

himself. "If this wasn't what Rider was talking about, what was it he thought I should know?"

"Ah..." My anger fled. "Well, it could be a few things." I wrung my hands together, and the moment I noticed, I forced them down to my side.

"What's wrong?" Vincent asked. His aggravation also seemed to have vanished.

"I'm not sure you'd say it's wrong. In fact, it's good news for you."

He looked confused and moved closer. It was good news for him, but for me, it still hadn't sunk in that I'd almost completely lost my abilities as a Reader.

"What is it, Cass?"

"I'm fixed," I said, blurting it out.

His confusion seemed to spread.

"My soul, I mean. The gremlins gave me something and they fixed it."

This didn't appear to fill in any blanks for Vincent. He moved to me, put a hand on my cheek, and stared into my eyes. But he didn't seem to be looking at me.

I half grinned. "Are you looking for it? It's there. I've checked. And rechecked."

He looked as though he searched anyway, not taking my word for it.

"You can't see it, can you?"

He shook his head and dropped his hand. "Not see, no. It's more of a sense. Getting a feel for it."

I looked away. "Well, like I said. It's there and all in one piece."

"You don't look happy about that. Cass, this is a good thing," Vincent said.

My eyes started to burn and I blinked hard. "Is it?"

"Of course," He took one of my hands in his and stroked my arm with the other. "It's a very good thing."

I sighed. "You saw me yesterday—in the fight with the changeling. I couldn't do anything."

"What are you talking about?" Vincent asked. "You sent him flying."

I rolled my eyes and shook my head. "Physically, but he did all the work for that."

"You mean you weren't using the Path?" Once again, there was that look of confusion, but it was fleeting.

"No. I don't have to use it for everything." I was being defensive and it was stupid. "Which is good," I added. "Because I don't think the Path is good for much of anything now."

"Your power is gone?" Vincent asked.

I shrugged. "Not gone. Not all the way, but it's diminished to the point I can barely trace a Path more than a few hours old. I'll be useless in the field."

"Useless?" Vincent shook his head and gave me a soft smile. "You'll never be useless. Not in the field or anywhere else."

That earned him another eye roll. "Anyway. I'm fixed." I sniffed and added the part I had been dreading. "You're off the hook."

"Off the hook?"

"Sure. You said you were staying to fix my soul. It's fixed now." I swallowed hard and tried my best not to tear up.

"Do you want me to leave?" Vincent asked.

"No," I said in a rush of air. "Never. I want you to—"

He kissed me. Hesitantly, at first, but harder as we got caught up in the moment. Passion flared and I fell straight into it. The world around me disappeared and only the two of us remained.

He pulled me to him, as close as two people could be without occupying the same space. When the kiss ended, he didn't pull away, but looked down at his arms wrapped around me.

There were stray tears which had worked their way out, but I was floating. I was also at a complete loss for words.

"We should talk," he said. Since he hadn't moved away, I knew he didn't regret it.

For some reason, doubt sprang up and I stepped back. "This wasn't because of my soul or because I lost my abilities, is it?"

He shook his head and closed the gap again. "This was something I should have done ages ago."

I let out a relieved breath. "I agree."

The second kiss came almost as unexpectedly as the first. It was hard and demanding, and turned my insides to jelly and had me trying to pull him even tighter to me.

Then I felt his hesitation and he pulled back again. "That's probably too fast." He looked concerned.

I didn't know if he meant too fast for me or for him, but I didn't care. "It's been over a year since you kissed me in the hall. Trust me when I say this isn't rushed."

His face was soft and he wore a smile. An actual smile that the whole world could have seen, except it was all for me.

"Cassie!" Gran screeched from downstairs.

Vincent's emotions fled from his face before I had a chance to turn away. There had been a trace of distress in his eyes.

Vincent and I tore out of the room. My own terror gripped my heart. Gran was scared. I've never heard my grandmother cry out in fear, and it put all other thoughts on hold.

Gran appeared coming from the kitchen. She looked pale and shaky.

"What's wrong?" Our footsteps thundered on the stairs, but she didn't look our way.

"We're about to have company in the kitchen and it doesn't look good," Gran said.

"Margaret, go to your bedroom and lock the door. Call Logan."

It was a testament to how scared she was that she didn't argue, but mutely left, grabbing the phone on her way.

"Where's your gun?" Vincent asked.

He already held his, but I couldn't think. I had just gotten home, so how was I supposed to know where my gun was?

"Where is it?" Vincent asked.

"I don't know. No one gave me back my gun or anything else."

In the kitchen, we heard the back door slam open.

"Stay behind me," Vincent said.

Logan walked into view. "Howdy, partner. You in a spot of trouble?"

What the hell was Logan doing there? I looked to the front door, making sure nothing came toward us in that direction. Vincent had his gun trained on Logan.

Rushing into the Path, I saw the truth of the person. Being this weak with my power, I knew there was no way I could have seen the Path of an elf.

"You're not gonna shoot me now, are you?" the changeling asked.

"Who are you and what do you want?" I asked.

"Now that hurts." The fake Logan put a hand to his chest.

"Don't move," Vincent said when the thing started to walk forward.

It didn't stop and Vincent didn't give another warning. He fired repeatedly, but the creature kept walking toward us. When the magazine was spent, the changeling grinned.

Vincent dropped the magazine and put another in place.

Something shifted in the changeling's face—its skin elongated and began to turn dark.

"It's you people." He slung the word people around as though it were an insult. "The humans are bad enough, but you people take something easy and make it complicated."

Gran's voice filtered into the room. The changeling shook his head.

Gran was in the house, but he wouldn't bother her, right? He had scared her. I knew that. What had she seen that could have made her go so pale?

"Is there anything you can do?" Vincent asked, not bothering to lower his voice.

Could I? Vincent was here and with me. Really with me. This thing couldn't come in here and wreck my life.

"I think so," I said. I took Vincent's arm and drew on the power of the tiny shard of my soul that lived inside him. Warmth radiated through me.

The front door banged open and Logan, the real Logan walked in. The changeling didn't waste any time, immediately launching itself at the elf. I don't know what it said. It sounded like a curse, but by then, the thing's face was a nightmare.

I took a deep breath, gathered my strength, and hammered straight through my soul.

"Dammit, not that," Vincent said under his breath.

Too late. The small stream of the Path started to grow. As my soul broke apart, the power amplified. The changeling made one swipe at Logan before I could grab it. I flexed the Path around the creature and squeezed, drawing it away.

The Path wouldn't work exactly the way I wanted, but it was the best I could do. The energy was raw and burned hot as a flame through my mind. I grabbed my head and vertigo swept over me. Logan yelled. His face contorted, and he balanced on the balls of his feet. He had stretched taller and his eyes grew larger as his features became sharper.

The power started to rip through me, and it felt like chunks of myself went with it.

Vincent gripped my arm and I looked up into slate-black eyes.

"I'm sorry," he said.

Before my brain could make sense of the words, he was gone. Vincent dove into the creature and they both disappeared. With the changeling gone, my power had nothing left to hold onto and fell in on itself.

CHAPTER
TWENTY-FIVE

"What?" I screeched. "No! Damn you!"

I tried to get a grip on my power. When Cole had tried to take Vincent between the worlds, I had dragged them back. It wasn't one moment they were here and the next they were gone. It had taken time, but I had pulled them back. It had to work now.

But there was nothing for me to grab. With two Walkers, one trying to leave and the other trying to stay, there had been something to work with.

I stared at the spot where he had disappeared. There was nothing there. Raw energy poured through me, but I didn't much care. It started to drain me dry. Still, I searched for something to grab hold of.

"Let it go, darlin'," Gran said.

"No," I cried. "If we couldn't fight the thing here, what made him think he could fight it there?"

"There's nothin' that can be done about it." She gripped my arm and I wavered. "He's gonna be upset if he comes back and finds you've done somethin' that got you killed."

"If?" I asked.

"That's all I have, sugar," Gran said. "Come on back."

I nodded and sniffed. Logan was back to normal. He looked human anyway. He was on the phone with Hank if I had to guess. Boone was on the phone as well. His eyes kept straying to where Vincent had disappeared and then to me.

I was making a spectacle of myself. It was stupid. Vincent knew what he was doing. If he did something crazy and got himself killed, well, I'd track down his soul and make sure it knew how angry I had been.

Closing my eyes, I took a few deep breaths and then began to push the Path away. The power ran coarser than it had before. It wasn't more difficult to handle per se. Before, I had trouble stopping when my power got out of hand. This was different.

"Time to come back," Gran said again.

Something brushed by me from the side. I turned, but there was nothing there. However, I saw the Path of something, although, not the flowing colors I usually saw. This was solid. It had substance.

Something jostled me from behind, but when I turned, again there was nothing there.

"Cassie, what is it? What's wrong?" Gran asked.

"I don't..." There was a hint of something which rounded the corner into the kitchen. I took one step to follow it, and then fell.

"Cassandra Anala Heidrich, don't make me tell you again. Get back here."

It was an automatic response, which was good because that was about all my brain could handle at the moment. It felt like I rode a boat on rough waters, but I pulled my focus back together and left the Path behind me.

It felt as though I had run a race.

"Rider's on his way," Logan said.

"I'm okay," I said.

"Yeah," Logan said, "you look it."

"I just need a minute," I said.

"Well, you can take a minute, but I need a few first. Paulson's coming."

I groaned and put my hand to my head, rubbing my temples.

"I need to know what happened and I need to know fast," Logan said.

I squeezed my eyes shut and pushed myself up. I wouldn't lie on the floor while they hovered over me. Sitting on the floor would have to do though. I wasn't up to moving much further.

"Gran," I said, staring at the spot where Vincent had disappeared, "do you want to start?"

Gran didn't have to talk long before Logan led her to the couch and had her sit down. By looking at her, you'd never have guessed she had been scared. Forcing myself to my feet took all my willpower, but I managed it and sat down next to Gran on the couch.

When she finished, she announced she needed to make a call and went back to her bedroom. Worried, I watched her go.

It didn't take me long to fill Logan in. At first, I thought there wasn't much to tell, but then I had to back up and explain things a few times. I had to tell him about the gremlins fixing of my soul before I could fully explain how I had torn it apart again.

He glanced at Boone a few times while I spoke, and he didn't look too happy, but Boone said nothing. I didn't care if Boone knew. I was too upset to care. Too tired to care.

Besides, I trusted Boone.

Logan, on the other hand, did not.

The third time he cast a not so friendly look at Boone, I

spoke up. "It's okay, Logan. Boone knows everything about what I've told you, except what happened today."

"He does, does he?" Logan said. "I'd like to know where he lands on this before we have company arrive."

Boone shrugged. "I saw a Walker take down a changeling. That's all I know."

I gave Boone a grateful look.

Logan didn't look like he believed Boone. "Did you hear what the changeling said?"

"I did hear him say something, but whatever language it was in, I don't speak it," Boone said.

"And you," Logan asked, turning to me. "Do you know what the changeling said?"

"I could barely make out that he was talking at all." I rubbed my temple again. "Something went wrong with what I was doing. There wasn't much else I could pay attention to."

"I wish one of you knew something about it. I understood the words, but not the meaning."

"What did he say?" I asked.

"He said I was a traitor to my kind and the bastardized humans were bad news."

"It was bad enough he tried to kill me, but he called me a bastardized human on top of it?"

"Was he talking about you?" Logan asked.

"He referred to me and Vincent as 'you people'," I said. "Like there was something wrong with us. He said humans were bad enough, but 'you people' make things more difficult."

"Coming from the source, that's not a bad thing," Logan said. "Paulson should be here soon. I think Hank'll be with him, maybe a few others. I don't want them upsetting Margaret, though. She's had a long week."

I nodded in agreement. She had been through so much

since she moved in with me. It was getting worse instead of better.

"Taylor's still in town. I think we should have him look in on her before Paulson talks with her."

"That's not a bad idea," I said.

"I think he needs to take a look at you as well," Logan said.

"Nothing happened to me." If you didn't count the fact that, it felt as though my heart had been ripped out. "I'm fine."

"Don't think I haven't noticed you've been getting headaches since you've been back. This one looks worse," Logan said.

Realizing I was still massaging my temples, I removed my hand from my forehead. "It's only a headache." But I said it half-heartedly.

Someone knocked, and before I could do more than glance in that direction, Rider strode in and looked around.

"I hurried over," Rider said. "Is everyone well?"

I drew my knees up to my chest, but didn't answer.

"Everyone here is okay," Logan said. "I need to call Taylor. I'll be back shortly."

Rider's forehead creased and his nose curled up at me.

"Don't even start telling me I smell," I said.

Rider nodded and didn't say anything, which was as good as telling me he thought I smelled odd.

"My partner?" Rider asked.

I looked away.

No one said anything, and Rider started moving through room. His nose would probably tell him more than we could.

A few minutes later, he dropped onto the couch. "I see. For the past month, since taking and releasing all the good souls from Einar, he has been lighter. Different. Less burdened. This may change things."

Rider was right. I had noticed it when we were in the

mountains, but I didn't know its cause. It made sense, though. He had taken in so many souls from the golem, Einar, but they weren't the monsters he usually dealt with.

What would he be like when he came back?

"We don't know he took the changeling's soul." I said it more for my own benefit than for anyone else.

"How will he fight the person any better there than he would here unless he takes their soul?" Rider asked.

"Funny, I had the same question," I said. "When he gets back, I intend to ask him." I thought about it for a moment. "In a loud voice."

Rider smirked, but he stared into space. "How long was he gone last time?"

"Do you mean how long was he out of this world? I know we didn't see him for over six months. Of course, I never really wanted to know how long he was gone. I knew the answer would tick me off."

"I think it was a week or more," Rider said.

"Why did he go last time?" Boone asked.

"Same stupid reason he went this time," I said. "Only then it was a vampire instead of a changeling."

"Vampire, as in the ones that have been here for a while or the ones that come over now?"

"I didn't know there was much of a difference." I could see Boone was going to fill me in, but I was too depressed to care. "This one was a new one, though. The demon we fought to get home? One of those opened a bunch of portals at once. Logan, Vincent, and I, ended up with the vampire."

Boone whistled under his breath.

"There was nothing we could do with the changeling here," Rider said.

"No," I snapped, "what you mean is we hadn't found anything yet."

"I haven't known Vincent long," Boone said, "but I get the feeling he can handle himself. I'm sure he'll be back as soon as he can."

We sat and listened to Logan's voice from the kitchen and Gran on the phone in her room.

"I'm sorry I brought this onto you all," Boone said.

"What?" Having been caught in my own little world where Vincent was able to come immediately back, I hadn't been paying attention.

"This thing was here because I was here," Boone said.

"No one blames you," I said. "This was the changeling's fault. We can't stop what we do because someone wants to kill us."

"You would never leave the house if that were the case," Rider said.

"Not everyone wants to kill me." I grinned, although I was thankful Rider was trying to lighten the mood.

"This is true," Rider said in all seriousness. "It is only the people that meet you."

I rolled my eyes and shook my head. "I can't help it if I rub people the wrong way."

"Actually, I do not believe you do anymore," Rider said.

"What do you mean?" I asked.

"With your soul put back together, I don't think you will have the same issue you used to have with meeting new people," Rider said.

"Maybe I should have thought about that before I broke it apart again."

Rider looked confused, so I told him what happened.

"That explains the smell," Rider said.

"I do not smell," I muttered.

Rider grinned. "You have a smell. Although the smell of you and Vincent being together is much more powerful."

The blush crept up and through my face. "Remind me to talk to you about boundaries again."

Rider's forehead crinkled in confusion. "Boundaries mean not walking in without knocking. It is the clothes thing."

Boone chuckled.

"You're not helpful," I said to Boone.

The crunch of gravel in the driveway announced the arrival of the agency and we all went silent. Sighing, I stood to get the door, but Logan came out of the kitchen, still on the phone, and waved at me to sit back down. He went to the door and ushered Paulson and his partner in. Hank arrived shortly after.

After that, work took over. Paulson stuck to the living room and questioned me, and then once Taylor had looked in on Gran, Paulson spoke with her as well.

There were reports, but there were always reports. This time, there were a few more. Apparently, the office had been upgrading their paperwork involving people going into other worlds. Not everyone thought going between the worlds counted, but to Paulson it did.

For hours, people from the office trampled through the living room and kitchen. They took readings on strange little machines, trying to measure something in the air. They tried to fingerprint everything that may have been in the changeling's Path in the kitchen. What they thought they could get from a changeling's fingerprint was beyond me.

Slowly, people started to filter away. The cleanup crew left, then Paulson and his partner. Boone hitched a ride with them, claiming he needed to arrange a few meetings. A while later, Hank went with Logan out the back door.

Taylor, Rider, Gran, and I sat around the kitchen table. Gran made hot chocolate, but I went for something a bit stronger. My head pounded, and I couldn't shut out the horrible knowledge Vincent had gone somewhere with a monster and I couldn't follow.

"This day has been somethin' else," Gran said.

"We should talk about it more," I said, not meeting her eye. "Work has come home with me a little too often lately."

"Well, I was going to wait till tomorrow to tell you, but I have been givin' that some thought."

My stomach clenched as I waited for the inevitable. It would be better if we didn't live together anymore, but I would miss it all the same."

"Tomorrow mornin' a friend of mine is comin' over."

"Okay," I said carefully, at a loss as to where the conversation was going.

"He said he has somethin' that's gonna solve the problems we've been havin' with strangers comin' into the house."

"What, like an alarm system?" I asked.

"I'm not sure. It's hard to tell with that old coot."

My eyebrows snapped together. "Is this the same old man you sent to find me?"

"One and the same," Gran said.

His answer to getting me home had been to put a demon into the same world as me and let it attack us. Since it worked, I couldn't really complain, but I hated to think what he would do to our house.

I shook my head. "What are you doing tomorrow, Rider?" I asked.

He still looked dejected. "I do not know. I am off work due to my arm."

"I'll be at the Farm again tomorrow to help Dr. Yelton," Taylor said, "but when I'm done, I'd like to invite you both to the city. There are a few things I wanted to go over with Cassie, and we have something we might need some help on."

"Sure. Do you want to stay the night?" I asked. "I'm sure it wouldn't bother Vincent if you use his room."

"I have a few patients at the Farm to work with tonight, but I'll give you a call when I'm back in the city."

I nodded, knowing I'd need whatever I could get to distract myself from Vincent's absence.

Want to read further?
Reliquary (AIR Series Book 7)

WRITING the AIR series has been a fun and amazing experience. There's more planned for Cassie and her partners!

IF YOU ENJOYED THIS BOOK, please leave a review on the site where you made the purchase. Leaving a review helps the reader and author in many ways. Your support is appreciated!

THANK YOU FOR READING!
Amanda Booloodian

COMPLETE WORKS

Complete works by Amanda Booloodian:

AIR Series (In Reading Order)
Stonecoat: Novella 0 (AIR Series Book 0)
Shattered Soul (AIR Series Book 1)
Redcap (AIR Series Book 2)
Broken Paths (AIR Series Book 3)
Stolen Sight (AIR Series Book 4)
Fenrisúlfr: Novella 3.5 (AIR Series 5)
Fractured Worlds (AIR Series Book 6)
Reliquary (AIR Series Book 7)
Never-Ending Nightmare (AIR Series Book 8)
Krampus (AIR Series Book 9)
Eclipsed Pathways (AIR Series Book 10)
Void (AIR Series Book 11)
Marked Soul (AIR Series Book 12)

AIR Series Box Set

AIR Series Books 0-4: Welcome to the Farm
AIR Series Books 5-8: Conspiracy Theory
AIR Series Books 9-12: Redacted

Spellbound Murder Series

Oath Bound (Spellbound Murder Series Book 1)
Grim Magic (Spellbound Murder Series Book 2)
Fallen Witch (Spellbound Murder Book 3)

Spellbound Murder Box Set

Spellbound Murder Complete Trilogy

AIR Series Audiobooks

Stonecoat: Novella 0.5 (AIR Series Book 0)
Shattered Soul (AIR Series Book 1)
Redcap (AIR Series Book 2)
Broken Paths (AIR Series Book 3)
Stolen Sight (AIR Series Book 4)
Fenrisúlfr: Novella 3.5 (AIR Series 5)
Fractured Worlds (AIR Series Book 6)
Reliquary (AIR Series Book 7)
Never-Ending Nightmare (AIR Series Book 8)
Krampus (AIR Series Book 9)
Eclipsed Pathways (AIR Series Book 10)
Void (AIR Series Book 11)
Marked Soul (AIR Series Book 12)

Spellbound Murder Series Audiobooks

Oath Bound (Spellbound Murder Series Book 1)
Grim Magic (Spellbound Murder Series Book 2)
Fallen Witch (Spellbound Murder Book 3)

ACKNOWLEDGMENTS

While editing Fractured Worlds, I started to get nervous. It's pretty common for me to get nervous around that point, but this time, it struck a little deeper. Taking Cassie into another world, introducing a new character, and changing relationships seemed like a lot of changes. My biggest concern was, will fans of the series like this?

For that very reason, I'd like to give a special thank you to Tamera Walton, who took the time to read the book and give me feedback in a few short days! I also need to thank JD Book Services and Frankie Sutton, my editors, for their feedback on the book which helped me get passed the anxiety.

Working with Deranged Doctor Design has been amazing. They've provided the entire series with wonderful covers and formatting. I love their work and their flexibility.

Many, many other family, friends, and acquaintances have been incredibly supportive.

For all the people who gave reviews online, you are amazing! Thank you so much for taking the time to leave a review.

ABOUT THE AUTHOR

Amanda Booloodian lives in Missouri with her loving, and often times peculiar, husband. She has been passionate about the written word throughout her life. Now, much of her spare time is spent at the computer, delving into worlds accessible only through vivid imagination. In warm weather, when she isn't pounding on the keyboard, she can often be found wandering through the wilderness. Occasionally she gets it into her head to SCUBA dive or to sit back at home and make wine, which can have interesting results and inspire her writing.

You can find out more about Amanda and her writing, including upcoming releases, on www.Booloodian.com. You can also find her on Facebook: Amanda Booloodian - Author and Instagram: AJBooloodian.